Critical Acclaim for *Glazed Murder*

"Jessica Beck's *Glazed Murder* is a delight. Suzanne Hart is a lovable amateur sleuth who has a hilariously protective mother *and* great donut recipes! Readers will have a blast with this book."   —Diane Mott Davidson

"A tribute to comfort food and to the comfort of small town life. With great donut recipes!"
          —Joanna Carl, author of
          The Chocolate Cupid Killings

"If you like donuts—and who doesn't?—you'll love this mystery. It's like a trip to your favorite coffee shop, but without the calories!"
          —Leslie Meier, author of the Lucy Stone mysteries
          New Year's Eve Murder and *Wedding Day Murder*

"The perfect comfort read: a delicious murder, a likeable heroine, quirky Southern characters—and donut recipes!"
          —Rhys Bowen, Agatha and Anthony Award–winning
          author of the Molly Murphy and Royal Spyness mysteries

"Jessica Beck's debut mystery, *Glazed Murder*, is a yummy new treat in the culinary mystery genre. Skillfully weaving donut recipes throughout a well-plotted story, the author proves that life after divorce can be sweet; all you need are good friends, your own business, and comfort food. Delicious!"   —Tamar Myers, author of
          Death of a Rug Lord and *The Cane Mutiny*

FATALLY FROSTED

A DONUT SHOP MYSTERY

Jessica Beck

St. Martin's Paperbacks

This is a work of fiction. All of the characters, organizations, and events portrayed in this novel are either products of the author's imagination or are used fictitiously.

FATALLY FROSTED

Copyright © 2010 by Jessica Beck.
Excerpt from *Sinister Sprinkles* copyright © 2010 by Jessica Beck.

For information address St. Martin's Press, 175 Fifth Avenue, New York, NY 10010.

EAN: 978-0-312-94611-1

Printed in the United States of America

St. Martin's Paperbacks edition / August 2010

St. Martin's Paperbacks are published by St. Martin's Press, 175 Fifth Avenue, New York, NY 10010.

10   9   8   7   6   5   4   3   2   1

For E & P,
And all the donuts we've shared together
through the years!

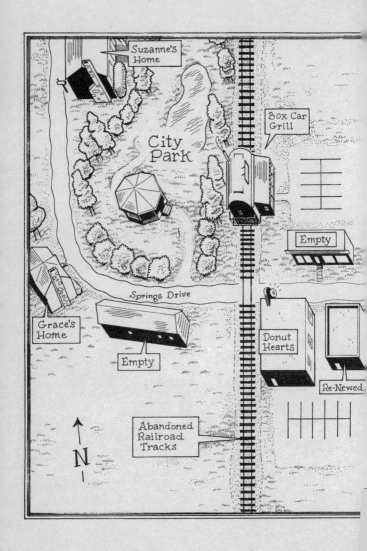

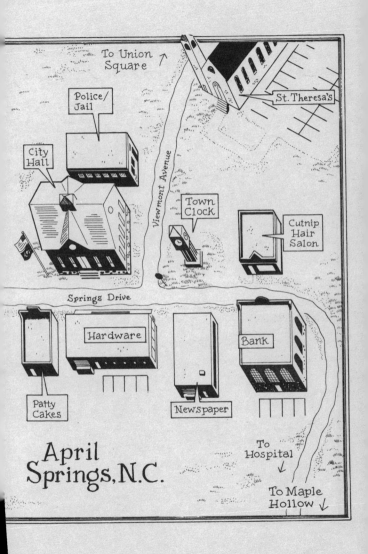

"Keep your eyes upon the donut, and not upon the hole!" —Anonymous

CHAPTER 1

I thought getting away from my business—Donut Hearts—for a few days might be fun. But when I agreed to make gourmet donuts for one of my friends, I had no idea it would put me right in the middle of yet another homicide investigation.

Just about everyone I knew in April Springs, North Carolina—population 5,001—was looking forward to the September Kitchens Extraordinaire home tour ever since it had first been announced in *The April Springs Sentinel*, including me. When my friend Marge Rankin suggested I demonstrate how to make something special in her newly remodeled kitchen for the tour, I'd jumped at the chance to show off just what I could do with some dough and a portable fryer. There wouldn't be a yeast donut or an apple fritter on the menu; I was going to pull out all of the stops and make something unforgettable.

"Jake, do you really want to learn how to make beignets?"

My boyfriend—a state police inspector named Jake Bishop I'd been seeing since March—smiled at me as we stood in the kitchen of Donut Hearts. He looked cute wearing one of our aprons, but I knew better than to tell him that. Jake was tall and thin, with a healthy head of sandy blond hair, and there was something about the man's presence that made me smile.

"Not as much as I want your company," he admitted. I didn't get to see him nearly enough, since his casework took him all over the state of North Carolina. I had to give him points for honesty, but I still had a job to do.

"I've got an idea," I said. "Why don't you sit over there and keep me company, and I'll let you sample the beignets I make? You can be my official taster."

He took off the apron as though he'd been pardoned for a crime he'd never committed. "That's the best deal I've had weeks."

"You don't have to look so relieved when you say it," I said with a grin.

"What can I tell you? I'm all about leaving tough stuff to the experts."

I frowned at the finished dough. It was close to the consistency I'd been hoping for, but the true test would be in the taste. "I'm not sure I qualify."

"Come on, you're the best donut maker in the world. You told me yourself beignets are just fancy donuts, and no one's better at making those than you. I'm a cop; trust me, I know donuts."

"I appreciate the sentiment, but I don't have time on the tour to make these with yeast, so I'm going to have to substitute baking powder instead. It's more chemistry than you'd imagine." It was true. While cooking recipes could usually be slightly modified with impunity, baking was another matter altogether. I needed enough baking powder to make the dough rise when it hit the hot oil, but not too much, or it would be a disaster, and if there was one thing I couldn't afford, it was to wreck my demonstration.

He laughed. "Don't sell yourself short. I know I couldn't do it."

I lightly floured the counter and rolled out the dough until it was somewhere between a quarter- and an eighth-inch thick, and then cut it into squares. For the demonstration, I'd be using my ravioli cutter, a scallop-edged tool that left perfectly shaped circles, but this test run was more about taste than appearance.

I dropped the first rounds into the oil and held my breath. After cooking two minutes on one side, I flipped them, and then pulled them out after another two. I had a plate ready, and dusted them with confectioner's sugar while they were still hot.

"Man, those smell fantastic," Jake said as I slid the plate in front of him.

"Now let's see how they taste," I said.

We both reached for the same one, and I laughed. "There's plenty for both of us."

"That's what you think." He took a bite, and I watched his expression. If his look of joy meant anything, I might have a winning recipe after all.

"Outstanding," he said as he reached for another one.

I was happy with his reaction, but I was a harsher judge myself. I bit into the treat, and felt the texture of the beignet in my mouth. The flavor was spot on, a hint of airy lightness that tasted something like a sophisticated funnel cake from a fair. I had to agree that it was good—there was no doubt about that—but was it as good as my yeast beignets?

"Are you sure?"

"Well, maybe I'd better eat the rest of these so I can be sure." He had a hint of powdered sugar on his nose, and I reached over and wiped it off just as his cell phone rang.

"Bishop here," he said as he answered, his voice becoming instantly serious. I had no idea how he turned it off and on like he did.

"Yes, sir. I understand. I'm on my way."

After he hung up, I asked, "Bad news?"

"I've got a case. It's on the Outer Banks, Suzanne. Looks like I'm going to have to miss the tour. Sorry."

"You've got a job to do," I said, a little sad that he wouldn't be there for my demonstration.

He shrugged, and then wrapped me in his arms. "I'll call you later."

"Liar," I said with a grin. When he was on a case, I knew how focused he could get, so I didn't expect daily, or even weekly telephone calls.

"You caught me," he said, and then to make up for it, he kissed me.

After he was gone, I could swear I could still taste the beignets on his breath.

The day before the tour, Marge stopped by Donut Hearts half an hour before we were set to close to go over my menu one more time. She was a petite woman in her early sixties, and her smile was always a little crooked, shifting slightly to the left whenever she grinned. You couldn't see it at the moment, though, since Marge wasn't anywhere close to smiling.

"Suzanne, are you certain you're ready for the big day? I don't mean to put any extra pressure on you, but this is important."

I nodded and did my best to reassure her. "Marge, I've got everything under control. I've been staying late an hour every day for a week to test my recipes and polish my cooking techniques with the portable fryer, and I've got it all down cold. Don't worry. It's going to be fabulous."

Marge Rankin had inherited a great deal of money from her father when he'd passed away a few years earlier. Rumors around town put her net worth at two million dollars on the conservative side, and all the way up to ten million on those hot summer days when no one had anything else to talk about. It was impossible to tell that Marge had money by the way she dressed, though; she bought her clothes from Gabby Williams's shop next door to the converted train depot that now housed my donut shop. ReNEWed was a clothing store that offered some of the best recycled clothing in our part of North Carolina, and Marge wasn't afraid who knew she shopped for her apparel secondhand.

"It just has to be perfect," Marge said, wringing her hands together with such force they were white. "I've dreamed about this kitchen for twenty years, and I can hardly believe I finally have it. I want everyone to know it, too."

I'd had the grand tour of her remodeled place the day before, and she had every right to be proud. From the Viking stove to the deluxe six-burner industrial cooktop, the lustrous marble countertops to the elegant hardwood floors, it was truly a thing of beauty.

"It's going to be the star of the show," I said. "Everyone will be talking about it when we're through."

Marge smiled. "I certainly hope so. Thanks again for making donuts for me."

The underlying theme of the exhibition was Working Kitchens, and everyone with a stop on the tour had hired a professional chef to show off their creations. I was the lone demonstrator who hadn't gone to culinary school, and I was beginning to feel the pinging of my nerves, something I couldn't let Marge see.

I tried to match her smile as I said, "Are you kidding? How often do I get the chance to work in such elegant surroundings? I'm looking forward to it."

She looked around the shop, then frowned softly. "I think your place is quaint. Who doesn't love an old train depot?"

I glanced at the painted burgundy floor, the large windows overlooking Springs Drive from one view and the abandoned railroad tracks from the other, and saw Donut Hearts in a different light. Sometimes I took it for granted, but it really was a welcoming place to spend my days, even if they did begin at one-thirty in the morning and end a little after noon.

"Don't get me wrong," I said. "I'm a huge fan of my shop. After all, it's named after me, isn't it?"

Marge nodded. "That was so clever, adding an E to your last name. Hart for Heart, it's perfect."

"I like it," I admitted. "Now, don't you have a thousand things to do to get ready for tomorrow? Do you

have the list of ingredients I asked you to get for me?"
Marge had insisted on supplying everything I'd need
for the day's donut making, and I hadn't fought her on
it. After all, it freed me to try some things that I'd
only read about in books before, and I wasn't going to
scrimp or substitute on second-class ingredients.

"I've got three of everything you requested, so
we'll be fine. I *do* have to see about the china,
though. I'd better go check to see if it's arrived at the
house yet."

As she started for the door, Marge hesitated, then
asked, "Have I thanked you recently for doing this
for me?"

"Just a thousand times," I said with a grin. "Just
remember to relax and have fun with it. Our stop is
going to be the talk of the town. Now shoo."

After she left, my assistant, Emma Blake, came out
of the kitchen. Emma was a pretty young woman
nearly out of her teens, with a cute figure and flaming
red hair. She'd been working for me a few years, saving to go away to college someday and taking classes
at the community college at night. Selfishly, I hoped it
wasn't any time soon. I'd grown to depend on her, and
had learned to trust her with my life. In a two-woman
operation, she was more important than my flour sup-
plier and all of my regular customers combined.

Emma looked around the room, as if not trusting
her eyes, as she asked, "Is she finally gone?"

"Don't tell me you don't like Marge Rankin," I
said. "She's got to be the gentlest woman in the world."

Emma bit her lower lip, then said, "Honestly, I'm
just tired of having her hover around the shop all of
the time."

"Don't worry, it's almost over. She's understandably just a little nervous about everyone in town parading through her place."

My assistant frowned at me. "You showed me pictures of her kitchen. What on earth does she have to worry about? It's absolutely perfect."

I shrugged. "Maybe so, but I know she's not going to sleep a wink until the debut tomorrow."

Emma sighed. "I wish I had her problems."

"I'm not sure you should," I said. "Just because she's wealthy doesn't mean she's got it made." It was time to change the subject, so I asked her, "Is everything set here for tomorrow? Do you have any last-minute questions?"

That earned me a frown from her. "Suzanne, I told you, I can handle the donut shop. Mom's coming in to help me, so we'll be fine. Don't worry, your place is in good hands."

I clearly surprised her by hugging her. "I know it is. I trust you completely." Though I made donuts alone once a week on Emma's day off, she'd never had to make them without me. But she'd been working for me for two years, and I'd taught her everything I'd learned since I'd bought the place. Donut Hearts had been my personal emancipation proclamation, bought with my settlement from the divorce from my cheating husband Max. Max was out of my life, though he still lived in town, and was constantly trying to get back into my heart.

Emma said, "I need to get back to those dishes."

A few minutes after she disappeared in back, a nice-looking man in his thirties came into the shop, and I had to keep myself from openly staring at him. It wasn't just because he had a full head of lustrous blond hair and the bluest eyes I'd ever seen in my life. There was something familiar about him, but I couldn't place him for the life of me.

"May I help you?"

"I'd like two black coffees to go," he said.

"Can I get you any donuts to go with them?"

He grinned at me as if I'd just said something amusing, then shook his head. "No, just the coffee, please."

As I filled two cups for him, I wanted to start a conversation, but I couldn't think of a thing in the world to say. When I glanced back at him over my shoulder, I saw him smiling at me, as if he knew something I didn't.

I told him how much he owed me, and as he paid for the coffee, he said, "I'll see you the same time tomorrow."

"I won't be here," I blurted out. Honestly, it was as though I'd never seen a nice-looking man in my shop before. Why was I suddenly acting like a girl in junior high school?

"More's the pity," he said, and then left.

Now what on earth had that been about?

The front door chimed ten minutes later, and I looked up to see who was coming into the shop three minutes before we were set to close.

I gritted my teeth the second I saw that it was Peg Masterson—the organizer of the kitchen tour—a woman with an amplified, nasal voice that could make a marble statue run away screaming. I knew her clothes were at best second-hand from Gabby's shop, but she still made me self-conscious about my blue jeans and T-shirt.

"Suzanne, I need a word with you," she said as she tapped her clipboard with the back of her pen. Peg was a short woman in her fifties, nearly as wide as she was tall. Her figure must have been a challenge to clothe, but I wasn't sure that justified the hand-made creations she sometimes made for herself to wear. What might look good on a fashion model that was a size zero certainly didn't seem to flatter her figure. She had black hair, and it was pretty clear to me that it wasn't natural.

"Hello, Peg. Come by for a donut?"

She looked at them for a second with longing. "No, I'm afraid I've decided to cut back on my sweets intake. They play havoc with my figure, you know."

"Not even a lemon-filled one?" I asked wickedly. They were Peg's downfall, and she usually ordered them from me by the dozen.

She looked tempted to break her abstinence, and I felt ashamed for my little jab, so I was more than a little upset with myself when she said, "Oh, why not? What's one going to hurt? You know, I've never been able to resist these little devils, even if I could stand to lose a pound or two."

More like forty or fifty, I thought to myself, again rather unkindly. Peg just seemed to bring out the worst in me, and I wasn't all that proud of it.

As she wolfed down the donut, I asked, "What can I do for you?"

She tapped the clipboard again. "I'm still not sure

about your exhibition. You assure me that it's going to be keeping in tone with the rest of the tour, correct?"

Now that she was firing back at me, I wasn't nearly as amused as I had been before. "Peg, I know you're not thrilled that Marge asked me to demonstrate donuts, but you really shouldn't be so narrow-minded. Donuts have been around since biblical times, they've been some of the favorite treats of presidents, and they're eaten all over the world. You really should respect them for their contributions to the world's happiness."

She rolled her eyes, and I knew it was a lost cause. "What exactly are you making tomorrow? It's the first day of the tour, and much will depend on how well it is received by the visitors who come tomorrow."

"I've been thinking about starting with beignets. You'll have to try one. They're delicious."

Peg frowned, then studied her clipboard again. "I have you down for donuts, which is fairly obvious since you own a donut shop. Why the change in offerings?" She added with a bite, "Unless simple donuts aren't good enough for you."

"A beignet *is* a donut, Peg," I said, trying to keep my temper in check. I didn't care what she thought of me, but if she was looking for an excuse to scratch Marge from the tour, I wasn't going to be the one who provided it. I'd been surprised to learn that Peg had allowed her rival a spot on the kitchen tour at all, and I had hoped that she'd finally put her petty jealousies behind her.

Apparently, that hope had been in vain.

Peg stared at me over the clipboard. "Whatever. Don't let all of us running the tour down, Suzanne."

"My part of it will be perfect," I said.

"Let's hope so," Peg said as she walked out the door, getting the last word in yet again.

I had one minute left before closing, but I couldn't face the idea of Peg popping back inside with "one more thing." I didn't think I could greet her again without screaming. The shop was empty, so I flipped the OPEN sign to CLOSED and started to dead-bolt the door.

Then I saw Max, my good-looking—though less than loyal—ex-husband come running up the street toward my door.

I was in no mood to deal with him at the moment.

"Sorry, we're closed," I said, as I pointed to the sign.

As he tapped his watch, Max grinned at me with the same smile that used to melt my heart. "I've got two minutes. You don't want to turn a hungry man away, do you?"

I thought about doing just that, but was it really worth having him complain all over April Springs that I'd locked him out on purpose?

I flipped the sign back and unlocked the door.

As he rushed in, I said, "Your watch is slow. You've got thirty seconds, and then I'm throwing you out."

"I just need twenty," he said.

"Donuts?"

"Seconds." He surveyed what was left in the case behind the counter. I never keep donuts overnight. I either give them to the church for folks who could use a treat, or I take them around the county to businesses who might like them enough to become regular customers. Today it was going to be a donation. I'd been working so hard at perfecting the beignets and some of the other donut recipe possibilities for the tour that I was in no mood to put on a smile and hand out donuts and business cards.

"I'll take them all," Max said.

"My, you are hungry," I said as I started boxing up the three-and-a-half-odd dozen donuts left in the display.

"It's for my theater troupe," he said.

"What's on tap this time? I have to admit that I enjoyed your rendition of *West Side Story.*" Max was a sometime-employed actor. He worked nationally just enough to get a commercial now and then so he could keep solvent, but his true love was directing. When he couldn't get anyone to pay him to do it, he volunteered at the senior center and put on plays whose only common thread was the need for young actors. It had been a running joke around town until folks had seen *West Side Story*, and now everyone was looking forward to his latest offering.

Max leaned over and looked at me with those gorgeous brown eyes of his. As he ran his hand through his thick auburn hair, I knew he was too handsome for his own good, and yet I still felt a tug from his attention.

He whispered, "It's still a secret, but I can trust you. We're working on *Romeo and Juliet.*"

I laughed out loud at that one. "Variations on a theme, wouldn't you say?"

"What can I say? They insisted, and I couldn't

very well disagree, since they're paying me for this production."

"Max," I said harshly, "you're not taking advantage of the seniors, are you?"

He shook his head. "No way. They're using some of the proceeds from the last show. You have no idea how much we took in."

"I still think you should volunteer your time," I said.

"Only if you promise to supply us with free donuts."

He had me there. I couldn't afford to give away my products on a daily basis any more than he could always donate his time and expertise.

Just to tweak him, though, I slid the boxes across the counter to him and said, "Done. Now give them back your salary."

He frowned. "Suzanne, are you serious?"

"I am for today. I'll give up the profit on these if you donate today's salary back to the seniors."

"I can do that," Max said grudgingly.

I put a hand on the stack of boxes. "That's what you say now, but how am I going to know that you'll actually follow through on it?"

"Come with me if you don't believe me," he said. "You can see for yourself."

I let go of the boxes. "No, I'll just have to trust you this time."

Max made no move to leave, though. "Now if I could just get you to forgive me for my mistake, we could be good again."

"Is that what you're calling Darlene these days?" His tumble with her was the main reason we'd split up, and I still felt the hair on the back of my neck stand up whenever I saw her around town.

"I keep telling you. There's nothing going on between us," he said.

"I've heard that record playing before," I said. "Good-bye, Max."

"Bye, Suze."

He knew I hated his pet name for me, but I was too tired to fight about it. I let him out, locked the door, then saw Emma come out through the kitchen.

"Is he gone?"

"Now you're afraid of Max?" I asked.

Her face reddened slightly. "I was trying to give you two some privacy."

I laughed bitterly, "You shouldn't have bothered. There's nothing between us anymore, and you know it."

She shrugged. "I still didn't want to interrupt you. I'm finished in the back. Are you ready to leave?"

I stifled a yawn as I said, "I'd love to, but I've still got a stack of invoices sitting on my desk, and if I don't write the checks, we can't make the donuts. I've been spending far too much time perfecting my beignets."

She wiped the front counter with her dishrag and said, "Suzanne, for once, just go home. Those bills can wait until next week, can't they?"

"I suppose so," I admitted. "You know what, Emma? You're absolutely right. Let's both go home."

She looked surprised by my compliance, then smiled and said, "There you go. That's the spirit."

I turned off the lights, then dead-bolted the door as we left.

Out on the sidewalk in front of the shop, I said, "See you tomorrow."

"No, you won't," Emma said. "You get to sleep in, remember?"

"It's been so long since I've been able to, I've forgotten what it's like."

Emma started toward her car, then turned back to me and grinned. "I've got a feeling it will come back to you pretty fast."

"If you need me, don't be afraid to call me on my cell phone," I said.

"Not a chance. Mom and I have it covered."

I nodded, then got into my Jeep and headed home. Gabby Williams had been out front, no doubt waiting to snare me into her gossiping trap, but I didn't have the time or the inclination to hear what she had to say today. I was going home to grab a quick nap, then I was going to find something fun to do. I needed a break. I'd been stressing out since Marge had asked me to cook for her, and tomorrow, I'd be put to the test.

I just hoped it was one I could pass.

I drove my Jeep home, hoping for a peaceful evening, but doubting I'd get it. After I'd found Max in bed with Darlene, I'd run home to my mother, and I hadn't left her house in the years since. We lived on the edge of the April Springs city park in a bungalow that sometimes felt two sizes too small for the both of us. Mostly we'd hammered out a good living arrangement, and I had to admit that it was nice to have someone to come home to, even if it was just my mother. It would be good to talk to her today about the pressure I was feeling from tomorrow's show. She'd find a way to reassure me.

To my surprise, the house was deserted.

After looking around the house, I found a note on the kitchen table, propped up against the mallard duck napkin holder my dad had made a few months before he died.

The note said, "Gone to Union Square. Back late. Fend for yourself for dinner."

I didn't really feel like eating by myself. If Jake were anywhere near April Springs, I'd call him, but he was working a case on the Outer Banks, as far away as he could go and still be in North Carolina. I grabbed my cell phone and called Grace Gauge, who was my best friend, even if she was three pounds within her ideal body weight while I hadn't seen mine since elementary school. Grace was a sales rep for a national cosmetics company, and her hours were extremely flexible, something that worked perfectly with my own odd work schedule.

She picked up on the second ring. "Hey, where are you?"

"I'm in Charlotte, stuck in traffic. Where are you?"

"I'm home, and without anyone to eat with tonight. Any chance you want to grab something with me? It's my treat."

Grace said, "Suzanne, how can you be that sure I don't already have plans?"

"I'm so sorry. I didn't think. Do you have a big date or something?"

Grace laughed, then said, "No, but I was just wondering how you'd know that. Actually, dinner sounds great." I heard a horn honking in the background, and she added, "No matter how many times I come to Charlotte, I always seem to get lost."

"I know what you mean," I said. "How does five o'clock sound? Will you be back in town in time?" One of the problems with my donut shop's operating hours was that I could never eat at six or seven, like most folks in town. With a bedtime at eight, it didn't leave a great deal of time for regular dating, not that it had been an issue with Jake's crazy schedule.

She paused long enough to blow her own horn, then said, "I tell you what. I'll leave right now. That way I'll be back in plenty of time."

"Don't do it on my account. As soon as we hang up, I plan to take a nap, then grab a quick shower before we go."

Grace said, "Maybe I'll make a few more calls, then. I'll see you at five. And Suzanne?"

"Yes?"

"Thanks for calling. I was just teasing before."

"I know that," I said. "See you soon."

After we got off the phone, I thought about taking a shower before I laid down, but that would probably just wake me up, and what I needed at the moment more than anything else was a nap. I'd have to live with the smell of donuts in my hair and on my clothes for now. Honestly, I'd grown so accustomed to the scent that I barely noticed it anymore.

Instead of going up to my room to sleep though, I sprawled out on the couch, feeling decadent grabbing an afternoon nap. I was looking forward to dinner with Grace. It had been too long since we'd just hung out together, and I'd missed it. Maybe I'd splurge and take her to Napoli's, the place Jake and I liked to eat whenever he was in town.

For background noise, I flipped on the television, stopped on a station with a benign infomercial before dropping the sound next to nothing, and found myself quickly drifting off to sleep.

A persistent knock on the door brought me out of my deep sleep, and as I jolted upright on the couch, I felt disoriented for just a second. I glanced at the clock on the fireplace mantel as I got up, and saw that it was two minutes after five.

Grace was at the door, dressed in her work attire, a suit that was worth more than my entire wardrobe. In my opinion, one of the joys of owning a donut shop was not having to dress up for work, but my friend differed. Sometimes I think she worked just to support her clothes habit.

Grace's smile faded slightly as I opened the door, still rubbing my eyes.

She said, "I woke you, didn't I? Have you been asleep the entire time?"

I nodded. "Sorry, it's been a hard week. I've been putting in some extra hours at the shop practicing my beignets."

"Suzanne, let's do this another time. You must be exhausted."

I grabbed her arm and pulled her inside. "Are you kidding me? I haven't felt this good in months. Give me six minutes, and I'll be ready to go."

"Where are we eating?" she asked.

"I thought Napoli's might be fun. Like I said before, it's my treat."

"That nap did do you good, if you're really willing to pick up the check at a place like that."

I stuck my tongue out at her. "Just for that, you're not having dessert."

She put a hand over her heart. "I'll manage, somehow." Grace glanced at her watch, then said, "You'd better get moving. You're on the clock."

"It might not be six minutes exactly," I said as I headed for the stairs.

She tapped the face of her watch. "One second too long, and I get dessert after all. Something decadent, I think, and I might not share."

"If you do, I promise to take seven or eight minutes instead."

"That's a deal. Now shoo."

I went upstairs, took a lightning-fast shower, then picked out a decent outfit to wear so it wouldn't look like Grace was slumming by eating with me. I owned one really good dress, something I'd bought at Gabby's secondhand clothing shop, but I wasn't about to dress that nicely. I'd worn it out with Jake a few times, but I didn't feel like wearing it with Grace now.

As I came down the stairs, Grace was frowning.

I asked, "What's wrong?"

"You beat the clock by thirteen seconds," she said.

"Then cheer up. In honor of my quickness, we'll get a dessert to celebrate."

"I'm feeling better already," she said. "Do you mind if I drive?"

"You're not a big fan of my Jeep, are you?"

She shrugged. "It's fine sometimes, but I like riding in my BMW better."

"Fine, if you're willing to drive, I'm willing to ride in your fancy car."

As we drove to Union Square—a town thirty minutes away from April Springs—Grace asked, "So, are you excited about the big event tomorrow?"

"I am, but it's tempered with equal parts of nervousness and anxiety. The kitchen home tour is a pretty big deal."

"You're telling me. Don't forget why you're doing it."

"I know, it's a favor for a friend."

She shook her head. "I mean the bigger reason. It should raise a lot of money for the town. At first I thought twenty dollars a ticket was a little high for April Springs, but from what I've heard, the tour's almost sold out for the first weekend."

"I didn't need to hear that," I said. "I'm jittery enough as it is."

"Suzanne, you make the best donuts in our part of North Carolina. I'm sure whatever you make will be wonderful."

I started to tell her beignets were on the menu first, but she stopped me. "Don't say another word. I want to be surprised when I walk into Marge's kitchen next weekend. She must be an absolute wreck. Marge Rankin isn't exactly the socializing kind, is she?"

"She's trying. This is her way of coming out into April Springs society now that she's inherited some money. To be honest with you, I think she used the idea of a kitchen tour as an excuse to gut her old layout and replace everything. It's absolutely stunning now," I said.

"I'm excited to see it," Grace said. "I won't be able

to come this weekend, though. I've got a quick trip for business I have to make, and I'm leaving first thing in the morning."

"Another one of those resort sales meetings?" I asked.

She smiled as she explained, "I can't help it if they're mandatory. We're going to the beach, and I don't play golf, so after the meeting, I plan to do a little shopping."

"I wish I could come with you."

"You know you're always welcome," she said, "if you can ever leave that shop of yours."

After a few minutes, Grace glanced over at me and asked, "So, is Peg Masterson driving you crazy?"

I laughed. "Are you kidding? She thinks I'm unworthy to be demonstrating on the tour, so she keeps checking with me to see if I'm ready to drop out. I wouldn't give that nosy old biddy the satisfaction."

"Good for you," Grace said.

As she pulled into Napoli's parking lot in Union Square, she said, "Stand your ground with her, Suzanne. If Peg is at Marge's place first thing, don't take any guff from her."

"Easier said than done, don't you think? Maybe I'll bring her a plate of lemon-filled donuts to keep her off my back. She can't resist those." I took a deep breath, then added, "Let's talk about something more pleasant. Are you ready to have dinner?"

"You bet," Grace said as we got out and walked to the restaurant.

I'd expected the place to be nearly empty, as was almost always the case when I ate there, but I was surprised to find the vestibule jammed with diners waiting for a table.

"Should we go somewhere else?" Grace asked as she looked at the crowd. "I know how tight your schedule is."

"Maybe we should," I said as I started to back out of the door.

Angelica DeAngelis—the proprietress and matriarch of her four-daughter staff—saw me before I could get away.

"Excuse me, people, I need to get through," she said as she made her way through the crowd toward us. "Suzanne, your table is ready."

That was a neat trick, since I hadn't called for a reservation, and she had no idea we were coming.

An older man with bushy gray eyebrows that threatened to take over his face, said, "Hey, we were here first."

"But you failed to call ahead for a reservation, didn't you?" she said, clicking her tongue at him.

"We didn't think we'd need to this time of day," he grumbled.

"Then apparently, you were wrong," Angelica said as she led us through the mass of people.

Once we were past the cashier's station, I was surprised to see that the tables in the dining room were mostly empty.

I frowned at her as I said, "Angelica, you know you didn't have to show us preferential treatment."

She beamed at me as she said, "I don't have to do anything I don't want to, do I? It's my place, after all, isn't it?"

Grace said, "Suzanne, don't argue with the nice lady who's going to feed us."

Angelica smiled at her. "There's the voice of reason I've been hoping for."

I touched the owner's shoulder lightly. "I don't want you to lose any of your customers on my account."

She laughed bitterly. "Are you kidding me? One of my brilliant daughters who shall remain nameless decided we needed a promotional gimmick for our early hours. She offered a twenty-five-percent discount before six PM in our *April Springs Sentinel* ad, and this is what we get for it."

"I must have missed it," I said.

"I wish *they* had," she said as she gestured to the waiting area. "We're not making a dime on it, and I doubt many of these folks are going to be long-term customers."

"How long are you going to keep them waiting?" I asked.

"I'm tempted to wait until six," she said. "But I won't." As she walked back to the front, she said, "I'll send Maria to your table, but don't tarry over the menu. Things are going to be crazy pretty soon."

"We won't," I promised.

Maria came by thirty seconds later, with a rueful smile. "Hello, ladies. What can I get for you tonight?"

"Oh, dear," I said. "Let me guess. The ad was your idea."

She nodded briefly. "I thought it was a good plan at the time."

I patted her hand. "Don't worry, you'll be able to handle all of them."

"The crowd isn't what I'm worried about," she said. "It's my mother I'm concerned about. She's got a way of hanging onto things like this."

"It's in the rulebook they get when they have us," I said.

"I'd like to get my hands on a copy," she said. "But no time soon," Maria added when she realized what that implied.

After we ordered, Angelica led the crowd in, depositing diners as she moved through the room. She'd tried to leave us with as much space as she could, but it still felt claustrophobic having so many other people around us.

"So, is this what eating out is usually like?" I asked after Maria brought us our water and a carafe of house red wine.

"It's not that bad," Grace said. "In fact, some folks actually like being around other people."

"To each his own, I suppose," I said.

Grace took a sip of wine, then said, "So, tell me about the tour. Can you believe Peg and Marge are actually working together on something? I thought their feud would last forever."

"I'm not even certain they remember why they're fighting anymore," I said.

"Well, they've buried the hatchet, at least for the duration of the tour." Grace ate a small bite of bread, then added, "Should we talk about your love life?"

"Jake and I are fine, though I don't get to see him nearly enough. Why don't we talk about yours, instead?"

"I'm afraid it would be a pretty dull story. What is

wrong with the men around here, and why can't they see how much I have to offer?"

I said softly, "I think they're all just a little bit crazy, Jake included."

Grace laughed so hard she garnered the attention of some of the other diners, but we didn't care. It was good being out with my friend.

Grace said, "Enough about my love life, or lack of one. Can we talk about something else?"

"Sure. Why don't we talk about him?" I asked as I pointed behind her with the breadstick in my hand to a man who'd just walked in. It was the mysterious customer who'd come into the donut shop earlier that day.

She turned to see who I was talking about, and he must have noticed the attention.

Our eyes met for just an instant, and he smiled broadly at me before placing a to-go order with Angelica.

When I looked back at Grace, she was frowning at me. "Suzanne Hart, what have you been up to?"

"What?" I asked, as innocently as I could muster.

"You've been holding out on me," she said as our food arrived. "I saw the way you two just looked at each other."

I smiled at Maria as she approached with plates of food for us. "Look, Grace, it's time to eat."

I reached for my fork, and Grace grabbed my arm. "Not one bite until you tell me who he is."

I laughed first, then I admitted, "He came by the donut shop for coffee this morning. That's all I know. I swear. He looks familiar, but I can't for the life of me figure out where I've seen him before."

She looked into my eyes and could see I was telling the truth. "He seemed pretty interested in you."

"Not enough to come over to our table and say hello," I said, dismissing the idea. "Now can I have that hand back? I'm hungry, and my lasagna's getting cold."

She released me, and as I took that first heavenly bite, I couldn't help wondering how the mystery man had managed to show up in my life twice in the same day, and why I couldn't remember when I'd met him before. I had a nagging feeling that our paths had crossed in the past, but I was no closer to knowing when that might have been than earlier that day.

For now, it was just going to have to remain a mystery.

I didn't have time for mysteries at the moment, though.

Tomorrow would arrive soon enough, and I had a feeling I was going to have my hands full with my stop on the kitchen tour.

I just didn't realize how true that feeling was about to be.

SUZANNE'S BASIC BEIGNETS WITH A TWIST

A flaky, delicious, and classy take on the normal everyday donut. These take a little longer to prepare, but they are well worth the time and effort! Some folks think they're reminiscent of funnel cakes, but it's a completely different taste and texture. While they might not technically be the classic New Orleans style of beignet, Suzanne likes them, and so does my family!

INGREDIENTS

- 2 packets active dry yeast ($1/2$ oz. total)
- $1^1/2$ cups warm water
- $1/2$ cup white sugar
- $1/2$ teaspoon salt
- 2 eggs
- 1 cup evaporated milk
- 6–7 cups all-purpose flour
- $1/4$ cup shortening
- $1/4$ cup confectioners' sugar
- Frying oil, 360 degrees F.

DIRECTIONS

Dissolve the yeast in warm water, then add the sugar, salt, eggs, and evaporated milk, and stir it all together thoroughly.

Mix in about half of the flour and beat the mixture again until smooth.

Add the shortening, and then the remaining 3 cups of flour. I like to break with tradition here and add enough flour to work lightly on a board, adding a little oil if the dough gets too dry.

Cover the dough and chill it for at least an hour, but you can wait until the next day if you'd like, though be warned, it will keep raising and might take on a life of its own.

Roll out the dough ¼- to ⅛-inch thick. Cut it into squares 2½ to 3 inches. Though it's not the traditional shape, I like to use my ravioli cutter to make rounds.

Fry them in hot oil for two minutes on each side, or until they're done, then dust with confectioner's sugar and eat. I like these best served warm. You can also add fillings like jam or pudding to these, but my family likes them plain.

Yield: 3–4 dozen

CHAPTER 2

"Suzanne, you're early," Marge said as she let me into her house through the back door the next morning.

It was true that I wasn't due to show up for another half hour, but I hadn't been able to wait a minute longer. I'd had the perfect opportunity to sleep in before the kickoff of the kitchen tour, but I'd lain in bed tossing for hours, waiting until a decent hour when most folks got up. By six AM I couldn't take it anymore, so I put on some sweats and a T-shirt and took a walk in the park that bordered our house. After a long shower when I got back home and more time spent picking out what I was going to wear than I'd ever taken in my life, I still had too much time to kill. Even dawdling over breakfast with my mother just killed an hour, and though I hadn't planned to be at Marge's until nine, I was knocking on her door at twenty-seven minutes past eight. I had to smile when I saw the fresh, oversized corsage pinned to her elegant dress. If her attire was from Gabby's shop, it had been very lightly worn.

"I'm sorry," I said as I glanced at my watch. "If you'd like, I can come back later. I'm sure I can find something to do in town." It had taken every bit of my self-restraint to keep from popping in on Emma at the donut shop, but I'd promised myself that I wouldn't do it, and I was going to keep my word.

Marge frowned at me for a second, but then her creased lips were wiped clean with a smile. "Now don't be silly. Of course you can come in. I've got a surprise for you," she added as she led me inside.

"I'm not certain I'm up for any surprises today," I said as I followed her into the house. Though the tour featured kitchens only, it was clear that Marge had realized she had to spruce up the rest of her house as well. There were fresh flowers throughout the place, and a shine on every surface.

I asked, "Did you buy all new furniture, too?" There were some pieces that I didn't recognize from my last visit, and an Oriental rug I knew was new. She must have spent a fortune.

"No," she said simply.

"Marge, I was just here a few days ago, remember?"

She shook her head slightly, then said, "Fine. If you must know, I contacted a staging company in Charlotte. They're responsible for all of this."

I looked around at the elegant antiques. "Are you trying to tell me that this furniture was all in a play?"

She laughed. "Not that kind of stage, Suzanne. The company helps sell million-dollar houses, and they stage each room with their own furniture to help their clients get top dollar. It was much more reasonable than actually replacing my things, and I didn't have to lift a finger to have it done." Marge bit her lip, then added, "Well, that's not entirely true. I wrote them a rather substantial check, but I think it was worth it, don't you?"

As I followed her into the kitchen, I added, "The entire place looks really great. I think it was money well spent."

"Thank you," she said shyly. "I wanted everyone to remember this stop on the tour. I hope you'll like what I got for you."

"You didn't get me a corsage, too, did you?" I asked, envisioning wearing a floral arrangement like hers on my blouse as I tried to cook. It was a step up from what I usually wore when I worked, but I wasn't ready for flowers.

"Of course not," she said. "Flowers wouldn't do at all, would they? I did get you something, though."

She reached into the pantry and pulled out a very nice chef's smock and hat—pristine white—starched and ironed without a wrinkle in sight. I shuddered when I thought about what would happen to it if I wore it working in her kitchen.

"I appreciate the thought, honestly, I do," I said, backpedaling for something to say. "I'm just not sure I could ever live up to it."

"Nonsense," Marge said. "I think you'll look delightful in it. I won't take no for an answer, Suzanne," she added as she shoved the garb in my face.

I couldn't stand there refusing to accept her offering, so I reached a hand out and took the smock and hat from her. I peeked inside the top and saw that unfortunately, she'd bought the right size.

"How'd you know my size?" I asked as I slipped it on over my blouse.

"I can't take all the credit. Your mother was most helpful."

"I just bet she was," I said. Funny, we'd just had breakfast together, but she hadn't mentioned this at all.

Marge must have seen my expression cloud over. "Now, Suzanne, don't blame her. I asked Dorothy for her help, and she was quite sweet about it." She frowned at the smock, then said, "It wasn't my idea in the first place. As a matter of fact, it was suggested rather strongly to me that I do this for you." She let out a deep breath, then said, "You don't have to wear it if you don't want to. It's fine with me."

As I slid the towering white hat into place on my head, I said, "Don't be silly. It's perfect for the tour."

"I'm so glad you like it," she said. "I do think it's rather smart."

I took the smock and hat off again, happy to be rid of it, at least for the moment. Before Marge could protest, I said, "It's much too nice to do the prep work in. Don't worry, I'll put it on when the tour starts."

"I thought you were supposed to demonstrate making the beignets during the tour," she said.

"I am, but since I'll be making them all day, I thought I'd get a jump on things by measuring out batches of some of the ingredients I'll be using to save time. Surely that's acceptable."

"I suppose," Marge said, as her doorbell rang. "Excuse me, I'll be right back. No one's supposed to be here yet. Who could it be?"

I left her to it, since I had problems of my own. Butterflies were starting to dance in my stomach, and I was beginning to regret the heavy breakfast my mother had forced on me. I didn't usually get nervous before I cooked, but then again, I normally didn't do it with an audience, either. There was just one solution; I needed to get to work so I could forget about the audience that would be coming soon enough. I was scooping out quantities of flour when Marge came back into the kitchen, trailing Peg Masterson, the entirely unpleasant head of the tour.

"Suzanne, why aren't you wearing your smock and hat? Marge, you did as I asked and bought them, didn't you?"

"Of course I did," she said defensively.

"I wanted to keep them pristine as long as I could," I said. "So, I have you to thank for my new outfit." It figured that Peg had butted into our demonstration, even down to the clothes I'd be wearing.

Peg looked at me as if I'd lost my mind, which I was starting to realize I probably had by ever agreeing to this in the first place.

She snapped, "Nonsense, those belong to your sponsor. I arranged to have all of the *chefs* wear them. It gives the tour a sense of continuity." I swear, she had to choke out the word *chef* when she looked at me, but somehow she managed to do it without flinching.

I shrugged. "I'll put it on once the tour starts."

"I suppose that will be all right," Peg said as she surveyed the granite countertop where I'd been working. "What's this?"

I held up each ingredient as I identified it. "This is flour, and this is sugar. Now this is . . ."

"I know what they are, Suzanne. What I don't know is why you are starting before we've opened the tour."

I couldn't believe this woman. Was she going to be hovering around me all day? "Peg, I'm just measuring out some of the things I'll need ahead of time. It will make the demonstration go smoother, trust me."

She shook her head. "I absolutely forbid it. The entire purpose of this tour is for our patrons to see the kitchens in real working conditions. You mustn't start anything until we open the doors."

"What if no one's here when I start?" I asked. "Do I have to sit around waiting for an audience before I start preparing my food?"

"Don't be ridiculous," Peg said. "You may begin precisely at ten A.M., and not a moment before."

"Fine," I said as I dumped some of the flour I'd already measured back into the container. "What am I supposed to do in the meantime?"

"I'd suggest you find a quiet place to relax and take full of advantage of it while you can. You're going to be on your feet constantly for six hours once the tour begins."

"I do more than that every day in my shop," I said. "Six hours is going to feel like a vacation."

Peg smiled cruelly. "Yes, but have you ever done it with an audience? I'm sure it's not as easy as it may seem."

I nodded. I hated to admit it, but she had a point. Then, I had a thought. "You're not staying here the entire time the tour's going on, are you?"

Peg laughed, but there wasn't an ounce of warmth in the sound. "Suzanne, as important as you must think you are, I have seven kitchens open on the tour today. I simply wanted to stop by to check on your setup, and to brief you one last time on the rules." As she looked around, she added, "It's a good thing I did, too."

I gave her my most artificial smile. "Well, you've done that, so why don't you move on to the next vic . . . I mean kitchen on your list."

I swear, I saw Marge stifle a giggle when she realized I'd been about to say victim. She'd been surprisingly quiet during my conversation with Peg, and I wondered how the tour organizer had managed to intimidate her so much.

After Peg was gone, I said, "Well, I for one am certainly glad we got all of that cleared up. It could have been an absolute disaster if I'd continued measuring out ingredients. What was I thinking?" I'd done my best to imitate Peg's nasal voice, but though I wasn't all that effective a mimic, Marge had understood the impression.

"She's certainly unique, isn't she," Marge asked.

"I'm kind of surprised you ever agreed to do this," I said. "How did you two manage to bury the hatchet?"

She waved her hand in the air. "Peg is harmless."

"That's not the first word to describe her that pops into my mind." Seeing coffee brewing on one of the countertops, I asked, "Is there any chance I could get a cup? I have a feeling Peg's right about one thing. It's going to be a long day, and I might not have much time for breaks once we get started."

Marge said, "Where are my manners? Why don't you sit over on the sofa, and I'll bring you a cup."

"I can get it myself," I protested.

"Nonsense. Let me wait on you. Now go sit."

I did as I was told, and sat on a sofa in the nearby

sitting area where I could look outside at Marge's landscaping. While it was true she skimped on buying things for herself, when it came to her flower garden, Marge hadn't held back. An explosion of blooms dotted the landscape outside, and a fountain centered on a delightful stone patio supplied a constant, aerated stream for the birds. Several feeders were arranged near my vantage point, and as I watched, a Carolina Chickadee swooped in for a quick black oil sunflower seed before darting off again.

"I think I found the best seat in the house," I said as Marge walked over with two thick mugs.

"I had the entire landscape in back designed just for that spot," she said as she took another seat.

"Then you should sit here," I said as I started to get up.

"Suzanne, you're here doing me a wondrous favor. Besides, I get to enjoy this view every morning. I can share it with you today."

"I appreciate that," I said. I wasn't about to fight her on it, especially when I noticed a bright red male cardinal come in for some seed of his own. Instead of making a hit and run on the feeder, though, this fella was obviously more interested in sampling a few of the offerings before giving up his spot in line.

"Who's that?" I asked as I saw part of the back of a head peek around the corner of the courtyard.

"Is someone out there?" Marge asked as she stared where I'd pointed. "They know they're supposed to wait at the front door."

She ducked outside, but was back just as quickly. It was clear that whoever had been out there was now gone.

"Suzanne, did you see who it was?"

"No, I just caught a glimpse of red hair."

"Was it a man or a woman?" she asked.

"Honestly, whoever it was had short hair, but that's all I could say from the little bit I saw."

Marge frowned. "Peg should be doing a better job of keeping people in line."

After she settled back down beside me, I said, "Marge, may I ask you something?"

She looked surprised, but nodded. "I owe you that much, at least."

I wasn't satisfied with her terse explanation about her relationship patch with Peg, and if I was ever going to find out what had happened, this was the time. I knew it wasn't any of my business, but that didn't keep me from dying to know the truth. I took a sip of coffee, then asked, "Why has there been bad blood between you and Peg for so long, and why did you ever agree to do the kitchen tour?"

"That's two questions," Marge said.

"Indulge me," I said as I sipped my coffee. It was a first-rate blend, and I wondered if she'd bought it and brewed it just for the tour.

Marge stood and started to pace around the large space. "I don't believe I even know where to begin. Peg and I have always been at odds over one thing or another. I suppose it all goes back to our fathers."

"They knew each other?" I asked as my attention was diverted from the backyard habitat for a moment.

"I should say so. They were business partners once upon a time, and I'm afraid it ended badly."

"What happened?"

Marge said, "Peg's father, Daniel, grew tired of the

investment house they were running, and from the way my father used to tell it, he'd done more than his part to run the company into the ground. One day Daniel came to my father and asked him to buy him out. My father agreed that it would be a good idea, but refused the outlandish price Daniel put on his half of the business. After much arguing, Father finally agreed to turn over the keys and title to his new car, a Cadillac that was the talk of the town. My father told me Daniel's share of the business wasn't even worth that, but he wanted to be rid of a partner who'd become dead weight. The papers were signed, the car exchanged hands, and my father proceeded to work eighty-hour weeks until he built his firm into a place he could be proud of. A year after the transaction, Daniel drove while he'd been drinking, and he crashed the Cadillac into a tree, totaling it beyond repair and killing himself in the process."

I'd heard stories growing up that Daniel Masterson had died in a car wreck, but I hadn't realized the history behind it.

"How awful."

"Not as bad as how Peg's mother acted. Shelly had to blame someone for her husband's death, someone besides the man himself, so she focused on my father. Peg must have grown up with stories of the evil man who'd stolen her father's business, so it's a wonder she speaks to me at all."

"It's tragic, though, isn't it?"

"On more levels than I can convey," Marge said. "Last year Peg talked me into serving on some of her favorite committees, but I don't have time for that anymore. My life these days is rather full without worrying about fundraisers and benefits." She glanced at her watch, then said, "Look at the time. We'll be opening in ten minutes! Suzanne, do you think anyone will come?"

"Of course they will," I said. "You're taking tickets at the front door, right?"

"If anyone shows up," she said.

"Why don't we go peek and see if anyone's out there waiting to get in?"

Marge looked surprised by the suggestion. "What if they see us?"

"Come on. It will be fun."

We slipped through the kitchen, and I started for the front door when Marge touched my shoulder. "Let's go into the living room. We can get a better view from there."

I followed her into yet another room of the big house, and she ducked behind the curtain first. When she came back out, she looked positively stunned.

I felt my heart start to sink. It was beginning to feel like I was going to be making beignets all by myself. "What's the matter? Did no one come?"

"Look for yourself," she said.

I brushed past her and glanced outside. There were at least sixty people on the sidewalk and stoop waiting in line to get in, all of them dressed in their Sunday best.

"I'd better go get ready," I said, more nervous than ever at the prospect of cooking in front of such a large audience.

Marge must have seen the terror on my face. She patted my arm as she said, "Don't worry, you'll be fine. Make me proud."

"I'll do my best," I said as I hurried back to the kitchen so I could don the smock and hat before my audience was admitted. As I settled the tall hat down in place over my hair, I gave myself a little pep talk. There was no reason to be nervous. I made donuts for a living, and the beignets I was about to prepare were very much donuts, despite their fancy name and appearance.

Taking a deep breath, I trotted out my brightest smile and prepared for the mob of visitors.

"If you'll all quiet down, I'll get started," I said. Even in the spacious kitchen and the adjoining sitting area, the room was packed with folks eager to see Marge's kitchen, and while they were there, watch me make a pastry.

Once they settled down, I said, "Today I'll be making beignets, and though they are traditionally made in the shape of squares, triangles, and even diamonds, though they lack the hole we're used to, they are donuts just the same. I've been told that even the name, in Cajun, means 'French donut.' Using flour, sugar, shortening, milk, eggs, salt, and yeast, the result is a spectacularly decadent treat, drenched in powdered sugar as it cools for a final touch of elegance." I held a photo I'd taken of some of the beignets I'd made practicing for today, and they looked suitably impressed. So far, so good.

I went on. "My recipe today uses baking powder instead of the traditional yeast. It's a shortcut I've come up with for our demonstration. When I make these in my shop, I prefer using yeast so they have time to rise, but these are quite tasty as well, as you all will soon find out."

As I laid the ingredients out on the counter, I was about to start mixing when a scream pierced through the room.

"She's dead," a voice cried out behind the crowd, and all eyes turned to the garden, visible through the windows where I'd watched the birds flitting in and out before. I didn't need to see the victim's face to know who was lying there beneath the feeder. I'd seen that outfit before; just that morning, in fact.

Someone had murdered Peg Masterson, and I knew that my time with the Kitchens Extraordinaire tour had ended before it had barely even started.

As everyone rushed to the window, I said loudly, "You all need to calm down. There's no reason to panic." I don't know why I said it, but it seemed to get their attention.

An older man in informal attire headed for the door to the garden.

"You shouldn't go out there," I said.

He barely slowed down as he said, "I'm a doctor. She might not be dead. I'm going to check on her."

I couldn't argue with that. "Fine, go ahead, but everyone else needs to stay right where they are." I said to the rest of the crowd, "Somebody needs to call Chief Martin and get him over here." That was one telephone call I had no desire to make. The police chief and I had clashed too many times in the past, and I had no desire to add anything to the list, though I knew he'd be cornering me soon enough.

A dozen hands went for their cell phones, and I looked around for Marge. She'd be shattered by a murder happening at her home, no matter how she might have felt about the victim.

But she was nowhere in sight.

I started toward the rest of the house to look for her when she bumped into me coming down the stairs.

"Where have you been?" I asked.

"I had to change my clothes. Silly me, I accidentally spilled coffee on my suit after I took up the tickets at the door." She noticed everyone staring out the window. "What's going on? Why aren't you making beignets?"

"I'm afraid there's been an accident," I said, not knowing how else to tell her that her chief rival was most likely dead.

Marge grabbed my hands and quickly looked me over. "Are you hurt? What happened? I've been worried about that hot oil all week. Oh, dear. Was it one of our visitors?"

I took my hands back from her. "Marge, I'm fine, and no one was injured during the demonstration. Something happened outside."

She craned to get a look out the window, but I stepped in front of her and blocked her view.

"Suzanne, move over. I can't see. Who is it? It's my house; I have a right to know what happened."

I couldn't argue with that, so I didn't try to stop her as she stepped around me. After a moment of silence, she asked softly, "Is that Peg?"

"It appears to be," I said.

"What happened to her?" Marge asked. The flat tone in her voice was something that caught me completely off guard. It was as if she'd just learned that oranges were six for a dollar.

"Marge, it looks bad."

My statement caught her attention. "For me? Just because it's my house? I didn't kill her, Suzanne. You can vouch for me. I've been with you all morning."

I hated myself for saying it, but I had to let her know what was on my mind before Chief Martin arrived. "Marge, I didn't see you while I was setting up, and you weren't there when I started my demonstration. There's at least fifteen minutes when you were out of my sight completely."

She looked at me as though I'd just stabbed her in the chest with a butcher knife. "What are you talking about? I was right here the entire time."

I shrugged. "I'm sorry, but I can't vouch for you with the police. You just told me yourself that you were upstairs changing your outfit."

Marge frowned. "Suzanne, if you're going to be that way, then I can't tell them you were with me the entire time, either, can I?" There was an odd expression on her face that I had trouble reading. Was she trying to imply I'd had something to do with what had happened to Peg?

"I've got a great alibi. I was standing in front of a crowd of sixty people," I protested, not believing that she was trying to turn the tables on me.

"They weren't here the entire time. You were alone in the kitchen when I started taking tickets on the front steps, and there's a French door that leads straight out to that patio. How long does it take to kill someone, Suzanne? You could have done it and I never would have even seen you slip out the door."

I shook my head. "This isn't getting us anywhere. I didn't kill her."

"Neither did I," Marge said.

I patted her shoulder gently. "Hey, I never said you did. Honest, I don't think you killed Peg, Marge."

Her eyes began to melt tears. "You don't? Truly? But I thought that was what you just said."

"No, what I said was that I couldn't give you an alibi for the entire time. I just realized that you're right. It works both ways. I guess the chief is going to have to look hard at both of us."

"You didn't have a motive, though, did you?" Marge asked softly.

"Everybody in town had a motive, when it comes down to it. Peg wasn't exactly Miss Congeniality, was she?"

Marge shrugged. "I know most folks weren't all that fond of her, but did anyone else really have a reason to kill her?"

That line of reasoning surprised me. "I don't know. Did you have a motive yourself? Is there something you're not telling me?"

She looked startled by the question. "Me? No, of course not. Peg had a beef with me and my family; it wasn't the other way around."

"Then that's what you should tell the chief," I said.

"Tell the chief what?" I heard a voice ask that was much too familiar to me. Chief Martin, our head of local law enforcement and a man who'd kindled his crush on my mother like a hearth fire, walked into the room. He'd put on some weight recently, though he tried his best to hide it with a jacket he didn't need.

The chief must have been a nice-looking man when he'd been younger, but the years had not been as kind to him as they had been to my mother. I couldn't imagine the two of them ever dating, but then that was ancient history, a time in their high school lives that was long gone, and never to be repeated, according to my mother.

"We were going to tell you that we've been waiting for you," I said.

"I got here three minutes after someone called," he said. "How much faster did you expect me to be?" He looked through the doorway into the kitchen and lounging area. "You pulled in quite a crowd," he said in disgust. "That isn't going to make it any easier."

I didn't know what to say to that. The chief and I had our differences, most of them stemming back to the time I was born. He'd resented my dad's presence in Momma's life, and I was a testament to the fact that she'd chosen someone else. Things weren't exactly all warm and fuzzy between us before my propensity to show up near dead bodies began.

Finally, he turned back and stared at me. "Are you telling me they all actually saw what happened?" I could tell in his voice that he was hoping this one would be wrapped up before lunch.

"As far as I know, no one saw a thing," I admitted. "They were all watching me."

He looked into the kitchen. "Then that had to give you the perfect view of the murder, didn't it," he said.

"If it happened while I was giving my demonstration, I didn't see it," I confessed.

"Suzanne, how could you not notice?" he asked fiercely.

"I was busy talking, measuring, and trying not to throw up," I said.

The chief turned to Marge. "I suppose you didn't see anything, either."

"Not a thing. Sorry," she said.

"Great. Why don't you two go on in with everybody else. I just want to have to say this once."

Marge and I walked in after the chief, and the second my audience realized that the police chief was there, they converged on us like we were giving out free samples of food.

As Chief Martin was being pelted with questions from a dozen different directions, he held up his hands. "Quiet, everybody. I need you to listen to me."

Everyone stopped talking, and I envied the chief's ability to silence them so easily. I looked over his shoulder and saw the doctor walking away from the body as he shook his head, and that's when I realized that Peg was indeed dead. Was there any chance it was from a heart attack, and not a homicide? I wanted to go out and ask, but I doubted that the chief of police of April Springs would have appreciated it. He tended to frown on my involvement with his police investigations, especially when it involved a dead body or two.

"First off, did anyone here see anything out on the patio?" he asked.

The silence continued. "Fine. If there are no witnesses, I'd like you all to give Officer Strickland your names and addresses, and then you can go."

"Is the kitchen tour canceled?" a well-dressed woman in back asked.

"It is at this stop," the chief said.

"What about everywhere else?" the man with her asked. "We've got tickets, and if we can't go to the other houses, I want my money back."

"I don't know anything at all about the kitchen tour. Why don't you all go find out? File out one at a time, and have some identification with you when you do. The officer will have to verify that each of you have a current ID."

"What if we don't?" an older woman dressed in her Sunday finest asked.

"Then I'll have to vouch for you myself if you want to get out of here before dark. Now form an orderly line, and we'll get you out of here as fast as we can."

The group started to do as they'd been told, but Marge and I followed the chief as he walked, not to the window, but to where I'd set up my cooking station.

As he stood there, he said, "Suzanne, are you honestly telling me you didn't see anything from here?"

I looked toward the window from what had been my vantage point, and clearly saw a police officer kneeling over the body taking pictures. "I'm sorry. There were a lot of people blocking my view. I realize it doesn't look good, but I honestly didn't see a thing."

"I've heard that before, haven't I?" Chief Martin said snidely.

I chose not to respond to that. Beside me, Marge asked, "Should Suzanne and I join the line?"

Martin shook his head. "Don't worry about it. You two are already at the top of my list."

"As witnesses, or as suspects?" I asked, before I realized that it wasn't the most delicate thing I could have said.

That got his attention. "Why, did either one of you have a reason to kill her?"

Before Marge could answer, I said, "You don't even know if she died of natural causes, or if it was murder. Aren't we all jumping the gun a little here?"

He stroked his chin, then said, "You know what? You're right. I need more information. Both of you should wait right here."

As the chief walked outside toward his officers, Marge took my hands in hers, and I could feel that her skin was clammy and icy cold. "Suzanne, I'm not afraid to admit that I'm terrified by all of this."

"It would be odd if you weren't," I said.

"Do you mean that you're afraid, too?"

I looked her in the eye. "I'm shaking like a leaf inside."

"You certainly don't show it," Marge said.

"Trust me, it's all bluff and bluster. I'm as scared as I could be, if that makes you feel any better."

Marge smiled sadly. "Oddly enough, it does."

"Good. I'm glad I could help, then."

Ten minutes later, the chief walked back in as the line started to dwindle to just a few people. He wasn't smiling, but then again, I could count the times I'd seen his grin on one hand in all the years I'd known him, so it wasn't necessarily a bad thing.

"Suzanne, we need to talk," he said gruffly.

That didn't sound good. "What about? What's going on?"

"You need to come outside with me," he said.

"Aren't you even going to tell me why?" His tone of voice was scaring me even more than it had before, though I hadn't imagined that would be possible.

"Outside," he repeated, and I followed him meekly through the door. I glanced back at Marge, and she was looking at me in a way I wasn't entirely comfortable with. Was that open suspicion in her gaze?

Once we were out in the garden, I found myself avoiding looking directly at the body, as if it were the sun, and I was in danger of being blinded by the sight.

"Does that look familiar?" the chief asked.

"It's Peg, I knew that when I was inside," I said, still not looking down at the body.

"That's not what I'm talking about," he said.

That must have been when he noticed that I was doing everything in my power not to look at Peg.

"Suzanne, no matter how unpleasant this might be for you, I need you to look at the body. More importantly, I need you to identify what's in her hand."

I took a deep breath, then steeled myself for an up-close view of the body.

I had to look twice when I saw what was clutched in her dead hand.

Hearing the trembling in my voice, but not being able to stop it, I said, "It's clearly from my shop. From the look of it, it's lemon-filled."

I saw that Peg was holding a donut with one bite missing that had to have come from Donut Hearts.

And I knew that at that moment, I was in more trouble than I ever had been in my life.

SUZANNE'S GLAZED YEAST DONUTS

These yeast donuts are delicious, and as a bonus, they're easy to make. Well worth a try in your own kitchen. I like to cut out donut rounds and holes, and sometimes I use my ravioli cutter to make round long johns that are perfect for filling!

INGREDIENTS

- ¾ cup scalded milk
- ½ cup granulated sugar
- ¼ teaspoon salt
- 1 packet active dry yeast (¼ oz)
- ½ cup warm water
- 4–6 cups sifted all-purpose flour
- 2 teaspoons nutmeg
- 2 teaspoons cinnamon
- ⅓ cup margarine
- 2 eggs, beaten
- Frying oil, 360 degrees F

Glaze Recipe
- 2 cups confectioners' sugar
- 6 tablespoons milk

DIRECTIONS

Scald the milk, then add the granulated sugar and salt, stirring the mixture until the dry ingredients dissolve. After the mixture cools, in a separate bowl add the cinnamon and nutmeg to the flour, then add two cups of the dry ingredient blend to the liquid and mix.

In a third bowl, dissolve the yeast in warm water, stir it into the milk and flour mixture, then add the butter and eggs. Add the remaining flour $1/2$ cup at a time. When the dough is firm, knead it 5 minutes on a floured surface. The amount of flour needed depends on many factors, so keep working it in until you have a firm dough. Place into an oiled bowl and cover for about 30 minutes.

On a lightly floured surface, roll the dough out to $1/4$- to $1/2$-inch thickness. Cut it into circles using a donut cutter, then set the rounds aside to rise for another 30 minutes.

Add the donuts to the hot oil a few at a time. Cook on each side until golden brown, then remove to drain on paper towels. Glaze while warm, or just sprinkle with sugar.

To make the glaze, stir together the confectioners' sugar and 6 tablespoons milk until smooth. Dip warm donuts into glaze, and then set them aside to cool.

Yield: 12–18 donuts

CHAPTER 3

"How can you be so sure it's one of yours?" the chief asked me.

"Believe me, when you've been making donuts as long as I have, you get to the point where you recognize your own work." I took a deep breath, then asked, "Is that what killed her?"

"We're going to have to leave that up to the medical examiner, but until I hear otherwise, that's the assumption I'm going to go on."

"I guess that makes me a suspect," I said.

"I'm not about to say that just yet," he said. "I just wanted to see if it was one of your donuts, or if it was something she bought at the grocery store."

"Now you know," I said. "Here's the thing, though, Chief. What possible reason would I have to kill her?"

"I'm not saying you did it," Chief Martin said, the ragged edge of his voice showing his exasperation with me.

"You're not saying I didn't do it, either."

He just shrugged, which wasn't a response that would have satisfied anyone, least of all me.

As I moved away, I stepped on something that made a crinkling sound. I looked at the bottom of my shoe and saw a cellophane candy wrapper on the ground. I started to pick it up when the chief grabbed my hand.

"What do you think you're doing?" I asked.

"Trying to stop you from contaminating the crime scene," he said. "Is that wrapper yours?"

"No, I don't litter," I said.

He got out an evidence bag and picked up the wrapper with a pair of tweezers.

"Is that important?" I asked him.

"I don't know yet. Right now, I'm still looking for any evidence I can find."

He had work to do, I knew that, but that didn't mean I had stick around any longer than I needed to. Being so close to Peg's dead body was really starting to get to me. "If that's all, can I go?"

"I'd like you to hang around a little, if you don't mind," the chief said.

"Fine, but can I at least go back inside the house?"

He thought about that for a few seconds, then said, "Okay, I don't see what that could hurt. Just don't wander off until I've had a chance to talk to you again."

"I'll be inside," I said as I rushed for the door.

Marge was waiting for me near the door. "What happened? Does he know what killed Peg yet?"

"He can't be sure, but it looks like one of my donuts did it." I couldn't believe how bizarre that sounded coming out of my mouth.

"She was poisoned?" Marge asked in a hushed tone of voice.

"The chief says it's too soon to tell," I said, fighting to hold onto the last shred of credibility that I could. "He won't know that for a while."

"So, what happens in the meantime?"

I said, "I'm supposed to wait here for him. You don't have to keep me company, though. I don't mind being by myself."

"Nonsense, there's nowhere else I need to be," she said, "Especially with the exhibition canceled."

"I'm so sorry about that."

"It's not your fault," Marge said softly.

"I didn't kill her," I said with a little more force than I probably should have used with her.

"I'm sorry, Suzanne. I didn't mean to imply that I thought you did."

I looked at her and saw that she was nearing tears. It was the worst thing that could happen to her much-anticipated coming-out party. "Marge, it's going to be all right."

"I wish I could believe you," she said.

I was thankful to have her there with me. If I was being honest with myself, I'd take any company at the moment over being alone.

After twenty minutes, there was no one left in the kitchen but me, Marge, and an April Springs police officer. He was a relatively new hire, and we hadn't gotten the chance to get to know each other yet. It wasn't the best circumstances for developing a bond today, either.

The chief finally came back in, and honestly looked surprised to find Marge sitting with me on the sofa.

"You can go somewhere else in the house, if you'd like," he said.

"If you don't mind, I'll stay here with Suzanne."

The chief shook his head. "There's no need. She's getting ready to leave."

That surprised me. "Where am I going?" I had visions of being led from the house in handcuffs, something that made me want to throw up.

He frowned slightly. "I don't care, but there's no need for you to hang around here. I'm done with you."

"For good?" I asked.

He shook his head. "I wouldn't say that, but I would say for now."

"Okay, I can live with that," I said.

I turned to Marge. "You don't have to stay here, either. Why don't you come to the donut shop with me? I'll treat you to cup of coffee and a bear claw."

Chief Martin interrupted. "Actually, that's the one place you can't go right now, Suzanne." He glanced at his watch, then said, "Give my men an hour, and then you can go back to your shop."

I hadn't been expecting that. "What? They're searching my business? I thought you needed a warrant for that."

"We do, and that donut was all it took to get one. Funny, I thought you'd welcome a search of your business. How else can we clear your name from our list of suspects?"

"You didn't have to get a warrant. I would have gladly given you my permission to search my shop."

"It's neater this way," he said.

I started for the door, but then I realized that Marge wasn't behind me. "Aren't you coming? I'm sure we can find a cup of coffee somewhere."

She shook her head. "I think I'll stay here, if you don't mind," she said.

I wasn't about to argue with her. I just wanted to get out of there. I walked out to my Jeep, got in, started it, then sat there wondering where I should go. I wasn't about to head home, for fear of the grilling I would get from my mother, and I'd been ordered not to go back to Donut Hearts. Grace was out of town on her business trip for a few days, so I couldn't call her.

I noticed the new policeman watching me, so I put the Jeep in gear and drove off. I might not be able to go back to the donut shop, but I could do the next best thing. I was going to the Boxcar grill to get some coffee, and keep an eye on what was going on in my shop from across the tracks.

The owner, Trish Granger, frowned when I walked into the Boxcar, an old train car that she had converted into a diner. One long wall offered booths, while the other sported a long counter for diners to sit while they ate. An attached structure housed the kitchen, so stepping into the train car was a little like stepping back in time. Trish was in her early thirties, neat and trim, with her blonde hair in a constant ponytail.

"You're having a hard day, aren't you?" she asked.

There were few customers in the diner at 10:30 in the morning.

It was a slow time for me normally at the donut shop as well. "Not as tough as Peg Masterson is having," I said as I slid onto a stool near her. "How'd you find out what happened so quickly?"

"Emma came over here when she couldn't get hold of you. She was pretty upset when the police shut the place down."

I'd wondered why she hadn't warned me about what was happening at my shop. "Why didn't she call me?"

Trish shrugged. "You tell me. She said her calls to you went straight to your voice mail. Is your phone on?"

I felt like such an idiot as I dove into my purse and pulled out my cell phone. I'd turned it off so it wouldn't interfere with my demonstration, and I'd forgotten to turn it back on in all the turmoil that had followed.

"Hang on a second," I said as I saw that I had two dozen voice mail messages since last night. That would take too long, so I punched in Emma's number, and she picked up before it had time to finish the first ring.

"Suzanne, are you all right?" she asked the second she answered. Emma had explained that she had a song for each of her callers to identify them with when they called. My song was "Ain't No Sunshine," because we worked most of our hours in the middle of the night.

"I'm fine. How are you doing?"

She started crying as she spoke, and I knew she was really upset. In the years Emma and I had worked together, I couldn't recall a time that I'd ever seen her cry. "I'm so sorry. They shut me down."

"It's okay," I said. "The chief told me what they were doing. I'm just upset with myself that I didn't call you to warn you about it."

"It's not your fault," she said as she fought her tears. "Suzanne, what are they looking for?"

"My guess is poison," I said softly, but evidently not quietly enough, because Trish's eyebrows shot upward when I said it.

Emma said, "Oh, no. Do they think you killed that dreadful woman?" She sniffled again, then added, "I shouldn't speak ill of the dead. Forget I said that."

"It's understandable, given the circumstances. I'm not sure what Chief Martin thinks, but I've got a hunch that if he has a list right now, I'm bound to be somewhere near the top."

"That's just awful," Emma said.

"Don't worry," I said, trying to keep my voice calmer than I felt. "He won't find anything there, and then he'll move to somebody else." If only I believed that. There were nooks and corners of Donut Hearts that I hadn't cleaned in years. Was it possible there was a box somewhere in my storage area that contained poison? If so, had someone come into my place of business to steal it before they killed Peg, or could they have hidden it after they'd dusted one of my donuts? My security system was pretty lax, and it wouldn't have been that difficult to plant something there, I was unhappy to admit.

"What are we going to do if he keeps focusing on you?" she asked.

"We can't do anything about that now. Emma, we'll burn that bridge when we come to it, okay?"

Her voice lightened a little as she said, "I've got to say that you're taking this awfully well."

"I can either laugh or cry, and I hate to ruin my makeup, since I don't wear it very often and it took me forever to get just right." It was true. I'd pulled out all the stops for my demonstration, even going so far as getting a manicure and breaking out some of the makeup my mother inundated me with every birthday, Christmas, and any other holiday she could use as an excuse to improve my personal appearance. It wouldn't surprise me to find a wrapped present on my bed on Arbor Day, the way she was going. I knew my mother's intentions were good, but that didn't mean I was willing to use the products she gave me. I was a lot more comfortable with a little bit of blush, some mascara, and a touch of lipstick than the layers I'd applied that morning.

"I feel better now," Emma said. "Thanks for calling me."

"Sure thing. And don't stress out about today. Nothing that happened is your fault, all right?"

"Okay," she said. "I'll be back at the shop as soon as they finish searching it."

I just couldn't do that to her after what she'd been through. "You know what? Why don't you take the rest of the day off. I'm at the Boxcar, so as soon as they leave, I'll take care of it myself."

"You don't have to do that," she said.

"I know I don't, but to be honest with you, I want to. It will give me something to do. I'll see you tomorrow, okay?"

"If you're sure," she said.

"Trust me. Take me up on my offer before I change my mind."

"Thanks," she said, just before she hung up.

Trish waited until I put my phone back into my purse before she said, "That was sweet of you."

"You weren't listening to my private telephone conversation, were you?" I asked her with a smile.

"Hey, if you want privacy, don't call anybody while you're in a train boxcar. There's not exactly a lot of room in here. Besides, I have to do something for entertainment. You wouldn't deprive me of my eavesdropping, would you?"

I laughed. "No, when you put it that way, I'm fine with it."

She slid a cup of coffee in front of me. "Can I get you something to eat? It's a little early for lunch, but I'll get Hilda to make you a burger, if you'd like one."

I was tempted, but I honestly didn't have much of an appetite. Just thinking about food made me visualize Peg sprawled out in the garden with one of my donuts clutched in her dead hand. Would I ever be able to look at another donut again without seeing that scene? I sincerely hoped so, or my business was in serious trouble.

I took a sip of the coffee, then said, "No, thanks. I'm good for now."

My gaze was on the donut shop the entire time we spoke, where two police cruisers were still parked. I half-expected them to drape the front of the converted train depot with yellow warning tape, but at least they'd spared me that indignity.

The train car's door opened, and I saw the good looking stranger come in. Instead of taking one of the booths in back, he surprised me by sliding onto a stool two spaces away from me.

"Mind if I join you?" he asked.

"Go right ahead."

Trish came out, and the second she saw him, one

hand went to her forehead to make sure her bangs were in place. I was surprised she didn't take her ponytail down and brush her hair.

"Coffee?" she asked as she slid a cup and saucer in front of him.

"That would be nice," he said, not paying much attention to her.

She made a show of placing a menu in front of him, though there was one wedged between the napkin dispenser and the pepper shaker.

He pushed it back. "Thanks, but the coffee's all I need," he said.

Trish collected the menu, then moved back a few steps where she could still see him.

The man turned to me and said, "What I really wanted this morning was one of your donuts. I couldn't get inside, though."

"Join the club," I replied. "That's why I'm here, too."

"What happened?" He looked honestly interested.

"I don't even know where to start," I said.

He nodded. "Got you. Health code violation?"

"Don't be ridiculous," I said, not realizing just how harsh it would sound until I said it. In a calmer tone of voice, I said, "There was an accident somewhere else, and the police are making sure I wasn't involved."

"So they're searching your shop? What happened, did someone eat a bad donut?"

It was clear that he'd been joking, but that was a lot closer to the truth than I was willing to deal with.

Suddenly, I had to get out of there before anyone could see me break down. I pushed my coffee away and slid a dollar under the saucer. "If you'll excuse me, there's somewhere else I need to be."

He said, "Hang on a second. I didn't mean anything by it. It was just a joke."

"I know," I said as I paused at the door. "It's just not all that funny right now."

I was outside walking with vigorous steps to my shop when I heard someone running in the gravel behind me.

I turned and saw it was the stranger, but I made no move to slow my pace.

He caught up quickly enough, then as he matched my stride, he said, "Hang on a second. I'd like to talk to you."

"It's fine, really it is," I said, hoping he'd get the hint and leave me alone.

He didn't. He walked with me toward the donut shop, matching my steps. When we got to the parking lot, I looked in through one of the windows, but it didn't appear the police were in any hurry to wrap up their search and leave.

"Now what?" he asked with a grin. "There's nowhere else you can run."

"I wasn't running," I said simply.

He frowned at that, then said, "We got off on the wrong foot today, didn't we? Is there any chance we could just start over? I'm really sorry about the donut crack. That was uncalled for." He offered a hand, then said, "My name's David Shelby."

I hesitated, then took it briefly. "You already know I'm Suzanne Hart."

"Donut Hearts is the perfect name for your place."

"I really like it."

He looked at the building, studying the muted mustard brick veneer, the cedar red trim, and the expanses of glass. "It's a fine old structure, isn't it?"

"You're not one of those purists who believe that every old, abandoned train depot should be restored to all of its earlier glory, are you?" I'd had such people come into my shop before, complaining about the lost history I'd destroyed, and I'd grown tired of defending my choice of locations for my shop.

"No, I'm just happy nobody tore it down altogether. If people can start over, why shouldn't a building get a second chance at life?" Then he did the most remarkable thing. He reached out and stroked a few bricks, as if he were petting a dog. There was obvious affection in his touch, and I felt my heart softening toward him. I wouldn't admit to most folks in April Springs, but I too had a love for the old building, and all of the stories it could tell, if only it could talk.

"That's what I think, too. So, tell me, David, is that why you're in April Springs? Are you looking for a second chance?"

The question was innocent enough, but his face suddenly darkened. "No, that's not entirely accurate. I'm here searching for my *last* chance, and that's something else altogether, isn't it?" He started to walk back toward the diner, then abruptly stopped and pivoted back toward me. "It was nice seeing you, Suzanne."

"It was nice seeing you too," I said.

I watched him walk down the abandoned tracks until he was gone. What had I said? Had I touched a nerve with my comment? And what did he mean by his quest for a last chance? Our conversation raised more questions than it had provided answers, but it was pretty clear that my curiosity wasn't going to be satisfied today.

I was about to call Grace when I remembered that she was out of town. I'd grown to depend on my friend for her strength, and it bothered me that I couldn't just run over to her place and see her when I needed to. I could always call her—I knew that— but it just wasn't the same talking over the phone.

I was wondering where Jake was at that moment when I heard the door to the donut shop open.

At least the two cops who came out didn't have any boxes of poison with them, though they were both carrying armloads of bags from the shop.

"What are you two taking with you?"

"Hang on a second, Suzanne," one of the cops said. It was an officer named Stephen Grant who frequented my shop in his off hours.

He turned to his partner and said, "Adam, why don't you call the chief and tell him we're through here. Ask him if Ms. Hart can get back in her building, would you?"

"Okay," his partner said.

After he was gone, Officer Grant said in a hushed voice, "We didn't find any poison in your shop, but the chief ordered us to take all of the donuts you had on hand for more testing. Sorry, my hands are tied."

"Then she really was poisoned with something from my shop?"

Officer Grant looked back at his partner, who was still talking to someone on the radio. "You didn't hear it from me, but yeah, somebody dusted the top of one of your donuts with rat poison, and we're pretty sure that's what killed her."

I said, "This is a real mess, isn't it?"

"We tried to be neat when we searched your place, Suzanne," he said. He could barely make eye contact with me. Officer Grant was a slim young man barely over the required five feet eight inch requirement to be on the force. It was pretty obvious that the search had bothered him.

"I'm sure you did your best," I said. "Don't let this bother you. I know this wasn't your idea."

He shrugged. "I tried to tell the chief that if you wanted to kill Peg Masterson, you were too smart to spike one of your own donuts, but he wouldn't listen to me."

"Thanks. I think," I said.

"Don't worry, it was a compliment. We didn't find anything that might incriminate you, but then again, I didn't figure we would."

His partner came back and said, "He said it was all clear."

"She's all yours," Officer Grant said.

"Thank you."

Once they were gone, I walked back into my shop. It was odd having the place to myself at eleven o'clock in the morning. The empty racks of donuts in the display shelves looked forlorn, and from the arrangement of the signs on the cases, I noticed that Emma had put the orange cake donuts where the maple frosted belonged. Out of habit more than anything else I remedied the miscue when I heard the doorbell chime.

"Sorry, we're not open," I said.

"Not even for me?"

I turned and saw state police inspector and boyfriend Jake Bishop standing there.

"I thought you were on the Outer Banks," I said as I rushed to him and threw my arms around him. "I'm so glad you're here."

After our hug, he pulled away from me and said, "I wrapped it up quicker than I thought I would. What have you gotten yourself into this time, Suzanne?"

"This wasn't my fault, Jake."

"Don't you think I know that? I had to see you, but I shouldn't even be here until I check in with Chief Martin."

This wasn't quite the support I'd been hoping for. "You should go, then. I'd hate for you to get in trouble because of me."

He shook his head and looked down at the floor. "You know what it's like when I'm working on a case. I'm sorry it has to be this way, Suzanne."

"So am I," I said.

I wanted him to apologize, to hug me and tell me everything was going to be all right. Instead, he gave me one last, sad look, then walked out of my shop.

It nearly broke my heart when he left, but I wasn't going to let him know how much it bothered me.

There was no reason to open again, and I knew it. That was one of the bad things about living in a small town. News—and more importantly, rumors—spread amongst the citizens of April Springs at an alarming rate, and there was no way I could stop everyone from thinking that one of my donuts had killed Peg Masterson.

I was rattled by my conversation with Jake, more than I was willing to admit even to myself. I should have been cleaning the donut shop over the course of the next hour since it was clear there wouldn't be any customers today, but instead, I sat at one of the booths and managed to feel sorry for myself as a way to pass the time. By the time noon rolled around, I was feeling a little better, and I knew that it was time to start cleaning up.

I started to lock the front door when Heather Masterson, Peg's niece, came charging up to the shop. She was a petite young woman with short, glossy black hair and eyes so dark that they nearly matched—just like her aunt's had been—and I'd known her for nearly fifteen years. One thing was certain: she'd grown into a lovely young lady since I'd first babysat for her long ago, though it was hard to see that with the rage now dominating her features.

"You killed my aunt," she screamed at me. "Why, Suzanne? What did she ever do to you?"

I knew Heather well enough to realize that she was hurting inside, and though she was usually a dear girl, the fire in her eyes in that instant was full of hate and pain.

"I didn't kill Peg," I said, trying to calm her down.

"Don't try to deny it, Suzanne. I heard a donut killed her, and it had to be one of yours. I thought we were friends."

Her face started to crumble then, and it was all I could do not to wrap my arms around her and comfort her. "Heather, I swear to you, I had nothing to do with it. I'm innocent."

She stared hard at me for a few seconds, then said, "I don't know what to think. I guess I just want to blame somebody, and you're the easiest target there is at the moment. What a horrid thing to have happen to her. She was so sweet."

I raised my eyebrows as I stared at her.

Heather frowned a little, then said grudgingly, "Okay, maybe sweet is going a little overboard, but I loved her, Suzanne. I know Aunt Peg could be a pain in the neck at times, but she was the last bit of family I had left."

Heather's parents had died while she was still in high school. They'd gone on a camping trip without her, and a heater had malfunctioned in their motor home, filling it with deadly carbon monoxide. And now, two weeks from her twenty-first birthday, she'd lost her aunt. The reason I knew Heather's birthday was approaching was because we shared the same day and month, something that had bonded us closer when she'd been younger.

No matter how grown up she looked like on the outside, this was a frightened and sad little girl standing in front of me. "I'm so sorry. I know it's got to be really hard on you."

Her tears started to slowly escape, though neither of us mentioned them. "I'm the one who should be apologizing. I shouldn't come charging in here blaming you. You're just about the only friend I have left in this town these days. Suzanne, I'm sorry I yelled at you."

"You don't owe me an apology. I just hope the police find out who killed her, and soon."

"Me, too." She wiped at her cheeks, swiping away the tears, then said, "I've got to go start planning her funeral. I'll be staying at her house until I get this all sorted out."

"You could always stay with Momma and me. You're welcome, you know that. You shouldn't be alone at a time like this."

"I'll be all right. It will give me some time to grieve by myself. But thanks for the offer, Suzanne. I really do appreciate it."

As she walked away, I saw Heather's shoulders slump. I knew losing her aunt had been a blow to her, and I realized just how much it must have shaken her. Seeing her like that gave me one more reason to find out who had killed her aunt, and why.

I locked the shop door, then I stared at the empty racks on the display shelves inside. There would be no food donation today, though I had promised Father Pete I'd have something for them at the church. The sad thing was, the folks who counted on my contributions and needed food would have nothing to eat from my kitchen that day, and there wasn't a thing I could do about it.

I called the church to tell Father Pete that I wouldn't be able to help after all.

The only problem was that his secretary, Roberta Dowd, wouldn't put me through to him.

"I'm sorry, Suzanne, but he can't be disturbed. His orders were most specific, and I mean to follow them."

"Roberta, I just need a second of his time. I won't take long, I promise."

She paused, then said, "I didn't want to come out and say it, but I should tell you that we're not interested in any of your food donations at the moment."

"Father Pete actually said that?" I thought we had a better relationship than that. What kind of minister ducked someone who was only trying to help?

"He shouldn't have to say it. Given what happened today, do you honestly think we'd want any contributions from your shop? How do we know that another donut isn't tainted as well?"

I tried not to scream as I said, "I wasn't calling about making a donation. I wanted him to know that I wouldn't be able to help out today after all."

"That's for the best then, isn't it?" she said smugly. "I'm still not certain it sends the right message to the people we're trying to help to hand your donuts out to them. We can't afford to drive anyone off. They have nowhere else to turn. You understand, don't you, dear?"

"Oh, I understand all right," I said as I hung up, afraid to stay on the line any longer because of what I might say. The nerve of that woman. If I could have talked directly to Father Pete, I might have been able to explain what had really happened, but with his secretary acting as a gatekeeper, I had a better chance of talking to the president of the United States. Another, more chilling thought struck me. Was there a chance she'd been blocking my call on his orders? Was I suddenly our town's very own Typhoid Mary?

It wasn't fair to Emma or her mother, either. They

had made me proud, and I was going to do my best to convince my assistant that she was the perfect donut-making substitute whenever I wasn't around, even though I had a bad feeling that after this, she wasn't going to be interested in the job anymore.

I hauled the trash out back to my Dumpster and was having trouble tipping it in when I heard someone behind me ask, "Can I give you a hand with that?"

I didn't even have to turn around to know that it was George Morris, a balding ex-cop in his sixties who was one of my best customers and good friends.

"I could use it," I admitted, and he took one handle while I took the other. We threw the trash away, and I wished I could clear me name that easily.

"It's a real shame, isn't it?" he said as he carried the can back inside for me.

"In more ways than one. I still can't believe some-one would use one of my donuts as a murder weapon, you know?"

George shook his head. "Suzanne, that donut didn't kill Peg Masterson. The poison on top of it did."

"Have you heard anything else about it?" I asked. Though George was retired, he still kept in touch with a lot of his friends on the force, and so far, Chief Martin had let him hang around the squad room as long as he didn't try to work any of the cases. His observations had been invaluable to me in the past, and I wanted to make sure he stayed in the chief's good graces.

George frowned, then said, "There hasn't been anything formal announced, but it's pretty clear that's what happened. How are you holding up?"

"I'm a wreck," I admitted.

"Don't worry, things won't stay this bad. I heard that the chief was calling the state police to see if he could get Jake to give him a hand."

"He's already here," I said.

George smiled at me. "See? Things aren't as bad as they might seem."

I admitted, "I'm not sure how good a thing it is that Chief Martin called him."

George shook his head. "Your luck's not running so hot right now, is it?"

"I don't know. I still have my friends. You believe me, don't you?" I asked as I bolted the door behind me.

"You shouldn't even have to ask," he said. George looked around the kitchen. While it was my habit to clean as I worked, apparently Emma had a different idea.

"So, where should we get started?" he asked.

I frowned. "On what? I'm not sure we should butt into this murder investigation, at least not yet."

George shook his head. "It's too soon, I agree. I was talking about getting this place cleaned up."

"You don't have to hang around and help," I said.

He grinned. "I know I don't have to, but I want to. Do you have an extra apron hanging around here?"

I walked to the storage closet and pulled one off a hook. "If you're serious, this should fit you just fine."

He put it on and tied it. "Don't you think I'm capable of washing a pot or two?"

"I know you can do it, I'm just not sure why you'd want to."

George said, "What else is there to do? Do you want to wash or dry?"

I laughed and gave him a quick peck on the cheek.

He rubbed the spot, then asked, "What was that for?"

"For being here," I said.

"Like I said before, it's no big deal."

"Well, it is to me."

It was so nice having company as we cleaned up Donut Hearts.

George and I had just finished washing the dishes when there was a knock at the front door. When I peeked out through the kitchen door, I could see who it was without them seeing me.

It was Jake Bishop, and from the scowl plastered on his face, I had a pretty good idea that he wasn't coming by to ask me out.

HOBO DONUTS

Kids in particular love these, and they're so easy to make, we do them all the time. The batter's kind of messy, but it's worth the trouble. Prep is easy to do while the oil's heating, so you don't have long to wait to enjoy these treats.

INGREDIENTS

Batter
- 1 cup all-purpose flour
- ¼ teaspoon salt
- 1 egg
- 2 teaspoons baking powder
- ¾ cup milk
- 2 teaspoons granulated sugar

Sift the dry ingredients together, then, in a separate bowl, beat the eggs and add the milk. Add the wet mixture to dry and mix well.

Additional Ingredients
- Slices of bread, any kind (but we use white)
- Jam or preserves (your favorite, cherry is one of ours)
- Cinnamon sugar or icing sugar
- Batter (the ingredients listed above)
- Oil for frying, 360–370 degrees F

Cut the crusts from the bread. Make jam sandwiches like you ordinarily would, then cut them into four squares each. Give each square a quick dip in the batter and fry them all until they're golden brown.

When they come out, dust them lightly with cinnamon sugar and eat.

Yield: 8–12 squares

CHAPTER 4

"Should I stick around?" George asked as he spotted Jake knocking on the door.

"I appreciate your support, I truly do, but I need to talk to him alone." I looked around the shop and added, "Besides, we've already taken care of this. The place looks great. I don't know how I can thank you enough."

"No thanks needed," George said as he put the apron in my hands. "I was glad to help. Any time, Suzanne, you know that. If you need me, I'm always just a phone call away." He paused, then added, "Better yet, I'll be across the road at the diner. Come on over after you're finished with him."

I hugged him, and then let George out as Jake waited to come inside.

After he was gone, Jake said, "What was that all about?"

"He came by to give me a hand cleaning up," I said.

"He's a good guy," Jake said.

"Is there something I can do for you?" I asked, keeping my voice level.

Jake frowned. "I'm sorry about what happened earlier. I know I need to try harder than I have been."

It was quite a concession coming from him, but I could tell from his eyes that he wasn't done. "There's something more, though, isn't there?"

He nodded. "You have to keep something in mind yourself. I've got a job to do, and I can't play favorites just because we're involved. I'm doing everything in my power to help you, so you've got to cut me a little slack."

I couldn't let that one go. "How exactly are you helping me?"

He got close enough to me so that I could smell his cologne. "You're not in jail, are you? If Chief Martin had his way, I've got a feeling you'd be sitting in a cell right now if I hadn't intervened."

"That's preposterous," I said. "What evidence could the man possibly have against me?"

"Suzanne, your donut killed that woman."

I couldn't believe what I was hearing. "Jake, you're acting as though I poisoned it myself! Somebody tampered with that donut after it left my shop, and I can't control that any more than an automobile manufacturer can keep folks from driving drunk after they buy a car."

"Hey, I'm on your side, remember?"

"I hope so," I said.

He glanced at the clock, then said, "I've got to be somewhere right now, but I wanted to stop by and make things right with us. I'd stay if I could, but I can't miss this."

He hugged me briefly, and then he was gone.

It appeared that Jake was going to bend over

backward to make sure no one thought he was playing favorites with me, and our chief of police was obviously already suspicious of me.

I hated butting into an ongoing murder investigation, but it appeared that I really didn't have any choice.

"Hi. Can I join you?" I asked George as I walked up to his booth in the Boxcar Grill.

"You know it," he said as he pointed to the empty seat across from him.

George was about to say something else when Trish came up with a glass of sweet tea and slid it in front of me.

"I haven't even ordered yet," I said.

"That's okay. If you don't want it, I'll drink it myself."

She started to pretend to drink my tea; at least I hoped she was pretending. There are a handful of things Southerners don't joke about, and sweet tea is near the top of the list.

"Not so fast," I said. "I'll take that."

Trish grinned at me. "I kind of thought you would." She looked at George and said, "Now that she's here, are you ready to order?"

"Absolutely. I'll take a cheeseburger and fries."

"That sounds good to me," I said.

After Trish was gone, I told George, "We need to find out who killed Peg Masterson. I was going to keep out of it, but from the conversation I just had with Jake, it looks like I'm not going to be able to count on him. Will you help me?"

George took a sip of tea, then he said, "I won't

say no, even though you know how I feel about interfering with an active police investigation. You know, the more I think about it, that was a pretty deliberate way to implicate you. There are a thousand ways to poison someone. Why use one of your lemon-filled donuts?"

"I can actually answer that," I said. "It was the only donut Peg would eat."

George nodded. "So whoever killed her must have known that."

"The murderer must have known her fairly well to use such a devious temptation," I said. I never would have believed that I'd ever call one of my donuts that. "I'm the first person to admit that no one should make a steady diet of them, but donuts are high on the list of most people's real comfort foods."

George smiled. "I can attest to that. The real question is, was your donut simply a convenient way to deliver the poison, or was there a darker reason the killer chose it?"

"Who would want to frame me for murder?" I lowered my voice when I noticed a few heads turn toward us, and I added, "Let's not be ridiculous. I'm a donut shop owner, not some international business tycoon. I can't imagine anyone wanting to pin this murder on me."

"Don't be so sure," George said. "Let's not forget when and where the murder occurred. It was thirty steps from where you were demonstrating donut making. That wasn't exactly random, was it?"

The weight of what he was saying was finally starting to sink in. It appeared that I had an even greater stake in finding the killer now, since someone had so diligently gone out of their way to frame me for their crime.

"I've got to admit that everything you've been saying makes sense. Where do we go from here, though?"

George said, "We come up with a list of people we need to investigate, and then we figure out ways to look into their lives." He looked at me for a second, then said, "Suzanne, I think it's pretty clear that the killer's tying this all in with you, and if you start doing something suspicious, or if he even thinks you're getting too close, you could be in danger yourself."

"I appreciate your concern, but there's no way I can sit by while you take all the risks."

Trish walked over to us with a tray loaded with food. "Here you go."

After she placed our plates in front of us, George and I started to eat. We were halfway through with our meals when the diner's door opened and Officer Grant walked in.

When our gazes met, I told George, "Excuse me for a second, would you?"

He nodded, and I approached the officer at the front counter. "You're not here looking for me, are you?" I asked, trying to keep the dread out of my voice.

"Not unless you're a steak sandwich," he said. Turning to Trish, he asked, "Is my order ready yet?"

"You just called it in three minutes ago," she protested. "Have a seat. It'll be ready in a jiff."

I rejoined George, and Officer Grant finally got his sandwich. After he paid, he saluted me with two fingers and left the diner.

I started to say something when he said, "This place isn't private enough. Any chance we can go to the donut shop and finish our discussion?"

"That's fine by me," I said. "Let me just pay this bill, and then we can go."

"Hang on a second. We're splitting this right down the middle," George said.

"Not this time. You're helping me, so I'm picking up the check, and I don't want to hear any fuss about it."

He didn't fight me, which was a nice change of pace, I had to admit.

I saw George slip his hand to his wallet, and added, "I've got the tip, too."

He laughed gently, but he didn't argue with me. "Then I thank you for a nice lunch."

As I stopped to pay our bill, George left ahead of me. I turned to Trish and handed her the bill, along with enough cash to cover it and a healthy tip as well.

She started to hand me my change, and I said, "The rest is for you."

Trish looked at the bills and whistled softly. "Sweet. I'm putting this in my Alaska fund."

Trish had been saving for the big trip for as long as I'd known her. "How close are you?"

"It varies, depending on whatever emergencies are happening in my life at the moment. But I'm going to make it one day, you just wait and see."

"There's no doubt in my mind about that," I said.

I walked out to find that George was nowhere in sight, and for a moment I panicked. Then I heard him calling me.

He was already standing in front of Donut Hearts, waiting to get in.

There was only one problem. As I got closer to him, I noticed that someone else had joined him while I'd been inside paying the bill, someone I most certainly did not want to add to our meeting.

"Hey, Momma, what are you doing here?"

"I just heard about what happened at Marge's place this morning," my mother said. "You poor child." Though she was a petite woman—a full six inches shorter than me—she managed to wrap me up in her arms and make me feel as though she was towering over me. In times like this, I knew how lucky I was to still have her in my life.

"It was bad," I said, wondering how I was going to explain to her what was going on.

Momma looked around and said, "Why isn't Grace here with you?"

"Momma, she doesn't even know what happened. She's out of town, and to be honest with you, in all the commotion, I forgot to call her."

That seemed to appease her, and it had the added benefit of being true.

She looked me in the eye. "Are you all right? Be honest with me."

"I'm not, but I will be."

"Is there anything I can do for you?"

I shook my head. "No, but I appreciate you coming by."

After pausing a moment, Momma asked, "Are you two hungry? I'm buying."

George said, "Thanks, but we just ate."

She nodded. "Then since you've eaten, and I'm starving, I believe I'll go have a bite myself. Suzanne, we'll talk about this again, yes?"

I hugged her. "Yes. Thanks for being here for me."

"You are my only child, and you are in distress. Where else on earth would I be, Suzanne?"

After Momma was gone, I asked, "Shall we all go inside?"

"Sure," George said, "But we'll have to keep it brief. I've got a feeling your mother's coming back."

"You've got good instincts," I said as I unlocked the door and let him inside the donut shop.

"How should we approach this?" I asked after we were settled in at one of the tables away from the windows.

George said, "We need to look into Peg Masterson's life, and figure out who would want to see her dead. I can dig around the police station to see if there's any buzz there."

"I don't think Peg had a housekeeper, but I can talk to her neighbors. Maybe they can tell me something I don't already know. Before I do that, though, I'm going next door and talking to Gabby Williams."

George asked, "Really? Is it worth it?"

"She's the biggest gossip in April Springs," I said. "If Peg was up to anything she shouldn't have been, you can bet that Gabby knows about it."

"That's brave of you, Suzanne," George said.

"Hey, somebody has to do it. So, should we talk again in the morning and share our discoveries?"

George stood. "I'll be here, bright and early."

After we said our good-byes, I took a deep breath and walked next door to ReNEWed, the classy secondhand clothing shop that Gabby owned, and the hub of her gossip network.

Gabby was with a customer when I walked in—though I couldn't see who it was—so I moved near one of the racks of clothing halfway through the store and pretended to consider a purchase or two. I heard voices that had been heated suddenly drop into whispers across the room, and the front door was hurriedly thrust open as the customer left in a huff. I only saw her a second, but it was pretty clear from where I was standing that it was Janice Deal, the woman who owned Patty Cakes, a cake and cookie shop on Springs Drive down the block from Donut Hearts. What on earth had they been talking about, and why had Janice left the shop so abruptly?

Gabby made a telephone call but she hung up quickly as I approached. "Are you all right?" I asked as I walked over to her. The woman's spirit was normally indomitable, but at the moment, she looked as if the weight of the world had crashed down onto her shoulders.

I asked quietly, "Gabby, have you been crying?"

"I'm fine," she said as she dabbed at her eyes with a well-used tissue. "It's these blasted allergies."

Funny, I hadn't heard anyone else complaining about them. "You're sure you're okay? I can come back later, if you'd like."

"Nonsense," she said, wiping her eyes again.

I wasn't going to let her get away with that. "Gabby, you can talk to me; you know that, don't you?"

She looked surprised by my offer to listen. "Janice was rude to me, and the sad thing is, she wasn't the only person to bite my head off today."

"Who else has been giving you trouble?"

I thought for a second she was going to tell me, but the notion clearly passed as quickly as it had come. Apparently, Gabby was finished sharing with me.

"What brings you next door?"

"I wanted to talk to you about Peg Masterson."

"What about her?" Gabby's voice was flat and devoid of any emotion as she asked the question. It appeared that I'd made exactly the wrong query.

"I've just been wondering who could do such a thing, no matter how abrasive the woman could be."

She stared hard at me a second, then without breaking eye contact, she said, "I've been wondering the exact same thing."

"Hang on a second. You don't think I had anything to do with it, do you?" I couldn't believe anyone who knew me could honestly think I was capable of such a thing, and yet I was getting the impression that most folks around April Springs were giving that thought much more merit than it ever deserved.

Gabby took a deep breath, then said, "She died with your donut in her hand, and you were five feet away from her at the time."

I shrugged. "Okay, I'm willing to admit it was one of my donuts, but I'm telling you, it was fine when it left my shop. And I never got within five feet of Peg. It was twenty feet, at least."

Gabby bit her lip. "You two didn't get along, though, did you?"

"Can you name one person who liked her?" I asked. "I mean really enjoyed being around her?"

"Me! I liked her. She was my friend, and now someone's killed her. If you didn't do it, who did?"

"That's what I'm going to try to find out," I said. "I'm sorry, I never should have come in here. I didn't realize you two were so close."

Gabby waved off my apology. "Some of us have to work a little harder to make friends."

She was openly glaring at me now, and I was glad her shop was empty so no one else was witnessing it.

I said as calmly as I could manage, "Gabby, I'm sorry you lost a friend, but I didn't do it. If you really cared about her, wouldn't you want to help me find her killer? Isn't that the best way to honor her memory?"

"You need to go, Suzanne."

I did as she asked, because really, what other choice did I have? If Gabby wanted to lash out at me because she'd just lost one of her few friends, I couldn't make her talk to me.

I walked out of her shop, and a few seconds later, I saw some movement inside. She slapped the OPEN sign over to CLOSED, then pointedly dead-bolted the door behind me.

It appeared that Gabby, a resource I normally depended on in my informal investigations, wasn't going to be available to me this time. I briefly thought about getting Grace to talk to her when she got back into town, but Gabby was too shrewd not to realize she would be asking questions at my bidding.

It was a dead end, and now it was up to me to find a new way into Peg Masterson's life, and to figure out why someone had decided to end it.

CHAPTER 5

"Janice, I'd like to order a cake," I said half an hour later when I walked into Patty Cakes. "I was wondering if you could help me with something special."

It was the only excuse I could come up with to spend some time grilling the woman about her relationship with Gabby, and to see if she knew something about Peg that I didn't. Janice's shop, which specialized in custom cakes for all occasions, had a large selection of cookies for sale as well. They were pretty enough to look at, but in all honesty, I'd never cared for the way they tasted, much too bland in my opinion. It wasn't very politic to bring that up at the moment, though.

"What's the occasion?" Janice asked. Her body type did nothing to help advertise her business. For a woman who made cakes and cookies all day, Janice was so thin that when she turned sideways, she just about disappeared. In my opinion, if you're going to own a shop where you're offering decadent treats, you should at least look like you enjoy indulging in them every now and then yourself. That was my excuse, anyway.

"It's for my mother," I said, lying on the spot. "It's her birthday soon, and I want to get her something special."

"Your mother hates cake," Janice said, which wasn't entirely true. Momma hated Janice's cakes, but she liked everyone else's just fine.

"How about a big cookie, then?"

The store owner put her pen down. "Why are you really here? We both know it has nothing to do with your mother. You overheard Gabby and me talking in her shop, didn't you? Admit it, Suzanne, you never were a very good liar."

"It was kind of hard to miss," I said. "What on earth were you two arguing about?" Was it really going to be that easy? Did I just have to ask the question to get the answer I was looking for?

"That's none of your business," Janice said.

So much for it being easy. "That's not a good way to treat your customers, you know," I said.

"I thought we already established that you weren't buying anything," she said as sweetly as she could manage, which wasn't very nice at all.

"Not at the moment," I said, "but that doesn't mean I might not be in the market for something in the future."

Janice began cleaning the display counter, though it already looked pristine to me. "I'll believe it when I see it. In the meantime, I don't have time for gossip and idle speculation, especially from you."

"Why me in particular?" I asked.

"Must we really have this discussion?" she asked.

I wasn't about to budge. "Yes, we do."

Janice threw her towel down on the case. "Fine, if

you insist on having this conversation, then we'll have it. You've been stealing my business, and we both know it. It's simply wrong. My shop was here long before you bought that donut shop of yours, and I'll be here well after you've moved on to something else."

I couldn't have been more surprised if she'd handed me a hundred dollar bill or a live chicken. "Janice, what on earth are you talking about?"

"Don't play dumb with me," she said.

"Who's playing? I haven't a clue."

Janice said, "The Jackson-Bright wedding."

Then I realized exactly what she meant. Robbie Jackson and his betrothed, Heather Bright, had decided that instead of a conventional wedding cake, they wanted donuts, and lots of them. I thought it was sweet, since they'd had their first date at Donut Hearts, and had wanted to commemorate the occasion appropriately. Emma and I had pulled an extra shift that day, making donuts long after our shop was closed in time for the late afternoon wedding. It had been a big hit with most of the folks who attended and knew their story, though a few relatives from out of town on both sides were perplexed by the nuptials being held in an old train station that now housed a donut shop.

"It was one wedding," I said. "They met in my shop, so it made sense. Trust me, I'm not going after your wedding cake business. I don't have the time, or the energy."

Janice was not appeased by my explanation. "Just know that if you do it again, I'm going to start making donuts and selling them here in my shop as well."

"You're welcome to make them any time you want," I said. I wanted to add that she'd better hope she made them tastier than her cakes, but I bit my tongue instead.

In a softer voice, I said, "I wasn't trying to poach your clientele, honestly."

Janice seemed to soften a bit, so maybe she actually believed me. "So you say."

I took a deep breath, then asked, "Can we talk about what happened to Peg Masterson today? Or would you rather tell me why you and Gabby were about to come to blows in her shop a little bit ago?"

"Suzanne, as I told you, I don't have time to stand around and talk to you. I have orders to fill and work that needs to be done."

"Go ahead. But be warned, I'm not leaving until you tell me," I said.

"Oh really? Let's just see what the police say about that," she said as she reached for the telephone.

I knew when I was beat. "Save yourself the call. I'll leave."

She had a smug expression on her face, one I wasn't going to let her keep for long. With my hand on the front door, I added, "Just remember one thing, Janice. I won't give up until I find the truth."

"Is that a threat, Suzanne?" she asked.

"No, ma'am. It's a promise."

I walked out of the shop, wondering where to go next with my investigation. So far, I was about as popular as a dog at a cat show, but I wasn't going to let that slow me down.

I just wish I knew where else to look. I'd told

George that I could talk to Peg's neighbors, but it was hard to tell what they'd be able to tell me about her.

I needed to come up with another plan.

My ideas, at least for the moment, were gone. I was ready to go home and grab a bite, then try to unwind before it was bedtime. I had George out scouring for clues, and I wouldn't do anybody any good stumbling around without at least some kind of plan. I'd had one day to sleep in, and it had turned out to be a disaster, so I was looking forward to getting back to my old schedule as quickly as I could.

In all honesty, I needed routine in my life more than I was willing to admit. Donuts were always the same; predictable, and steady. I could make them in my sleep, and sometimes it felt as though I did. I found great comfort in knowing what tomorrow would bring. At least most days.

I drove home the few short blocks, and as I pulled the Jeep into my parking place, my cell phone rang.

I checked the caller ID and was surprised to see who was calling me. What on earth did Trish Granger want?

There was only one way to find out, no matter how tired I was.

"Hey, Trish. How are you?"

"Oh, dear. You sound tired. Maybe I shouldn't have called."

I glanced at my watch and saw that it was barely past five. "Nonsense. I'm fine, though I will admit that it's been a long day."

"This isn't really all that important," she said.

"Why don't you call me tomorrow and we'll talk then."

"Trish, I assure you, I'm fine."

"Okay, then. I caught enough of your conversation with George at the diner to know that you two are investigating what happened to Peg Masterson. It's not like I mean to," she added quickly. "But you know how small that place is, and voices tend to carry."

I'd dodged enough direct questions for one day. "I admit it. We're both afraid the police are going to focus solely on me, and we know I didn't do it. There really isn't much choice but to find out what really happened to Peg ourselves, is there?"

"I agree with you completely," she said. "That's why I'm calling. I overheard something that might be useful to you."

"I'm listening," I said.

She paused, then admitted, "Two minutes ago, I could swear I heard someone say that Burt Gentry at the hardware store isn't as upset as he should be about the murder."

I'd known Burt all my life. "Why should he be any more affected than the rest of us?" I asked.

"Didn't you know? He and Peg were dating, at least until she broke up with him last week. I thought everyone in town knew about the two of them."

"Apparently it was a better kept secret than you thought," I said. None of my friends had said a word about Burt's relationship with Peg, and I thought we knew everything that was going on in April Springs.

"Maybe so. Do you think the police know about the relationship? It might give them a suspect in her murder. Besides you, I mean."

"You could always tell them yourself," I said.
"Why don't you?"

I sighed, "Trish, if I tell them, they'll immediately assume that I'm making it up to get myself off the hook. You're a lot more credible at the moment than I am."

"I don't know, Suzanne. I hate to get involved," Trish said.

"How do you think I feel? I'm in the middle of a murder investigation, and I'm as innocent as a spring lamb."

"Okay, I'll do it. I'll call the chief right now."

"Let me know what he says, okay?"

"I'll do it."

As I hung up, I looked up and saw Momma standing on the porch.

As I got out of the Jeep, she said, "I was beginning to wonder if you were ever coming in."

"I had a telephone call I had to take," I said.

"I heard that Jake was back in town," she said. "Will he be joining us for dinner?"

"No, ma'am. He seems to think that it would look bad to go out with me while he's investigating Peg Masterson's murder, so I don't see that there's much of a chance we'll be dating again anytime soon."

Momma frowned. "That's just nonsense."

"You want to know the truth? I've had some time to think about it, and I'm starting to think he's right."

As I walked inside the cottage, I smelled the air, and was suddenly enveloped by the aroma of my mother's famous meatloaf. "Besides, if Jake were here, I'd have to share my dinner with him."

"I made an entire meatloaf, I believe we have enough to spare for some company, don't you?"

"You don't know how hungry I am," I said. "Is it ready yet?"

"We can eat whenever you'd like."

I took my seat at the table, and helped myself to meatloaf, mashed potatoes, and green beans, one of my favorite meals of all time.

After we said the blessing, I had a forkful poised for my mouth when my cell phone rang.

"Let it ring," Momma said. She hated it when our meals were interrupted by telephone calls, and though she couldn't ban them from the table, she managed to show her disapproval if I took a call while we were eating.

I looked at the caller ID and saw that it was Trish. "Sorry, Momma, I've got to take this."

"Not at the table then," she said.

I frowned, jammed the bite I had poised ready to go into my mouth, then got up and walked out onto the front porch.

"Hey, Trish. What did he say?"

"You were right. He thought I was trying to help you," she said. "I used to think you were paranoid thinking the chief was out to get you. I'm not so sure anymore."

I wished I could tell her that I was surprised by his reaction, but I couldn't. "You tried, and that's what counts. Thanks for believing in me."

"Suzanne, we've been friends forever. I'll always look out for you, you should know that."

"I do," I said, then hung up.

If Chief Martin wasn't going to talk to Burt, that

meant that I had to do it myself. The hardware store was already closed, though, and I couldn't just show up on his doorstep without a really good reason. It would have to wait until tomorrow.

I planned to go to his store to find out what was really going on.

After the delicious meal, I'd just finished doing the dishes when my cell phone rang again. Momma was on the couch working her way through our complete set of Agatha Christies yet again. I put the last dish in the drying rack, then answered the call.

"Suzanne Hart, I'm going to shoot you," I heard Grace say.

"Is there a particular reason this time, or is it just out of sheer meanness?"

"You didn't call me after what happened to Peg Masterson. I had to hear it from Emma."

"Why on earth did she call you?"

"Don't take it out on her. She's worried about you. Don't worry. I'm coming home in the morning."

"You shouldn't cancel your trip because of me," I said.

"Nonsense. We had our meeting this morning, and I spent the rest of the day shopping at Barefoot Landing. There's nothing going on tomorrow, except for a golf outing at Myrtle National. Honestly, I was planning on coming home early anyway. I'll see you around lunchtime," she said.

"That would be wonderful," I admitted. It would be good having Grace nearby. She was more than just a dear friend. She was a rock I could lean on if I needed to, and a partner in my earlier unofficial investigation. While she wasn't all that interested in coming up with lists of suspects and motives, Grace was a whiz at play-acting, and there wasn't a role she wouldn't tackle to help me find the truth.

"See you then," Grace said, and hung up.

I thought Momma had missed the telephone call altogether, but she looked up from our copy of *The Murder of Roger Ackroyd*, putting her finger on the page to mark her place, and asked, "Who was that?"

"Grace just found out what happened today," I said.

"I thought she was out of town," Momma said.

"She was. I mean, she is. But she's coming home tomorrow."

I got that look from her again. "Suzanne, you're not going to drag her into this, are you?"

"Momma, I don't drag anyone anywhere they don't want to be. She's my friend, and she wants to be here to support me."

"She's a good girl," Momma said, then went back to her book.

I slipped off to my bedroom upstairs. Tomorrow was another big day of making donuts. Some folks in town gave me grief for being open on Sundays, but it was my biggest day of the week, what with Sunday schools and other folks indulging in a little weekend decadence. I'd made a conscious choice to stay open seven days a week, and I found most of my regular customers appreciated the convenience.

As I got ready for bed, I kept staring at my telephone, not even aware at first that I'd been doing it. Was I actually expecting Jake to call? He'd made it pretty clear that he was busy at the moment, and if he was thinking of me at all while he was back in April Springs, it was probably as a murder suspect.

To keep myself occupied until bedtime, I decided to follow my mother's lead and read a good book. For the rest of the evening, I was going to spend a little time with one of Carolyn Hart's books. The adventures of Annie Darling were just what I needed to take my mind off my own troubles.

I had finally dozed off when my bedside phone rang. I'd forgotten to turn off the ringer, and as I grabbed it, I found myself hoping it was Jake.

No such luck.

"Hi, Suzanne. It's Heather Masterson."

"Hi, Heather," I said, fighting a yawn.

She said, "Oh, dear, I'm calling too late, aren't I? I guess I'm used to college time. Wait, it's only ten."

"Yes, but I get up every morning at one," I said.

"I should have realized that someone had to get up to make the donuts you sell every day. I'm sorry I bothered you. Go back to sleep."

"No, it's fine," I said as I rubbed my eyes. "I can talk. What's up?"

"I wanted to ask a favor from you, but I surely didn't start off on the right foot by calling this late, did I?"

"What is it? I'll do anything I can. You know all you have to do is ask."

She hesitated, then said, "I've been going through Aunt Peg's things, and there's a lot I'm not sure what to do with. Do you know anyone who could help me sort through her clothes and things and tell me what's worth keeping? I'm afraid I have no talent for it at all, and I don't want to get rid of something valuable by mistake."

"I understand," I said, as I thought about who could help.

She must have misunderstood my delay, because she added quickly, "I can't bear to be here any longer than I have to, you were right about that. The memorial's planned, and the sooner I can put this all behind me and get back to school, the better. I just can't stand being surrounded by all of this sadness."

"Why don't I help you myself?" I asked as inspiration struck. The best way to learn more about Peg might be going through her things.

"I thought you had a shop to run."

Making it up as I went along, I said, "I can get my assistant to fill in, as long as I make the donuts myself. Tell you what. I have an even better idea. If you wait until noon, I can come over after work and she won't be alone at all."

"That's too much to ask of you," Heather said. Her voice caught as she added, "I can't pay you much."

"Don't worry about that all. I'm perfectly willing to do this as a favor to you."

"Thanks, Suzanne. I don't know how I'd get through this without you."

"You'd be fine, I'm sure."

After we hung up, I tried to get back to sleep, but it was no use. I suddenly realized I'd forgotten to talk to Peg's neighbors, but it really didn't matter any more. After all, tomorrow I'd be inside the woman's house, and if there was anything to learn from it, I planned to take full advantage of the opportunity.

I knew that if I picked up my book and started reading again that I'd never manage to fall back to sleep, so instead, I lay there in bed in the dark, trying to drive the thoughts of what had happened that day from my mind.

I was only partially successful, but I still managed to drift off to sleep before it was time to get up again and start another day from scratch.

I woke up the next morning a little before one AM. My alarm clock was due to go off in ten minutes, but it was the sound of thunder that had brought me awake. I looked out the window, and through the gloom, I saw rain pounding down in the night.

It was going to be one of those dismal days we sometimes got in the foothills of the Blue Ridge Mountains, and I hoped it didn't keep customers away from Donut Hearts. I figured with the poisoning, I was going to lose some regulars anyway, and I didn't need a downpour to keep other customers from coming in. It might just be Emma and me today when we opened up, but I couldn't worry about that. I had donuts to make, and if folks bought them or not, I still had to be ready.

I dressed quietly, grabbed a yogurt from the fridge, and left the house, hoping the rain would have let up by the time I was ready to go. No luck. It was coming down in sheets, and the small umbrella I'd chosen was no match for it.

In twenty paces, I was soaking wet.

I crept along in the Jeep toward the shop, and finally made it without having an accident. At least there hadn't been any other traffic on the road.

To my surprise, Emma was waiting for me inside the shop when I pulled up.

She ran outside with a huge golf umbrella one of our customers had left, and escorted me into the building, though I was already soaked to the bone.

"It's amazing, isn't it?" she said with too much enthusiasm for that time of night as we walked inside. "I just love thunderstorms, don't you? There's something so romantic about them."

I dabbed at my wet hair with one of our towels. "Yes, it's absolutely magical," I said with a deadpan voice.

"Come on, you'll feel better once you've had your coffee," she said. "I've already made a pot."

I took a mug from her and sipped it gratefully. "How long have you been here, anyway?"

She grinned. "Honestly? I never went to bed. I had a date with Paul Simms, and he dropped me off here an hour ago. He wanted to keep me company until you showed up, but I told him that wasn't going to happen."

"He's new in your life, isn't he?" I asked her.

"Tonight was our first date. I just love the start of a relationship, don't you?" Emma paused a moment, then added hastily, "Not that what you have with Jake isn't still special, too."

I looked at her a second, then said, "Listen, I'm happy for you, honestly, I am. But my love life is not a topic of conversation we're going to be covering. Agreed?"

"That's fine," she said. I hated to step on her grand mood, but I didn't particularly want to be around her when she was in her giddy stage of the first blush of romance.

"What are we making special today?" Emma asked.

"It's business as usual. After we get the cake donuts made, we'll go to work on the yeast ones."

We worked through the variations of our cake donuts first—turning out plain, old-fashioned, pumpkin, orange spice, apple cinnamon, and lemon—and after they were finished and dripping in glaze, I turned the fryer up to 365 degrees, an easy temperature to remember. As I added twenty pounds of flour to the mixture of yeast and water already in the stand mixer, I turned it on to blend the mix and set the timer to five minutes.

When the timer went off, I turned off the mixer, removed the beater, and put a cloth over the top of the mixing bowl while it was still in the stand. I reset the timer to forty minutes, and it was finally time to stop for a while. Emma and I enjoyed our breaks outside, where the world was still dark and quiet and we felt as though we had it all to ourselves. Not even the rain, still pouring down in prodigious amounts, could keep us inside, since the awning over the front of the shop was enough to protect us from anything short of a hurricane force wind. There were a pair of modest tables with accompanying chairs outside for those who liked to eat their donuts alfresco, but the seats were wet, so we stood under the awning together and watched it rain.

"Are you really going to eat that?" she said as she pointed to my modest treat. Emma always had a power bar with her coffee, while my snacks were varied, depending on the current state of my diet. Today I was having a rice cake, after getting on the scale a few days before and being alarmed by what my donuts were doing to my waistline.

I nodded. "Sadly, until I can stop sampling our wares, I'm going to have to. Walking doesn't seem to help as much these days as it used to."

Emma took another bite of her power bar, then said, "I read that as women get older, our metabolisms start slowing down, so it's harder and harder to lose weight."

"Fascinating. Did the article also mention that rain is wet, and fire burns?"

She said softly, "I didn't mean anything by it, Suzanne. I just thought it was interesting."

I laughed gently. "I'm sorry. I guess I'm just concerned about how the town's going to perceive me as some kind of killer, and I don't even want to talk about what Jake is thinking."

"Don't worry. He'll come around," Emma said.

"We'll see, won't we," I said. I glanced at my watch and saw that we still had a few minutes left, but the tone of the conversation and the pelting rain were depressing me. "I'm going on in, but feel free to stay out here a few more minutes."

She said, "No, I'm ready to go back in, too."

Three minutes after we were back inside, the mixer timer went off again, and it was time to get back to work. I moved the dough to my counter, punched it down, and waited another ten minutes before touching it again. After the timer went off yet again, I divided it into sections, and got to work. Rolling a section at a time out on my floured board, once I had it about a quarter-inch thick I was ready to make donuts. Now was the fun part. I don't know who the genius was who thought of the cutting wheel, but I'd buy him a cup of coffee if I could. An aluminum contraption that looked like a children's game, it featured a continuous circuit of donut and hole cutters on a hand-held wheel. The process of cutting out donuts was simplicity itself. Starting on the edge closest to me, I rolled the cutter across the dough, leaving perfectly formed donut rounds behind, with the holes separated as well. Any dough that was left was kneaded a little, then added to a big bowl to be used again later. I loaded the donut rounds onto trays, then handed them to Emma, who slid them into the proofer. There are much fancier rigs on the market, but ours worked just fine, though it wasn't much more than a glorified box with a light bulb in the bottom and a humidifier. Twenty-five donuts fit on each tray, and we liked to put a hundred holes on one. After the first round was in the proofer, I set the timer to twenty-eight minutes and got to work on the scraps of dough I'd collected. I rolled these out again, made more donut cutouts, then went through the process again. This time though, I used the bismark cutter, a long-john-shaped rectangular grid that cut out perfect forms. With this cutter, we made long johns, honey buns, twists, pinecones, and whatever else I was in the mood to create. Finally, there was just a little dough left, now too tough for anything but fried pies and fritters. Fortunately, I had customers who liked both, so by the time we were finished, there wasn't a scrap of dough left.

After the proofing, it was time to add the donut rounds—eighteen at a time—to the fryer. Forty-five seconds per side, and they were ready to drain and glaze. The donut holes went in for their hot bath next, and while they were frying, Emma took a bread pan and scooped out enough glaze to drench the yeast donuts. The excess ran down the slope back into the pool, and she moved the finished donuts to display trays and put them in the holding rack, just as I dumped out donut holes on the cooling rack so she could repeat the process with them. The specialty items went into the hot oil next, a continuous process of frying, glazing, and traying up. There wasn't a lot of time to chat when we were working at this stage, but as soon as we had the front display cases stocked, we could take a breath, clean up a little before it was time to open, and take a well-deserved break. A lot went into making donuts, and not many folks knew just how much effort we put into producing each one. I didn't care. The only thing that mattered to me was that they enjoyed eating them, and I knew from the satisfied smiles that they did.

We were cleaning up some of the racks in back when Emma glanced at the clock. "It's just about time to open."

I shrugged. "Do you honestly think we'll have any customers?"

"Absolutely," she said. "I have faith in our friends."

"That makes one of us," I said as I finally got up the nerve to peek outside. To my surprise, there was a line of people standing in the rain, all sporting umbrellas and waiting to get in.

I told Emma, "You're not going to believe this. Come look."

My assistant looked as though she wanted to cry. "Okay, I'm sorry. I was putting a brave front on for you. Don't worry, Suzanne. Business will pick up."

"I hope not," I said. "If it does, I'm going to have to hire somebody else."

Emma looked thoroughly confused. "What are you talking about?"

"Come look."

She walked through the door with me, and saw the masses waiting to get in.

Emma stared at me and said, "I can't believe it."

"Well, you'd better. I'm going to unlock the door, so you should get ready for a hard morning."

"There's nothing I'd like better," she said as she took a place behind the counter.

When I opened the door to let my customers inside, each one had a kind word for me as they entered.

George was just about the last one in.

As he stepped in and put his hat into his pocket, I asked, "Did you have something to do with this?"

George said, "Hey, you've got more than me as a friend."

I wasn't sure if I believed him or not, but I said, "Thanks for coming, and for believing in me."

As he slipped into the last open booth, I hurried back to help Emma. The display of affection I was receiving was more valuable to me than all of the money in the world. The only real currency I counted was friendship, and from what I was seeing at that moment, I was one of the richest women in all of North Carolina.

DESSERT PUFFS

These are a nice change of pace from regular donuts. They have a different, almost cake-like texture, and if you use your ravioli cutter to make whole rounds, they puff up nicely for any fillings you might like.

INGREDIENTS

- 2 cups all-purpose flour
- 2 teaspoons baking powder
- 2 teaspoons nutmeg or cinnamon
- $1/2$ teaspoon salt
- 2 tablespoons canola oil
- $1/2$ cup water

DIRECTIONS

Sift the flour, baking powder, and salt together, then add the oil and water to the bowl, mixing it all together well. Take the dough out and knead it lightly, then place the dough in a buttered bowl, cover, and set aside in a warm place for about an hour. Roll the dough out to $1/8$ to $1/4$ inch and cut into any shape you'd like. We like round shapes, but diamonds and squares around 2 inches each side work just as well.

Fry these until golden brown, turning them halfway to cook both sides.

Drain and dust your treats with powdered sugar, and they're ready to eat.

Yield: 8–14 depending on size

CHAPTER 6

By eleven, we were completely sold out, something that had never happened in all the time I'd owned Donut Hearts. I'd sent Emma home for a well-deserved rest ten minutes before we were due to close. She'd earned the time off. George had left with a promise to return later, but I wasn't going to wait around for him. I had a suspect to interview, and I'd been thinking about what I was going to say to Burt Gentry all morning. I just hoped the hardware store owner had some answers for me. I had about an hour before I had to catch up with Heather to start working on Peg's place, and I planned to take advantage of it while I could. It was hard to tell how long I'd be there that evening.

I was just showing the last customer out the door when a man barged through the open door.

"Sorry, we're closed," I told him.

"This will just take a second," he said as he brushed past me.

I was getting ready to tell him that we were out of donuts when he tapped on the window, which had our hours posted. "I've got an hour left, anyway. Does the owner know you're closing up early?"

"She's got a pretty good idea about what's going on," I said.

He smiled at me. "I doubt she knows what time you're locking up. Don't worry, I won't tell her you're bugging out early. I need three donuts, and then I'll be out of your hair."

"Sorry, I can't help you."

He looked at the empty display cases behind the register for the first time. "You've got to have something in back."

"No, like I said, we're closed. We just sold out of everything."

The man shook his head. "I don't see how this place stays in business if there isn't enough stuff to sell to customers."

I leaned over and said, "The woman who owns this shop is an eccentric old bird. She likes fresh donuts every morning with her coffee, and anything else we sell is just icing on the cake as far as she's concerned."

He shook his head as he started for the door. "If I live to be a thousand, I'll never understand life in a small town."

"I'm willing to bet you didn't grow up in one, did you?"

"No, ma'am. I'm from Chicago."

"Tell you what, Chicago. Come back tomorrow, and your first donut's on the house. How's that for small-town charm?"

"Aren't you afraid your boss will fire you for giving out free stuff?"

I smiled at him. "No, she can't live without me. See you tomorrow."

"If I'm still in town, I'll take you up on it," he said with a smile as he left.

I hastily scrawled a note on the front door that told any more customers that we'd closed early, then started off for the hardware store. It was time to speak with Burt and find out what he had to say about his clandestine relationship with Peg Masterson.

"Is Burt around?" I asked a clerk as I walked into Gentry Mercantile & Hardware. The building was ancient, sporting weathered bricks outside and scarred wooden floors within, everything testifying to over a hundred years of service. Besides a typical hardware store's usual fare of items for sale like bins of nuts and bolts, metal baskets brimming with nails, and garden tools hung like stockings at Christmas, Burt also catered to a clientele that liked model trains, dollhouses, and hobby kits for just about every kind of enthusiast that existed. It was the most eclectic place I'd ever been in my life, and I usually reveled in the chance to visit it, but today was lacking any real joy.

"He's back in his office, Suzanne," the young man said. It took me a second to recognize him.

"Pete? I thought you were still in school." Pete Evans was a tall, gangly blond, though he was finally starting to fill out.

"No, ma'am. I graduated in June, and started work here full-time a week later."

"How are your folks?"

"They're fine. I'll tell them you asked about them."

"Please do," I said. "I'll see you later."

As I walked back to Burt's office, I marveled at

how time seemed to fly by. With every year I got older, the speed seemed to increase, and I wondered how it would feel in twenty or thirty years. I could remember Pete playing one of the shepherds in the town's Nativity Scene the year they'd decided to use real animals. The donkey had taken off in the middle of the play, and the sheep, being true to their nature, had followed suit. There was a mad rush to corral them all, but by the time they were gathered together again, the players rushed through an abbreviated version of the approved script, and everyone met in the basement of City Hall for hot chocolate and Christmas cookies.

Had that really been six years ago?

I tried to clear my mind of those images from the past and focus on the present. I needed to talk to Burt, not as an old friend, but as a man who just might have committed murder, though I still couldn't bring myself to believe it.

"Burt, do you have a second?" I asked as I leaned in through his open office door. Burt Gentry was nearing sixty, and his thick red hair was clearly still a source of pride to him. Burt was still a handsome man, and from some old photos he had posted in his office, he'd been a real heartbreaker back in his youth.

"Suzanne, what brings you by? You didn't close the donut shop early just to talk to me, did you?"

"No, believe it or not, I sold out my entire stock today."

He grinned as he leaned back in his chair, an old wooden roller with arms that bore the scars of its years. "I wish I could pull that off. I'd be on the next plane headed for the Florida Keys if I could clear my inventory."

"Really? You don't seem the type to just pick up and go," I said.

"The wanderlust bug bites me every now and then, but I can't imagine living anywhere but our little part of North Carolina."

"I can't either. Even when bad things happen here."

Burt sat back up in his chair. "That's a pretty awkward segue into what happened, isn't it? I can't believe she's gone."

"You knew each other pretty well, from what I've heard around town," I said, carefully studying his expression as I spoke. If he was hiding something, though, I couldn't see it.

He chuckled softly. "Folks like to talk, don't they?"

"Is it true? Did she break up with you recently?"

That got his attention. "Is that what they're saying? I shouldn't be surprised. The rumor mill never was more than half right on its best day."

"What's the truth, then?"

Burt rubbed his forehead, then asked gently, "Why are you so concerned about it? It doesn't really involve you, does it?"

Though his words were spoken softly, there was an underlying edge to them, not of anger or guilt, but of animosity.

"She was killed with one of my donuts," I said. "I've got a stake in this if I'm going to clear my name and save my business."

"I thought you said you sold out today," he said as he played with a bit of raw copper no bigger than a quarter that was sitting on his desk. "Business couldn't have been hurt that much."

I shrugged. "That's today, when my friends came out in force to support me, but what happens tomorrow, or the next day? Where am I going to be if this doesn't get wrapped up quickly? I can't afford to wait for the police to solve it."

Burt nodded, his gaze still drawn to the copper. "How about your young man? I understand he came back to town yesterday. Surely he's doing his best to clear you of suspicion."

Burt had somehow managed to shift the conversation from himself to me, and it was time to turn it back.

I decided to ignore the statement. "Which part of the town gossip isn't true, then? Did you break up with Peg, or were you even dating?"

Burt shook his head. "I never cared for that word, dating. It doesn't seem to fit two seniors spending time together, does it? Peg and I had been seeing each other, though it was all quite casual. It ended amicably enough, though."

"What happened?"

For a second, it appeared as though he wasn't going to answer the question, but after a moment, he said, "I met someone else, and that was that."

"Who was it?"

Burt shook his head. "Suzanne, I'm not the type of man to kiss and tell. I never have been, and I'm not about to start now."

"All I'm looking for is a name," I said, pressing him a little harder than I liked.

"Well, you're not going to get it from me," he said

as he stood. The genial old man I'd known so many years was gone completely now. I'd somehow made him mad enough to drop his "aw shucks" demeanor.

It was pretty clear the interview was over, and I was about to leave when Pete came back to the office. "Burt, Marge is on the phone. She wants to know if you're still coming over for dinner tonight."

Burt looked mad enough to spit nails. "Pete, who's at the front register?"

"I am," the young man said.

"Really? Cause it looks to me like you're standing back in my office."

"Sorry. I'll get right back on it," he said.

After Pete was gone, Burt looked at me and smiled a little. "I don't suppose there's a chance in the world you missed that, is there?"

"Sorry, I don't want to get Pete in trouble, but it was kind of hard not to hear. Marge? Really?"

"She's a fine woman, a nice person to spend some time with, and a pretty good cook. I make her laugh, so I bring something to the table myself. Suzanne, we're in our sixties, we're not dead."

"I never said you were," I said.

"Don't bother her with your questions," Burt said as we walked out of his office together. "She's a little more sensitive than I am about being grilled about a murder."

"I wasn't grilling you," I said hastily, though that was exactly what I had been doing.

He just laughed. "Then why do I feel like I've been under your microscope since you walked in? Let me put your mind at ease. I didn't do it, and neither did Marge."

"Thanks for your time," I said as we reached the front door.

"So, I'm trusting you'll drop this?"

I gave him my best smile. "There's not a chance in the world of that happening, and you know it."

Burt returned my grin with one of his own. "No, I didn't figure there was. You always were a stubborn little girl."

"Just think how much truer that is now that I'm a full grown woman," I said.

Burt just nodded, and I walked back to Donut Hearts to meet up with George. I'd learned something valuable from our conversation, that Burt had indeed been dating Peg. I hadn't known he'd taken up with Marge until Pete had spilled it, and that added something else to the mix. Was Burt telling the truth? I couldn't imagine him lying to me, but then again, I couldn't see him as a cold-blooded killer either, and that was a possibility I couldn't afford to ignore. He certainly had access to plenty of different poisons in his hardware store, and no one would miss the slight quantity used to kill Peg. But what was his motive? If he'd dumped her, he had no reason to kill her. But what if she'd dumped him, and he'd felt more rage and anger than he'd showed me? I'd seen a hard edge to him I'd never noticed before. Could there be more of that he kept hidden from the world? Could he have killed her out of a sense of betrayal?

I'd never really thought that someone in his sixties could get so heartbroken that they might commit murder, but added years didn't necessarily mean more patience, more understanding, or better control over emotions. Whether he liked it or not, Burt had to stay on my list of suspects until I could confirm his version of things. Marge had to be added to the list as well, no matter how much I liked her. If Peg was a rival, and Marge was afraid of losing her boyfriend, it might drive her to do something desperate. I'd just added two people I genuinely liked to my list of suspects, and there was nothing I could do about it.

I had a visitor waiting for me outside of Donut Hearts. I almost turned around in time, but it was too late to get away. Jake spotted me before I could duck into a shop, but I was in no mood to see him. At least the rain had finally stopped.

"Hang on a second," he said. "I need to talk to you."

"What's going on, Jake?"

He stared at me a few seconds, then said softly, "I just came across some information I thought you might like to know. None of the donuts the police pulled had any traces of poison in them."

It was a relief to have my belief confirmed. "Thanks for letting me know," I said. "I knew in my heart that someone doctored it after it left my shop."

Jake stood closer and said, "You know that, and I do too, but now it's official. I came by and saw you'd closed up early. What happened, did everyone stay away?"

I smiled at him, remembering the warm glow of having my friends and customers embrace me earlier. "No, as a matter of fact, I sold out my entire morning's production in record time," I said.

"Good for you," Jake said. "Listen, don't be so

hard on me, okay? I care about you. This is hard for me, harder than you can imagine."

It was the most tender thing he'd ever said to me, and from the hurt look in his eyes, I could see that he meant it.

I touched his cheek lightly. "I'm sorry if I've been testy with you. You just can't imagine how much I need you as a boyfriend right now, and not as a state police inspector."

"I wish I could be both," he said.

"But we both know how impossible that is," I replied.

"I promise that as soon as this investigation is over, we'll make time for each other."

I was about to respond when I heard a car horn. It was Grace, and as she parked and approached us, I turned back to Jake, but the moment between us had passed.

"Hello, Jake," Grace said.

"Grace," he said, then turned to me. "I'm sorry, Suzanne, but I've got to go."

"Thanks for stopping by," I said. I wasn't even sure that he heard me as he ducked back into his car.

"What was that all about?" Grace asked as we watched Jake drive away.

"Jake was trying to smooth things over with me," I said.

"Good." She grabbed me by the shoulders and looked deep into my eyes. "So tell me, my friend, how are you holding up?"

"I've been better, but I'm going to figure this out, trust me."

"You mean 'we,' don't you?"

I shook my head. "Grace, I don't want to pull you into another investigation."

"You're not pulling, I'm pushing. If you have someone to talk to, let me go with you. I'm good at it, and you know it."

I agreed, then told her about helping Heather go through Peg's things. "You don't have to come with me, but you're welcome to join us if you'd like."

"Try to stop me," she said. "Just let me go home and change, and we can get started."

As Grace changed in her bathroom, I sat on her bed and brought her up to date on what I'd learned. "Believe it or not, it appears that Peg Masterson was smack in the middle of a love triangle."

"Why would you find that hard to believe?" Grace asked. "Surely not because of her age."

"Honestly, that has a little to do with it, but mostly it's because of what kind of person Peg was. Any guesses about who her boyfriend was?"

"You've got me, unless it was Max."

I laughed at that response. "You're not even close. She was dating Burt Gentry before they broke up."

"Sweet old Burt from the hardware store?" Grace asked.

"One and the same," I admitted.

Grace poked her head out of the bathroom and said, "You know what? I can see it. He's still a handsome man, and he treats women as if we matter." Grace frowned, then asked, "You said triangle. Who's the third side?"

"Marge Rankin," I said.

"Now that I find hard to believe. Suzanne, I hope this is more than just idle speculation."

"She called the hardware store while I was talking to Burt, and he confirmed it. The thing is, Burt claims that he broke up with Peg, and someone else told me it was the other way around."

"Who's your source?" Grace asked.

"I'd rather not say just yet. She told me in confidence."

"It was Trish," Grace said.

"How could you have possibly known that?" I asked.

"It just makes sense. Who else could your source be?"

I shrugged, then said, "I wonder if Peg had any money."

"I don't know, but we can find out," Grace said as she came out wearing blue jeans and T-shirt. It was the same kind of outfit I wore every day, but somehow she made it look special.

We were getting into Grace's car when my cell phone rang.

After saying hello, George told me, "I had one of my buddies run a check on Peg to see if she had a record. She was clean, but something interesting popped up. It turns out her second ex-husband was arrested for assault. From what I understand, he has quite a temper, but I can't really see it as a motive for murder. They've been divorced for six years. It's a little long to wait to get even, wouldn't you think?"

"Who knows how some people's minds work?" I asked. "Thanks for calling."

"I'll keep you informed," he said, and then hung up.

We pulled up in front of Peg's house and saw Heather's old car parked in the driveway.

As we walked up the steps, Grace asked, "Do you think Heather will mind that I tagged along?"

"Are you kidding? She's overwhelmed with the job. I'm sure she'll take whatever help she can get."

I rang the doorbell, and Heather came out, already looking tired and defeated. "Hey, Suzanne. It's worse than I thought."

I said, "That's why I brought reinforcements. Heather, have you met my best friend Grace?"

"No, it's a pleasure," Heather said as she shook Grace's hand. "You must be a good friend to be willing to do this."

"There's nothing I like better than cleaning," Grace said.

It took everything I had not to laugh.

As we walked inside, I asked, "So, where would you like to get started?"

Heather looked around trying to figure out where best to put us to work, and that gave me a chance to size up Peg's place. It was decorated impeccably, something that shouldn't have surprised me. Peg wasn't afraid to spend money on herself, and the furnishings proved it. Thick Oriental rugs covered hardwood floors polished to a bright shine, while antiques were everywhere. Crystal candy bowls were everywhere, filled with butterscotch candies, peppermints, and wintergreen lozenges. There was a nice selection of art hanging on the walls, and I realized that whoever inherited this from Peg was going to find themselves with a windfall. If her beneficiary was her niece, Heather was going to find it easier to pay for college than she ever could have imagined.

"Why don't one of you start on the master bedroom and the other one take her home office. I'm up to my ears in the kitchen, so any help you can give me will be greatly appreciated."

"What exactly is it that you want us to do?" Grace asked.

"I'm looking for any papers that will help me figure out what I should do next. The lawyer told me I'm her executor, but I haven't been able to find much in the way of paper trails. Too, if you run across something that looks valuable, set it aside." She must have realized how that sounded, because she quickly added, "I'm not treasure hunting. I just have to have the house ready to sell in a week, so anything that's not worth much has to go. Once I've sorted through everything, I can figure out what to do with the rest."

"Were you her only beneficiary?" I asked. It might have been an indelicate question, but it was something I needed to know.

"I haven't even seen the will yet, so I don't know. I was just told to do this, so that's all I'm concerned about at the moment. Honestly, I won't mind if I don't get a dime. There are some old photographs I'd like to have and a few other keepsakes, but other than that, I don't really care who gets it."

I nodded. "Then we'll do our best to help you sort this all out."

Grace and I walked down the hallway, and I asked, "Which room do you want?"

"I'll take the bedroom," she said. "You know how I feel about paperwork."

"Then I'll handle the office." I lowered my voice as I added, "If you find anything that's of interest to us, show me first."

"Right back at you," she said, and we split up.

While the public part of the house had been pristine, the office was a train wreck. Papers were stacked everywhere, and it would take a forensic accountant to figure out Peg's ultimate worth. But that wasn't going to stop me from my search.

An hour into it, I hadn't turned up any clues about what might have happened to Peg, but I did have a much clearer picture of her financial status.

The woman had been loaded. It all became clear once I found her investment log buried under a pile of grocery store receipts and take-out menu flyers. The first entry in the log showed a $50,000 entry as a divorce settlement from her angry ex-husband, and I could see a reason why he'd been so mad. Peg had parlayed that initial investment into stock, which she soon sold at a huge profit, and then split into more stock, then real estate investments in town, and a pretty healthy pile of certificates of deposit to boot. Who knew she was so well off? It wasn't a million dollars when it all added up, but it was within shouting distance of it. I had to wonder what her will said. Had she left her money to Heather, or had she given it to someone else? Say a boyfriend like Burt. Then again, it was just idle speculation at this point. Peg could have left every dime to the Society to Outlaw Daylight Savings Time for all I knew.

I needed to find out exactly what that will said. I had a hunch it might lead me to another suspect.

I jotted down some notes on a separate sheet of

paper, and was just closing the log when the office door opened.

I quickly folded the sheet up and tried to stick it in my pants pocket.

"If that's a grocery list, don't forget eggs," Grace said. "People are always forgetting them."

"Hey," I said. "Come and look at this."

I showed her the log, and she whistled softly when she saw the bottom line. "That's a motive in my book."

"I know, but who gets it? That's the question."

"I'd love to know," I said as I shut the book and buried it back under the papers I'd been riffling through.

"Maybe we can find out. Don't you have a contact at the courthouse?"

"I used to, but I don't know anyone there now," I said. "Who could we ask?"

"Why don't you call George? He's working part-time there, isn't he? Maybe he can find out."

I bit my lip, then said, "I don't know. I've been asking him so much lately, I hate to push it."

"Don't worry about it. We'll come up with a way to find out," she said. Grace's eyes lit up as she added, "I almost forgot why I came in here."

She shoved a well-worn note into my hand.

"What is it?" I asked.

"Open it. I found it in one of Peg's jacket pockets."

I did as she asked, and began to read it. In a strong hand, it said,

Peg,
  There's no use trying to change my mind.

I won't allow it, and you should be prepared for the consequences.

There was no signature, just a torn bit of paper at the edge.

"Where's the rest of it, Grace?"

"It's all I could find, but I'll keep looking." I shoved the note into my pocket, then said, "You know what? I have to give Heather the log I found. It's exactly what she's been looking for."

"You're right." Grace looked around the room, then said, "This must have been the only messy room in her house."

"You mean the bedroom isn't like this?"

Grace laughed. "No, it's as neat as a pin. Not the bathroom, though."

"What's it like?"

"Did you know that Peg dyed her hair? I found a freshly opened box of hair dye in her bathroom, but it wasn't a brand I'd ever heard of. In fact, there were generic items everywhere, from her toothpaste to her shampoo."

I thought about the incongruity to the log, then I said, "Maybe that's the reason she had so much money when she died."

I dug out the financial log just as Heather came in.

The hope in her voice was just about gone when she asked us, "Did you find anything?"

"We were just coming to get you," I said.

I handed her the log, and as she opened it, I watched her read the numbers as they continued to grow almost exponentially.

She looked like she was going to faint by the time

she got to the bottom line. "Are you all right?" I asked.

"I had no idea she was worth this much," she said.

"I doubt anyone else knew, either."

Heather nodded absently. "I'd better get this to her lawyer's office. This is one of the things he asked me to find."

"Can we give you a ride?"

"No, Mr. Crenshaw works in Union Square. I wonder why Aunt Peg didn't use someone closer to home?"

"Maybe she didn't want anyone in town to know how much she was actually worth," Grace said.

I'd thought it, but I wasn't going to say it. "We'll be glad to keep working while you're gone." There was still a great deal more hunting I wanted to do in the house, and without worrying about Heather popping up, Grace and I would be able to do it much quicker.

"I'd better not," Heather said. "I trust you completely, but Mr. Crenshaw was pretty specific. No one can be here unless I'm here, too. Thanks for your help in finding this."

"We were glad to help," I said as Heather walked us out, the log tucked safely under her arm.

Once she was gone, Grace said, "We could always break in."

"I don't think so. Think how happy it would make Chief Martin if he could lock me up. I'm certainly not going to give him any reason to." I added, "She's going to be rich, isn't she?"

"Heather? Probably. That's a lot of money we're talking about."

I bit my lip, then I said, "I wonder if she's telling the truth."

"About what?" Grace asked me.

"Knowing about her aunt's money. It's enough reason for a great many folks to commit murder, wouldn't you say?"

Grace shrugged. "A hundred dollars is enough motivation for some people, but I don't think she's a killer. Do you?"

"I'm just not sure," I said after giving it a little more thought.

As we got into Grace's car, she asked, "Did you notice anything odd in the house?"

"Besides what a wreck the office was?"

"Think about it. There wasn't a single photograph anywhere in the place."

"Maybe she didn't like pictures," I said.

"But didn't Heather say that's what she was looking for?"

I shrugged. "Who knows? They could be in a box in that office and no one may ever find them. I can't believe how wealthy Peg was."

"You never can tell, can you?"

I took the note out of my pocket again and re-read it.

"Is it from Burt?" Grace asked.

"That's my guess," I said. "But the problem is, I don't have a sample of his handwriting to compare it to."

"That shouldn't be hard to get," Grace said. "I can get him to place an order for something for me, and we'll be able to compare his handwriting with that."

"Just don't let him know why you want it," I said.

"Trust me, he won't have a clue."

As Grace started to drive away from Peg's house, she said, "What do you have planned for the rest of our afternoon?"

"What makes you think I have a plan?"

"I know you, Suzanne. There's got to be something else we can do."

I admitted, "I need to talk to Marge to see if her story matches Burt's about their dating history. I hate to interrogate a friend, but I don't have any choice."

"I'll come with you," she said.

"To be honest with you, I'm not sure Marge will speak as freely in front of you, Grace." I hated to hurt my best friend's feelings, but this was something I had to do alone. Knowing Marge, if I brought reinforcements with me, she'd clam up and wouldn't say a word. But if I could convince her that we were just having a chat between two friends, she might open up, and I could learn something.

"While you're doing that, I'll go ahead and see if I can get Burt to give me that writing sample."

"I'm starting to have second thoughts about that," I said.

"Don't worry about me. I'll be careful, Suzanne."

"I'm just afraid that if you start asking questions randomly, you're likely to spark the wrong kind of interest. Don't ever forget that there's a killer out there, and one of us could be next on his list."

Grace looked as if my words had stung her, and a part of me regretted being so blunt, but if anything happened to her while she was trying to help me, I'd never be able to forgive myself.

I took her hands in mine and said, "Promise me you'll be careful."

Grace nodded. "I promise." She added, "Call me after you talk to Marge, okay?"

"You call me if you find something first."

"It's a deal." She held out her hand.

"What?"

"It might help me compare handwriting if you let me have that note I gave you."

"Fine," I said as I took it out of my pocket and handed it to her.

Grace offered me a slight laugh as she dropped me back off at my car in front of the donut shop.

"Talk to you soon," she said.

Grace drove off in her fancy new BMW, and I got into my banged-up old Jeep. As we split off in different directions, I didn't envy her the nice car she was driving, because it came with a price tag I wasn't willing to pay, answering to bosses I didn't care for, doing something that didn't matter all that much to me in the long run. I was fairly certain Grace wouldn't trade with me, either. She enjoyed a healthy and steady income, had a great deal of flexibility in her hours, and could take a vacation whenever she wanted. I was still waiting for a real day off, but I enjoyed making donuts, and satisfying a sweet tooth now and then was all I cared about.

I thought about driving straight to Marge's, but then I realized that I was dirty from working at Peg's, and I still smelled like donuts from the day's production, so I knew I had to go home to shower and change before I spoke with her. That plan of action carried a pitfall of its own. It meant that I had to talk to my mother, which was not generally an odious task, but with my unofficial investigation going at full speed, I had a feeling she knew what I was up to. And if she did, I was going to get lecture #134 on letting the police handle murder cases and sticking to making donuts.

CHAPTER 7

"I love seeing you in that dress," my mother said as I came back downstairs after my shower. She hadn't been there when I'd gotten home, and I was just beginning to think I'd make a clean getaway when I found her sitting in the front parlor.

"Thanks," I said. "I thought it would be a nice change of pace from my usual blue jeans."

She shook her head and smiled at me. "Suzanne, don't try to fool me. You're up to something."

"Can't a gal dress up and look nice now and then without any particular reason?" I asked.

"Some can, but not you. Where are you going?"

"Out," I said.

It hadn't worked when I'd been a teenager, but maybe it would work now.

"Out where?" she asked.

So maybe it wasn't going to work after all.

I was trying to think of how to couch my answer when she suddenly smiled. "Are you going to see Jake?"

"I might be," I said, not entirely lying. We could bump into each other by accident, couldn't we?

"I think that's a wonderful idea," she said. "This

situation has put entirely too much stress on your relationship."

I know there are times when I need to stand my ground, moments when I should tell the complete and unvarnished truth, and take the consequences, no matter what they are.

This wasn't one of those times.

I smiled at her, showed her my crossed fingers, and said, "Wish me luck."

"You know you always have it all," she said.

I drove to Marge's, wondering about the conversation I'd just had with my mother. We could go weeks and not have an odd word between us, but then something would happen that would trigger us, and we'd be back to our old roles of mother and daughter again, with her trying to guide my way through life, even though I was a grown woman with a marriage—and a divorce—under my belt.

I supposed that would never entirely change as long as we lived under the same roof, and I thought about moving out for the thousandth time since I'd shown up on her doorstep after finding Max with his paramour, but I just couldn't bring myself to do it.

At least for now, I was going to stay right where I was.

"Don't you look nice," Marge said as I walked into her living room. After how we'd left things the last time we'd been together, I wasn't sure how she'd react to me. That was why I'd just shown up, hoping that she'd have a harder time turning me away in person than on the telephone.

"Thanks. You do, too."

Marge said, "Would you like some tea? I was just about to have some myself."

"That would be nice," I said.

Marge was wearing a peach-toned dress with shoes that matched exactly. As she readied the pot, she said, "Unless I miss my guess, I saw an outfit just like that at Gabby's once."

"This is it," I admitted. "It's the only place I shop for my formal wear." It was true, too, since the dress I was wearing was the only thing I had in my closet that I couldn't wear to Donut Hearts.

"It just makes sense, doesn't it? Why pay full retail for something when Gabby has such a wonderful selection at such good prices. So, what brings you by?"

I bit my lip and wondered how to bring Burt into the conversation. It was a delicate situation, one that could easily be made worse, if I didn't handle things just right.

"I need your help," I said, surprising myself with the suddenness of the statement. Long ago I'd learned the best way to approach most people who were reluctant to speak candidly to me was to ask for some kind of assistance, if I could. It tended to make folks more receptive to me.

She nodded. "Of course. Whatever I can do, you can count on me."

"It's about Peg Masterson. With the way she was killed, there's a great deal of talk that I might have had something to do with it, and I'm trying to clear my good name."

"I haven't said anything," Marge said, putting a hand over her heart. "I swear to you, Suzanne, I wouldn't."

"I wasn't accusing you," I replied hastily. "It's just that I need to find out why she was killed, and I can't do it if I don't ask some indelicate questions."

Marge nodded. "I've spoken with Burt, and I understand you know about our relationship. We'd hoped to keep it quiet, but these things do seem to get out in a small town, don't they?"

"It's tough keeping any secrets here," I agreed. "But then again, I didn't know about Peg and Burt, either."

She waved a hand in the air. "From what I understand, there was nothing really to know about it. They shared a few meals together, saw a movie or two, but that was the extent of it."

"But when you came along, he stopped doing even that, is that right?"

Marge handed me a cup of tea, and I couldn't help notice that her hand was shaking slightly as she did. The echoed circles on the cup's surface magnified her case of nerves. "As I said, there wasn't anything to stop, really. He was never really all that serious about her."

"So he told you," I said as I took a sip.

Marge frowned. "Why should he lie to me?"

"I don't know," I said. "It just seems odd that your new boyfriend's old girlfriend was murdered in your garden."

Marge shook her head. "Don't give her the title. She had the nerve to try to scare me away from him, can you believe that?"

"What did she say?"

Marge looked angry as she admitted, "Peg told me Burt was after my money, not me. She said he'd drop me just like he'd dumped her when he got what he wanted."

"Is the hardware store in some kind of financial trouble?" I hadn't heard any rumors to that effect, but I didn't hear every bit of gossip in town.

Marge shook her head. "Burt said it's seasonal, that things will pick back up soon enough and he'll pay me back, including interest." She looked almost triumphant as she said it.

"How much have you given him?"

Marge must have suddenly realized that she'd told me something she hadn't meant to. She said abruptly, "Suzanne, I'm not sure I like your line of inquiry."

I tried to soften my position. "I'm not making any claims. I'm just thinking how all of this must look to the police. They've spoken to you about Peg, haven't they? Surely they must have."

She nodded. "I discussed the situation with Chief Martin, and then again with a state police inspector named Queen."

"Do you mean Bishop?" I asked.

She said, "I knew it was a chess piece, I just couldn't remember which one. Now that you mention it, yes, it must have been Bishop. Either way, neither one of them seemed to put much credence in any clash I might have had with Peg."

"But did they know about Burt?" I asked.

"How on earth would I know that? Suzanne, is that why you're here, to grill me like a common murderer? I don't think I want to talk to you about this any more."

"And you shouldn't have to," Burt said as he came

into the kitchen. "Why are you asking these questions?"

"I'm just looking for the truth."

Burt answered, "Suzanne, we appreciate the fact that you're trying to find Peg's killer, but you're wasting your time with us. Now if you'll excuse us, we're late for a movie."

Marge looked startled for a moment, but then nodded in agreement. "We really must be going. I'd nearly forgotten about it."

They walked me out to my Jeep, and we all drove off at the same time. The interview hadn't been particularly illuminating, but watching them together had been. Burt was extremely protective of Marge, something I hadn't really expected if they'd just been seeing each other such a short time. Was there more to their story than either one of them was willing to admit? It was a possibility I had to consider, no matter how much I liked each of them. This wasn't a popularity contest, which was a good thing, because if it had been, I was certain to come in last place.

So, now I was dressed up, with no place to go. It made perfect sense to go home and change clothes— since the dress wasn't exactly my first choice in apparel—but then again, it wouldn't hurt to be seen around town in something besides the blue jeans I typically wore. My cell phone rang, and I was relieved to see that it was Grace.

After saying hello, I asked her, "What did you find out?"

"You first," she said.

"It's too involved to go over on the phone. I don't

know about you, but I could use some pie. Do you
have any interest in meeting me at the Boxcar?"

"I'll be there in four minutes," she said.

I figured Trish would get a kick out of my attempt
to dress up, and I was sure she could make me laugh,
something that was sorely missing in my life at the
moment.

I parked in the gravel lot, then I walked up the
steps into the converted dining car.

"You shouldn't be here," Trish said as she approached me. I'd barely made it through the door, and
her tone was a surprising one to hear coming from a
friend.

"What did I do? Don't tell me you're afraid of
anyone seeing me eat here when some folks are suspicious of me."

"Don't be ridiculous," she said. "This is for your
own good."

"I'm a grown woman, Trish. I don't need to be
shielded from anything."

"Suit yourself," she said. Trish took in my outfit,
then added, "I'll say this for you. At least you look
good."

I wanted to smile, but I had a hard time coming
up with one. "Hey, I always look good. Today, I just
look a little better."

She was called to the register by a customer wanting to pay, and I started looking for a place to sit.

Then I saw why she'd tried to warn me off. Sitting
in a booth near the back was my ex-husband Max, as
handsome and charming as ever. I was used to seeing him around town, but it was his dining compan-
ion that threw me off step.

He was with Darlene Higgins, the woman he'd slept with the day he'd thrown our marriage away. I didn't like her and took pleasure in the fact that although her blonde hair was natural, I suspected her curves were not. For just a moment, I wanted to duck out, but then, steeling my nerve, I walked straight toward them.

"Hi, Max," I said. "Hello, Darlene."

To Max's credit, he looked like he wanted to crawl into a hole and die. Darlene, on the other hand, appeared to want to take out a front page ad in the newspaper.

"Suzanne, hi," Max said. "I was having lunch, and Darlene just came over and sat down. Would you like to join us?"

She looked as though she'd rather eat glass than share a seat with me, and I thought about joining them just to spite her, but that was more than my stomach could take. "No, thanks," I said. "I just came by for some pie to go." There was no way I was going to sit there with Grace while my ex-husband was on a date.

Darlene said, "I admire you for that. It's awfully brave of a woman your age to just let herself go and eat whatever she wants."

I looked at her half a second, then said, "I have to admit, it's certainly a great deal easier once you stop trying to hold onto someone who doesn't want to be with you. But then you'd know all about that too, wouldn't you?"

Before she could rebut, or Max could protest, I added, "You know what? I've suddenly lost my appetite. Good-bye."

I left the grill, and was surprised to find that Max had followed me out.

"That wasn't what it looked like," he said.

"Max, were you under the impression that I still cared? You don't owe me any explanations anymore. We're divorced, remember?"

He nodded. "I'm not likely to forget. I didn't invite her to lunch, I didn't ask her to sit down, and I was trying to get rid of her when you walked in."

"You didn't look like you were trying that hard," I said as I continued walking toward my Jeep.

"You look really great," he said as he watched me move away.

"Oh, Max," I said as I laughed, though there was no joy in it. "You're losing your touch. In the old days, you would have led with that."

I got into the Jeep and drove away, and as I turned the corner, I glanced back and saw that Max was still watching me.

What was wrong with me? I hadn't handled that situation well at all, and I knew it. Why should I care who Max chose to eat with, and why was it bothering me so much? I was finally free of him. Or was I? I hated to admit it—and would have denied it if confronted with the truth—but my first reaction upon seeing Max with Darlene was jealousy, pure and simple. I wasn't sure if that meant I was still carrying a little torch for him, and if I was being honest about it, I wasn't at all certain I wanted to find out.

Leave the past to the past, I told myself and dialed Grace's number to ask her to meet me at home.

It would be easier said than done, though, and I knew it.

When she walked up onto the front porch, Grace took in my outfit, and then said, "Did you get dressed up for Marge, or was there another stop on your list?"

"No, I was just trying to impress her." I wasn't going to tell her about running into Max and Darlene, at least not yet. I wasn't sure myself what it meant, and didn't want to have to explain it to her.

Grace nodded. "Go on, tell me what happened."

"Why don't we go inside? Give me two minutes so I can change into jeans, and I'll join you in the living room."

"If you don't mind, I'll stay out here. It's a beautiful day," she said.

"Momma's out walking, if you're worried about that."

"No, I just don't get enough fresh air in my life," she said.

"That sounds good. I'll be back soon," I said. Good as my word, I came back out in five minutes, with blue jeans and an old football jersey on, my hair pulled back into a ponytail.

"That's the girl we all know and love," Grace said the second she saw me.

"Can I help it if I'm more comfortable this way?"

"Are you kidding me? There are days I'd be willing to take a pay cut and trade places with you, just so I wouldn't have to dress up."

I smiled at her. "Anytime you want to swap career paths, just let me know."

"You don't mean that, and neither do I," she said with a laugh. "Tell me how Marge reacted to you grilling her. I've been dying to know."

"She was fine, at least at first," I admitted. "When

I started pushing her, though, she wasn't too pleased with me. Burt showed up, if you can believe that, and he practically threw me out of her house. The thing is, I can't be sure he wasn't there the entire time, eavesdropping on us."

Grace stared out at the park for a minute, then said, "It sure sounds like they've got something to hide."

"I'm starting to think so, too."

I hesitated, thinking about telling her about my encounter with Max right then, but decided not to. Grace wasn't my ex-husband's biggest fan, and I didn't want to add any fuel to the flames. She could tell I was holding back on her, though. "Suzanne, what else happened? Are you sure you didn't see Jake?"

"Not since I got dressed up."

She stopped us swinging. "If it's not Jake, then who is it?" Grace frowned for a moment, then said, "Tell me it's not Max."

I couldn't keep it from her any longer. "I would if I could, but you know how much I hate lying to you."

Grace shook her head sadly. "He's no good for you, Suzanne."

"I saw him at the Boxcar grill with Darlene," I said flatly.

"No. They're together again? I thought that was a one-time thing. At least that's what Max has been telling everybody."

Staring down at my hands, I said, "He tried to tell me they weren't together, but they looked pretty cozy."

"I'm amazed Trish didn't stop you before you saw them."

I shrugged. "She tried to, but I was too dense to pick up on what she was trying to tell me. Don't worry, I'm not going to waste any more tears for Max ever again, not if I can help it."

Grace put a hand lightly on my shoulder. "That's best, and deep in your heart, you know it."

There was no way I was going to tell her how I'd felt when I'd seen Max and Darlene together. I was certain it would do nothing more productive than generate a lecture I didn't want to hear. "Can we not talk about my ex-husband anymore?"

"I'd be thrilled if we never mentioned him again," she said. Grace reached into her purse and pulled out an order sheet for Christmas lights.

"New lights? Really?" I asked.

"I couldn't think of anything else to buy," she said as she handed me the note I'd seen earlier at Peg's.

"They don't match," Grace said as I examined them. I could be wrong, but I didn't think there was any way both of those notes had been written by the same person. Since Burt was ruled out, who did that leave?

At the moment, I didn't have a clue. It might not even be a break-up note. I'd just assumed it was when I'd read it.

"If you don't mind, I'll hold onto this," I said as I tucked the note into my pocket.

"Where do we go from here?" Grace asked.

"I'm not sure just yet," I said.

I looked out onto the park and saw my mother fast approaching. "Let's drop it for the moment, okay? She still doesn't know what I'm doing."

Grace laughed. "Don't be so sure about that. That

woman has some kind of radar when it comes to you and misbehaving. Remember the time we put Tide in the fountain out in front of the courthouse? How long did it take her to find out, and make us clean up the mess ourselves?"

"Okay, we should have bought a new jug instead of draining hers, I admit that. We weren't exactly master criminals back then, were we?"

"No, but think how much trouble we could get into now, if we really put our heads together."

Momma approached, and before she could say anything, I fired one of my preemptive strikes. "Did you have a nice walk? It's a beautiful day, isn't it?"

"It was lovely. How was Jake?"

"I didn't get a chance to see him," I said.

Momma nodded. "Don't give up." She studied each of us in turn, then she said, "You two are up to something."

"Do you automatically assume that Grace and I are doing something we shouldn't be doing?"

"Based on your past history, it's really not that great a leap of reasoning, now is it?" she said with a smile.

I started to protest again when Grace began laughing beside me. "She's got us there, and you know it." Then she turned to my mother and said, "We were planning another bubble assault on city hall."

"Let me grab my purse and I'll help," my mother said.

"Mrs. Hart, I didn't know you had it in you."

She looked at Grace and smiled. "There's a great deal you don't know about me, young lady."

"I'm beginning to realize that," she said.

I said, "On second thought, if you two are planning a bubble run, count me out. I'm in enough trouble with the chief of police as it is."

Momma asked, "Anything recent, Suzanne?"

"Do you mean besides being at a murder scene where one of my donuts was used to kill someone that nobody in town really liked? I guess if you discount all of that, he doesn't have a single motive in the world not to like me."

My mother clicked her tongue at me. "You're problem is that you never learned how to deal with Phillip Martin."

"You know what? I couldn't agree with you more."

Momma gave her head a brief shake, then she said, "I'm going inside for some lemonade. Would you two like to join me?"

Grace stood as she said, "Thanks, but I've got to be going."

"Don't rush off on my account," Momma said.

"I'm not. I just have a few more things to do today."

My mother nodded. "This time, be sure to get a soap that's environmentally friendly."

"I promise. See you at the church bell tower at midnight."

After Grace was gone, my mother asked, "She wasn't serious, was she?"

"Honestly, with her, you never know."

My mother took in my new, more casual outfit, then said, "I didn't want to say anything in front of your friend, but I must say, I'm disappointed you changed out of your dress so quickly."

"I felt like a lawyer in it," I said. "This is the real me."

My mother shook her head. "That's exactly what I'm afraid of. Are you hungry at all?"

"I'm starving," I admitted. "What did you have in mind?"

"I was thinking we could thaw out that leftover lasagna we had last week. With a salad and some garlic bread, it should be all right. I just don't feel like cooking."

"Hey, lasagna sounds great. You heat it up, and I'll set the table."

After we ate, I turned on the television, flipped through the stations twice, then shut it off again. My mother wasn't a big fan of cable, so we had what we could get from Charlotte and were limited in what we had available to watch. We did have a nice collection of movies on DVD, but I didn't feel like watching one of those, either.

Evidently my mother noticed. "You're restless tonight, Suzanne. Is there something on your mind?"

"No, for some reason, I'm just out of sorts."

She sat beside me. "I know you have friends you can talk to, but I'm here, too. If you need a sympathetic ear, I'm always available."

I patted her hand. "Thanks for the offer, but tonight, I wouldn't even know where to begin. I think I'll call it an early evening and head upstairs."

"Suit yourself," she said. "Good night."

"Night," I said as I started toward my room. Before I left, though, I turned to her and said, "Thanks, Momma."

"For what?" she asked as she picked up her novel.

"For offering to listen to my problems. One of these days I might just take you up on it."

"Any time, Suzanne."

I walked into my room and shut the door tightly behind me. I picked up the novel I was reading, but it just couldn't hold my interest. Staring at my cell phone, I willed it to ring, with Jake on the other end, but it appeared that I lacked those particular powers and it remained mute. At least I could leave him a message.

"Hi, Jake. It's Suzanne. I'd like to see you tomorrow, if you can make some time for me. It would be great if we could have a chance to talk."

I'd given up on waiting for him to call me. I got his voice mail, which didn't really surprise me. I knew firsthand how focused he could be when he was working on a case.

I checked the phone's battery level, then noticed the inbox indicator flashing in the lower left-hand corner of the display. I'd forgotten all about the calls I'd missed the day Peg had died. I didn't have anything else to do, so I decided to clear them out, just in case there was something important I may have missed. I was deleting them almost as fast as they were playing when my finger suddenly hesitated over the delete button.

One of my calls was from Peg Masterson herself, a voice that sent shivers through me as it seemed to reach out from the grave.

In her unmistakable timbre and tone, she said, "Suzanne, if you insist on doing this, you should know that if you don't perform up to my expectations, I'm going to get rid of you without a second of hesitation. You will ruin this kitchen tour over my dead body, do you understand me?"

It took me a second to realize what she was talking about, and then I knew that she must have left the message right after she'd left Marge's kitchen, and just before she'd been murdered.

I knew how it would sound to Chief Martin, who was clearly already suspicious about me.

Without hesitation, I hit the delete button, glad that no one else had heard that particular message.

SUPER EASY DONUTS

These are a fun and fast alternative when you just don't have the time to wait for yeast donuts to rise twice. Delicious, and ready to eat fast!

INGREDIENTS

- 1 tablespoon white vinegar
- ½ cup milk
- 2 tablespoons shortening
- ½ cup white sugar
- 1 egg
- ½ teaspoon vanilla extract
- 2–3 cups sifted all-purpose flour
- ½ teaspoon baking soda
- ¼ teaspoon salt
- 1 quart oil for deep frying
- ½ cup confectioners' sugar for dusting

DIRECTIONS

Stir the vinegar into the milk, then let the mixture stand for a few minutes until it thickens slightly.

In another bowl, cream the shortening and sugar together until smooth, then beat in the egg and the vanilla until everything is well blended.

In another bowl, sift together the flour, baking soda, and salt, then combine the dry ingredients with the wet, adding a little bit at a time until it is all well blended.

Roll the dough out on a floured surface to 1/4- to 1/2-inch thick. Cut out donut rounds and ravioli-sized pieces and let them rest for 10 minutes.

Add the donuts to the hot oil, turning them once as they brown. Drain them on a rack or paper towels, then dust them with confectioners' sugar while they are still warm.

Yield: Makes 8–12 donuts

CHAPTER 8

My alarm sprang to life much too early for my taste, and I struggled to shut it off before it managed to wake Momma up, too. She always claimed to not hear it, but I knew that sometimes it roused her from her sleep. As I got dressed and hurriedly ate a bowl of cereal, I turned my telephone on to see if Jake had called me after I'd left him a message. There was a zero on the display when I checked for any new messages, and I wondered why he hadn't at least tried to get in touch with me.

As I walked out to my car, I realized that it was a beautiful night—the temperature was somewhere in the mid-fifties and the humidity almost nonexistent—and thought about walking across the park to the donut shop. It was an impulse I squelched, though. There was too much darkness, too many shadows for evil to hide in, and my nerves were tight bands that vibrated with every slight breeze.

Donut Hearts was dark, as I'd expected it to be, but there was something wrong about the place. It took me a second to realize what it was, and then I noticed that there was something sitting on one of the tables I kept out front for customers.

As I got closer, I saw that it was one of my lemon-filled donuts, and there was a green miniature plastic sword embedded in the middle of it. Some of the lemon filling had oozed out of the puncture wound, and I was very glad they hadn't used cherry or raspberry instead. I wasn't sure if I could handle a filling that looked like blood.

And that was it. No threatening note, no one lurking in the shadows, just a sad little donut with a skewer jammed into it. If it was a joke, it was in extremely bad taste, and if it was a warning, it was too silly to be frightening. What were they trying to say, stop nosing around or the donut gets it? As threats went, it wasn't much of one. Probably it was a group of teenagers who thought it would be funny to throw a scare into me.

Still, just in case it was more serious, I grabbed a plastic glove from inside the shop and put the donut, along with its skewer, safely on a tray and took it back to my office and set it on my desk. Should I call the chief, or maybe one of the local officers more sympathetic to me, or should I go straight to the top and let Jake know what I found?

I wasn't sure what to do, so I put the tray on top of the bookshelf, and started getting things ready so we could make the donuts for another day.

Emma was ten minutes late, and I'd already started making my preparations without her.

I glanced at the clock as she walked in, and Emma said, "I know, I know. I'm sorry. I came as fast as I could."

"Another late-night date?" I asked as I continued preparing the ingredients for the day's cake donuts.

She frowned as she said, "No, Paul dropped me off at my house at nine."

"Don't tell me the bloom is wearing off the rose already?"

"I'm afraid it might be," Emma said, and when I looked at her, I could see that she was really concerned about it.

"Come on, I was just teasing you," I said.

She shrugged. "I know that." After a moment's pause, she said, "Suzanne, could I ask you something?"

I nodded absently as I weighed out the ingredients for my brand-new modified pumpkin donut recipe.

"What do men really expect in a relationship? And what makes them want to stay?"

I couldn't help myself; a hearty laugh escaped my lips before I could rein it back in.

Emma frowned at me and said, "I'm serious. It's not funny."

"The question's not, but you have to be able to pick someone better to give you advice about men. I'm not exactly the world's leading authority on relationships."

"You've been married, though," she said.

"Need I remind you that it failed, and pretty miserably at that?"

Emma wasn't going to let me off the hook that easily, though. "I've seen the way Max looks at you when he comes in here. He still has feelings for you, and that's even after you divorced him."

"Not without cause," I said. I stopped what I was doing and looked hard at Emma. "My friend, there aren't any easy answers. You're going to have to find your own way. We all do, you know."

"I guess," she said with a frown. "I just didn't think being a grownup was going to be all that hard."

"It's one of the toughest jobs there is," I said. When I saw the gloom intensify, I added, "Don't worry, it's not all bad. There are a lot of fringe benefits, too."

"Name one," she said.

"You can have dessert for breakfast, if you want. That's kind of what we do for the world, isn't it?"

"I guess so," she said.

I reached for her apron and threw it to her. "Then we'd better get to work, or we're going to disappoint half of April Springs."

"We wouldn't want to do that, would we?"

"Don't worry," I said as I hugged her quickly. "Everything will all work out in the end. Trust me."

"I can't help wondering if Peg Masterson felt that way too, and we both know what happened to her."

I said, "Emma, we can't feel guilty about that. Someone killed her, but it wasn't our fault they used a donut to deliver the poison to her system. All we can do is move on, and do the best we can with what we've got."

"Is that what you're doing?" she asked. "I thought you were looking for Peg's killer yourself?"

"That's different. There are good reasons for what I'm doing." I dusted my hands together, then said,

"Now, we can talk, or we can make donuts and earn a little money today. Which one is it going to be?"

"I vote for the money," Emma said.

"That gets my vote, too, so let's get started."

As we worked on preparing today's offerings, I couldn't help wondering if Emma was right. Maybe I should let the police handle things and get on with my life. Then again, if I took a passive approach to the way things turned out, I never would have gotten where I was today. Which, come to think of it, was being locked into a marginal business that barely paid its way most days.

Those thoughts were too dark for such a happy task as making donuts, so I buried them and focused on making the best treats I could. Just because my life was suddenly covered in clouds was no reason not to try and brighten my customers' existences.

By the time were ready to open the doors at 5:30, I was close to coming to terms with what had been happening around me lately. And then I saw Jake standing there waiting to get in, and it all came flooding back to me.

"Hi," I said as I stepped aside to let him in.

"You have a second?" he asked.

I pretended to look around the empty shop. "At the moment, I've got all the time in the world."

"And an assistant who likes to eavesdrop," he said softly.

From the kitchen, Emma said, "I do not."

Jake shrugged, and I said, "Point taken." I turned and said, "Emma, you've got the front."

She came out wiping her hands on one of our towels.

"Spoilsport," she said to Jake, but he was already halfway outside.

"I'll just be a minute," I said.

"Take your time. I think I can handle the place on my own."

I walked outside, and breathed in the chilled air. The promise of the day was heavy in the darkness, and I knew sunrise wasn't far away. "What's up?"

"You called me, remember? I hate it when a woman says we need to talk. I'd rather face down three angry thugs."

I nodded, fighting to keep my smile to myself. "That's probably a good call. Listen, I know you're in town with a job to do, but to be honest with you, I miss you. Can we have dinner together tonight?"

"There's nothing I'd like more, trust me, but you're still one of my prime suspects in the case I'm working on, Suzanne."

I grinned at him. "So, if anyone asks, you can say you were interrogating me. I've been craving spaghetti. Why don't we go to Napoli's?" That was the scene of our first real date and maybe, if only for a few hours, we could forget about everything else.

He returned my smile with one of his own. "Yeah, I've been dreaming about that place." Then he hastily added, "You, too, of course."

"So, what do you say?"

He was going to say yes, I could see it in his eyes, and then his telephone rang. "Hang on one second. I've got to take this."

He turned away from me, whispered something for a few moments, then turned back to me. "I'm sorry, I've got to go."

"What happened? Is there a new development in the case?"

"No, it's nothing like that. It's something personal," he said as he headed for his car.

"What is it?" I asked.

"I'll call you later," he said as he got in and drove off like he was being chased by the devil himself.

What was going on? Was he lying to keep me from knowing something that was going on in the investigation, or was there truly a personal emergency he was facing? If he was, why hadn't he at least given me a hint what it was about? I was a part of his life, after all.

I was still standing there on the sidewalk when Max walked up. In all the years I'd known him, I'd never seen him awake before nine AM, and here it was not even six yet. I asked, "Have you been out all night?"

He shook his head. "No, ma'am. I got to bed at a reasonable hour so I could come by and talk to you before things got busy here."

"I don't have time to talk to you right now, Max."

He looked over my shoulder at the deserted donut shop. "Yeah, I can see you're really jammed up."

"Okay, maybe I've got the time, but I've long since lost the inclination." What was it with men? When I wanted them around, they were as scarce as hen's teeth, but when I was through with them for good, they wouldn't leave me alone.

"Hear me out. I was not out on a date with Darlene yesterday."

It was all I could do not to shout at him. "Max, it doesn't matter what I think anymore, remember?"

"It matters to me, and I'm not leaving until you tell me 'I believe you.'"

I looked him dead in the eye. "Fine, I believe you."

"You don't mean it," Max said.

I let out a sigh, then said, "Have it your way. If you say you aren't dating Darlene, then I believe you. You don't have any reason to lie to me anymore, do you?"

"Good. Now that we've got that settled, have dinner with me tonight."

I walked up to him and put my face within two inches of his. "No, and stop asking. My answer isn't going to change. Now go away."

He laughed. "I'm leaving, but I'm not giving up."

I couldn't take his smugness. "Max, be serious. Why are you so interested in getting back together with me, anyway? I'm nice enough looking, but as handsome as you are, we both know you could do better than a donut maker."

"You don't get it, do you? It's you, Suzanne. It's always been you."

"Maybe at one time that was the truth, but not anymore. Find someone else, Max. Anybody else but me, because I'm not interested."

I walked back into the donut shop and saw that Emma was staring strangely at me.

"What's wrong with you?" I asked her.

She looked at me carefully, then said, "I don't see a gun."

"Emma, what are you talking about?"

She shrugged. "Like I said, I'm looking in vain for some kind of weapon, but whatever you just said hit him harder than a bullet would have. I thought he was going to collapse on the sidewalk. So I can't help wondering, what exactly did you just say to him?"

"I told him the truth," I said flatly.

"No wonder he looked like he wanted to die," she said.

"Don't you have dishes to wash in back?" I asked her.

"I'm getting on it right now, ma'am," she said as she ducked back into the kitchen.

I looked back outside, but Max wasn't anywhere in sight. I'd bludgeoned him with the truth on purpose, trying to get his attention so he'd stop acting so foolishly. I just hoped that I really wanted to let him go in my heart of hearts—once and for all—and move on with my life.

George was conspicuously absent as the morning wore on, and many of the people who'd been so kind the day before were missing as well. It appeared that the show of support I'd enjoyed was over, and reality was starting to rear its ugly head. It wasn't that we had no customers, but there wasn't enough flow to break even if we kept going at the rate we were facing.

Promptly at ten, my donut shop book club group came in. I'd become a member almost by accident, but I loved the one hour every month when I could discuss the latest mystery pick with my new friends. I'd thought about inviting my mother, and maybe some-day I would, but for now, I wanted this all to myself.

The three older women were fast becoming fa-vorites of mine. Sure, they sported expensive cloth-ing and had regal postures, but beneath it all, they were a lot like me.

Jennifer, the redhead and leader of the group, smiled warmly as she saw me. "Hello, Suzanne. Are you going to be able to join us today? We're going to have to keep it to half an hour, but we'd love to have you."

"Let me get Emma up here," I said.

After she was safely ensconced at the front, I grabbed my copy of A *Sudden Deadly End* and joined them after pouring four coffees and grab-bing some huge cinnamon buns.

"I've got treats," I said as I joined Hazel and Elizabeth.

"You know you're welcome without them," Eliza-beth said as she took one of the coffee cups.

"But it's ever so nice with them," Hazel added as she went straight for a bun. She noticed the other two women staring at her, then added, "Suzanne knows I'm teasing." As recompense, she reached into her purse and pulled out a fifty.

"That's too much," I said.

"Please, I'd gladly pay twice that for just one of these creations." After a moment, she added thought-fully, "I shouldn't have admitted that, should I?"

We all laughed, and Jennifer got out her notes. "The first question I have is why would any woman go in that house after she hears the gunshot in chap-ter one?"

"I'd dive in the bushes," I admitted.

"Or drive away," Hazel said.

"Sure, but then he could see you leave, so he'd know you were there. I'd wait until I was sure he couldn't see me, then I'd leave."

Jennifer nodded. "I hadn't thought of that. Sometimes I think authors have their characters do foolish things just to advance the plot."

I smiled. "It wouldn't be a very big book if the heroine called the police at the first sign of trouble, though. I think we have to suspend our disbelief while we're reading, don't you all agree?"

There were solemn nods, and I felt right at home.

Too soon, it was time to break up for another month. "We hate to go, but Hazel's uncle is in the hospital, and we promised to visit. You're welcome to come with us," she added brightly. "We can continue our discussion in the car on the way over."

"I'd love to, but I'm afraid I have to stay here. Thanks for asking."

Jennifer put a hand on mine. "Suzanne, you're a member of our group. Wherever we go, you're always welcome to join us."

After the ladies left, I felt so fortunate to be included in their group. I enjoyed being among bright and energetic people. It had been a lucky day for me when they'd first stumbled into my donut shop looking for a place to hold their meeting.

When the door chimed a little just after eleven, I would have welcomed a band of first-graders, if it meant selling them each a donut.

Instead of a customer, though, it was Janice Deal, the owner of Patty Cakes, and I wondered what was on her mind this morning.

"Hello, Suzanne."

"Hi," I said, trying my best not to show that I was cringing inside. Janice had an attitude that was accompanied by a chip on her shoulder that barely fit through doorways, and I wasn't in the mood to spar with her today. "What can I get you?"

She looked around the deserted shop, then said, "I don't suppose you'd give me some advice," she said.

"Concerning what in particular?" I asked. This was uncharted territory for us, and I wasn't sure I liked covering new ground with her.

"How do you glaze your yeast donuts after you make them? Krispy Kreme has a waterfall system, but I can't imagine you being able to afford something that complex, and glazing them one at time looks like it would take forever."

"Why do you want to know?" Emma asked as she came out of the kitchen. "You're making donuts yourself, aren't you?"

"Emma, be nice," I said.

"Yes, you should learn how to at least be polite to your customers," Janice snapped at her.

"Funny, I didn't hear you order anything," Emma said.

"Go back to the kitchen," I said to my employee.

"But she's . . ."

I wasn't about to have that conversation right now. "Emma. Please do as I ask."

"Fine, you're the boss," she said as she walked back through the door to the kitchen. I noticed that it hadn't closed all the way, and I was certain she was still listening. Good, I wanted her to hear what I had to say next.

"It's good to know that you understand how to keep your employees in line," Janice said.

I took my apron off and slammed it on the counter. "How dare you come in here and insult my staff. She's not just an employee, Janice, she's my friend, and she was only looking out for me."

"What's the matter? Is it possible that you're afraid of a little competition?" Janice asked snidely.

"From you? Hardly. You might as well try to learn to make a decent donut, since your cakes taste like sawdust, and your icing resembles toothpaste. Would you like to discuss your cookies? I've got notes somewhere we could go over if you've got an hour or two."

Her face had paled during my diatribe, and she left my shop without another word, nearly knocking David Shelby over as she stormed off.

As he walked in, Emma started applauding.

"Wow, that's some greeting," he said. "Do you clap for every customer who comes through the door?"

Emma walked out and said, "It's not for you, it's for Suzanne. She just spanked Janice Deal."

I shook my head. "Emma, I'm not exactly proud of the way I handled that," I said. "But she deserved it. I can't believe she thought she could get away with talking to you like that."

"She won't make that mistake twice," Emma said.

My assistant looked at David, then said, "Excuse me; I've got dishes to wash."

After she was gone, David asked, "What exactly did you say to her, anyway? She left like you'd just flayed her alive."

"I attacked her baking skills, or lack thereof, which is pretty much the same thing," I said. "Sometimes I wish the gear between my mouth and my brain worked a little better at shutting me up."

He laughed. "What kind of fun would that be? What did she say to get you so riled up?"

"She wanted some tips on making donuts," I said. "It's bad enough that she wants to put me out of business, but it takes some kind of nerve to ask me for my hard-fought knowledge to do it."

David frowned out the window toward her place. "Just for that, I'm not going to shop in her store."

"Have a big need for decorated cakes and cookies, do you?" I asked.

"No, but you never know what might come up." He looked around the shop, then added, "Do I even need to ask how business is going?"

"The full trays and the empty seats say it all, wouldn't you agree?"

"Tell you what," he said as he studied the case. "I'll take a dozen donuts to go. Mix and match them for me, would you?"

"Having a party?" I asked as I got out a box.

"No, but this way I'll have something to snack on as I work."

Ordinarily I wouldn't have accepted his obviously pity-inspired order so willingly, but I really didn't have much choice. A sale was a sale, and he was getting good donuts for his dollars. Still, after I put twelve donuts in the box, I added a handful of donut holes as well.

As I took his money, I said, "You never told me what you do for a living, did you?"

He grinned as he took his change. "No, I sure didn't."

I was about to push it when my mother walked into the shop. She took one look at David and said, "You're new in town, aren't you?"

"Yes, ma'am, I am."

"Are those donuts for your family?" Momma asked.

"Actually, I'm single. Have a nice day."

"You do the same," she said.

After he was gone, my mother said, "Suzanne, if your relationship with Jake founders, you could always go out with a nice man like that. He dresses well, he obviously likes donuts, and from the way he was looking at you when I walked in, I'd say he's fond of the donut maker as well."

"Momma, don't you torment me enough at home?" I said with a laugh. "Do you honestly have to come down to the shop and do it, too?"

"I've got a life myself, believe it or not. But I'm here to deliver a message. Jake Bishop called the house a few minutes ago."

"Why would he do that? He knows I'm working."

"Suzanne, perhaps you should check your cell phone for messages."

I reached into my pocket, and to my surprise, found that it wasn't there.

She held it up, and asked, "Is this what you were

looking for? It was at home, sitting on your dresser and laughing like mad at me. I thought you were going to change that ringtone to something more civilized."

"I kind of like it," I said as I took the phone from her. "That explains why he didn't call me on my cell phone, but why didn't he try me here at the donut shop?"

"He didn't have time to track down the number," Momma said. "When I picked up your phone, he asked me to tell you why he had to leave so abruptly."

"What did he say? What was the emergency?" I asked.

Momma frowned as she said, "It's about his niece, Amy. She's the oldest child of Jake's sister Sarah, and apparently she's had a rather bad time of it this morning."

"What happened to her? Is she all right?" Jake had often talked about his oldest sister and her kids. Since he had no children of his own, they acted as surrogates for him. Since Sarah's husband had left shortly after Amy's brother Paul had been born, Jake had told me she'd been delighted by the male attention for her kids.

Momma said, "I'm afraid she's in the hospital."

"He must be going out of his mind with worry. What happened to her? Was it a car accident?"

I remembered Jake's story of losing his own family, and prayed fervently that this incident wasn't parallel.

"No, apparently she has a dangerously high fever, and they rushed her to the emergency room."

"That's terrible. I hope she's all right."

"He said he'd call when he learned more about her condition."

"Thanks for coming over to tell me," I said.

"It was my pleasure." She looked at me another few seconds, as if she wanted to add something else, but then obviously thought better of it and walked out of the shop.

Emma came back out, wiping her hands on a towel. "Wow, sometimes it sucks being you, doesn't it?"

"Have I ever had a conversation in this shop that you haven't eavesdropped on, Emma?"

She pretended to think about it, then said, "I don't think so, but I'm trying my best to make sure it never happens."

I couldn't help myself and laughed at her expression. "Why don't you finish washing up in back, and then you can take off. I doubt we're going to get many customers in here today."

"You're not just trying to get rid of me, are you?"

"Emma, if I were, I'd fire you instead of sending you home with pay. Why do you ask me that?"

"No reason," she said as she scurried into the back to finish her last duties.

After ten minutes, she popped back out, this time wearing her jacket and missing an apron.

"That was fast," I said, "even by your standards."

"What can I say? I was motivated. Have a good day, Suzanne, I'll see you in the morning."

"See you then," I said.

Once she was gone, I realized that Emma hadn't pushed me about helping with my investigation surrounding Peg Masterson's murder. Had she lost her curiosity, or had her father discouraged her from helping me? He was the editor-in-chief of the county's only newspaper, and I found myself wondering what their conversations at home sounded like when they talked about her work. Emma's loyalty to me was unflagging, and I knew if I needed anything from her, all I had to do was ask. I was going to try not to, though. While my crew and I were older, I felt—whether rightly or wrongly—that we didn't have quite so much to lose as Emma did.

At three minutes before noon, the door chimed, and George walked in. He sat at the counter, ordered a pair of pumpkin donuts, then said, "Peg seems to have left very little tracks of her existence in the world. Aside from the charity fundraising events she's spearheaded over the years, she didn't make an awful lot of impact. I have heard she's got money, more than most folks around April Springs would ever suspect." He studied me a second, then asked, "What have you been up to?"

I brought him up to date on what Grace and I had uncovered about the accounting log and the note Grace had found, but I'd forgotten it at home, so I couldn't show it to him.

"That's something, anyway," he said after taking a bite from one of the donuts. "Where do you think we should go with this investigation now?"

"I keep wondering about Burt Gentry's involvement with Peg and Marge. Is there any chance one of your buddies knows about that?"

"I could ask around," George said. "Or I could talk to Burt directly. Knowing him, he's liable to crow about his conquests."

"Burt?" I asked. "That doesn't sound like him at all."

"Believe me, I'll take him out for a drink after work, and he won't be able to keep it to himself. He's always fancied himself quite the ladies' man, and I've sat through enough of his stories in the past to prove it."

I looked at him and asked, "Are we talking about the same sweet old man from the hardware store?"

George laughed. "Suzanne, some men don't like to kiss and tell, but I haven't met many of them in my life. I'm willing to bet if I guide him a little and get a drink or two into him, I can get him to open up."

"It's worth a try," I said.

"As a matter of fact, I think I'll go take a run at him right now."

After he was gone, Grace came by as I was just getting ready to lock the place up. I had eight dozen donuts to take to the church, since the day had ended up being even slower than I suspected.

She took one look at me and asked, "You're not taking those all home with you, are you?"

"I don't know, I might feel a little peckish later."

She smiled. "At least let me have a dozen."

I handed her the box on the top. "Take it. The rest are going to the church."

"I can't do that," she said. "Besides, I was only kidding. What are you going to do after you drop them off?"

"I'm coming straight back here," I said. "If you're up for it, we have something pretty challenging to do."

That got her excited. "What do you have in mind? Are we going to slip into police headquarters and eavesdrop on the chief?"

"No, it's much more dangerous than that," I said as I flipped off the lights.

"Don't keep me in suspense, Suzanne."

I took a deep breath, then said, "We're going to talk to Gabby next door and grill her for information."

Grace frowned. "To tell you the truth, I'd rather go spy on the chief."

"So would I, but this will do us more good. Gabby's hiding something, and we need to know what it is. Right now, I feel like we're stumbling around in the dark bumping into walls. If enduring Gabby for an hour is what it takes to set us back on the right course, then we'll just have to get through it."

"An hour? Really? That's just cruel."

I nodded. "At least there will be two of us."

After stowing the donuts in the back of my Jeep, I dead-bolted the door behind us. Grace said, "I don't suppose you'd believe me if I told you that there was somewhere else I had to be."

"Not a chance," I said as I locked my arm firmly in hers. "If I'm going in there, I'm taking you with me."

After our quick donut delivery, we were parked back in front of my shop. Father Pete had been happy to get our offering, something I hadn't been sure of, given my earlier reception from his secretary. Upon querying him about her, it turned out that she was taking a day off, and I made a mental note to schedule my drop-offs on the same day she'd be gone.

Soon enough, though, it was time to brace Gabby in her shop and see what we could find out about her relationship with Peg.

SUZANNE'S FUNNEL CAKES

This recipe is reminiscent of the county fair, and makes for a quick, light snack that always leaves the kids begging for more. We don't use our portable fryer for these, because the batter gets stuck in the wire cage before it can fry. Instead, we opt for a big pot of oil on the stove where this isn't a problem. The family especially likes it when I use a large plastic funnel to add the batter directly into the hot oil!

INGREDIENTS

- 2½ cups all purpose flour
- 2 eggs
- 1¼ cups 2% milk
- ⅓ cup granulated sugar
- 1 teaspoon baking powder
- ¼ teaspoon salt
- Powdered sugar for topping
- Canola oil at 360 degrees F

DIRECTIONS

In a bowl, beat the eggs lightly, then add the milk and sugar, mixing it all together thoroughly.

In a separate bowl, sift together 1½ cups of the flour, baking powder, and salt.

Gradually add the dry mix to the wet and combine it all to get a smooth, batter consistency.

Next, add the mix to a large funnel (with an opening about ½ inch), putting your finger over the opening as you do. Carefully drop a string of the batter into the oil, but be cautious here, since the oil is extremely hot, and the addition of the batter can cause it to spatter. You can add it as a swirl, long lines, or any pattern you like.

Check and turn when gold on one side, then remove onto paper towels to shed excess oil. Add a dash of powdered sugar, cocoa, or jam, and eat it while it's still warm.

Yield: Makes 3–6 funnel cakes

CHAPTER 9

"Ladies, I don't appreciate you coming into my shop so that you can gang up on me. I'm not some defenseless little lamb. I'm fully aware of what you're trying to do."

It hadn't taken Gabby long to figure out that we were there to question her, and not shop in her store. Once she realized why we were there, the courteous shopkeeper was replaced by the indignant interview subject.

"Gabby, we keep telling you, we're here for your help, not to accuse you of anything," Grace said. My friend, normally deft when it came to dealing with people, had somehow managed to raise Gabby Williams's ire from the very start, and the more she spoke, the more defiant Gabby became.

"Forgive me if I don't believe either one of you," Gabby said harshly.

It was time to step in and see if I could make things any better. Chances were good that I couldn't make them any worse, which gave me a certain freedom to try a different approach, namely, the truth.

I held up my hands. "Okay, fine. I admit it. You've got us. We need to know some things that have been going on around town, and you're the only one who can help us."

Grace's cell phone rang, and after she glanced at the number, she said, "Excuse me. I've got to take this."

After she stepped outside, I told Gabby, "That wasn't fair of us to gang up on you like that," I said simply. "I apologize."

She looked at me skeptically. "Why should I believe that you're being sincere?"

"Why shouldn't you?" I countered, trying my best to convince her of my sincerity. "I'm putting all my cards on the table. Will you help me?"

I watched her struggle with how to respond to my plea, and even when her mouth opened to speak, I still wasn't sure how she'd react.

Finally, she smiled. "I must say, I do appreciate your honesty. I'll help you if I can. What is it you want to know?"

Pay dirt. "Tell me about Peg, Janice, and Marge. I'd like anything you know about Burt Gentry, and how they all may be interconnected."

"You're not asking much, are you?"

I laughed. "I know I'm being pushy, but you're the best shot I have at clearing my name. You've got to know how important my reputation is to me."

She nodded. "I understand." Gabby thought about it for a minute, then she added, "Janice is the vice chairperson of the kitchen tour. Were you aware of that?"

"No, I had no idea," I confessed, wondering what that had to do with anything.

Gabby went on. "Peg often had someone take the

second chair on paper, but it was always strictly an honorary position." She studied me for a moment, then asked, "Don't you find that odd?"

"I don't know. Should I?" Where was this going? I had no choice but to play along and see where she was headed, but I had to admit, I was baffled by this new line of information.

"Suzanne, most honorary positions are at the head of the committee, while underlings do all of the work. Peg was just the opposite, zealously guarding her charitable functions like they involved state secrets. She withheld all the responsibilities from everyone, demanding that she do all of the work herself."

"I still don't understand," I said, sounding like the dullest knife in the drawer, but not knowing what I could do about it.

"It was almost as if she were hiding something," Gabby said, watching me closely to see if I was finally getting it.

"Ah," I replied, still not sure of what she meant. What could Peg have been hiding?

"Naturally, Janice has been concerned about the situation, so she came to me the morning the tour was to begin. She thought I could help her, since I'd dealt with Peg before myself."

Gabby sniffed again. "I told you Janice was quite rude about it."

"You also said someone else was mean to you that day, remember?"

Gabby frowned. "I'm not about to forget."

It was time to push her a little harder and see what she'd tell me. "It was Peg, wasn't it?"

Gabby looked at me as though I'd slapped her. "What makes you say that?"

"It makes sense, that's all."

"Our last words were an argument," she said, regret thick in her voice.

"On the day of the murder, you mean," I said.

She couldn't bring herself to speak as she nodded in agreement. After a moment, she said, "I told her we needed to talk, but she called me a bad name, and then hung up. That's when you approached me."

She looked at her hands a few moments, then added quietly, "I decided to have a word with Peg again myself, to see if I could clear the air a little. I wanted to give her the opportunity to explain herself before anyone else was involved."

"Are you saying she was doing something she shouldn't have been doing?" I was starting to see where she was going with this now.

"That's exactly what I'm saying."

"When did you two speak again?" I asked, barely able to contain myself.

"Just before she left for Marge's house," Gabby admitted.

"Do the police know about this? Have you spoken to them?" I couldn't believe Gabby had held back any information, not even considering how important this might be.

"I wasn't sure how it would look," she admitted. "We shared some harsh words, and I know how Chief Martin can be when he finds a suspect he likes."

I touched her hand lightly. "What exactly did you talk about?"

Gabby frowned. "She was angry, accused me of butting into her business. She threatened me, if you must know. I didn't understand her overreaction; it was completely over the top in response to the simple questions I was asking."

"Gabby, you've got to tell the police."

She looked at me as though I were insane. "I can't. I just told you, if I do that, it's going to make me look guilty."

I wasn't about to let it go, though. "Just think how bad it's going to look if you don't come forward on your own, and someone else tells Chief Martin first."

She pulled back from me. "Suzanne Hart, is that a threat?" There was an icy stillness in her eyes that made me shiver.

"No, you've misunderstood me. I would never tell him without your permission. I won't violate your trust. But someone else might have seen you two talking. Do you really want the chief coming after you?"

"I suppose not," she said reluctantly. "You're probably right. Every time the door opens here or the telephone rings, I think it's going to be the police. I haven't slept a wink since the day of the murder."

"Gabby, would you like me to be here when you talk to Chief Martin?"

Her look of horror was easy enough to read. "Why on earth would I want that? I'm a grown woman. I can speak with him myself."

I looked at my watch, then said, "Why don't you call a lawyer to be beside you, then?"

"I don't need an attorney. I'm not the one who did something wrong." She hesitated, then added, "You are right about one thing, Suzanne. It's best to resolve this, and to do it quickly. I'll call Chief Martin right after you leave."

I felt bad leaving her alone to face the police chief, but her negative reaction to my suggestion that I should stay was pretty apparent, and I didn't feel like getting shot down again.

"It's the right thing to do," I said as I walked toward the door.

She said so softly I could barely hear her, "Thank you."

"You're welcome."

I walked outside, and Grace was pacing back and forth in front of the used clothing shop. "What happened?"

"Why didn't you come back in after you were finished with your phone call?"

"I thought you might have more luck in there without me. Did you?"

I smiled softly at her. "As a matter of fact, I did. She's calling the police right now."

"Why on earth would she do that?"

"It appears that Gabby had an argument with Peg the morning she was murdered," I said lightly.

"How did you find that out? Did she actually tell you that? You're good, Hart, I'll give you that."

I kept looking for a police cruiser, but as the time ticked past, I was beginning to wonder if Gabby had undergone a change of heart.

"How did you get her to talk to you?" Grace asked.

"I told her the truth, and then I just stayed there and listened," I admitted.

She nodded. "I never thought to try that with

Gabby." As her gaze matched mine out the front window, she asked, "What were they fighting about, did she say?"

"It appears that Peg made sure that her position as chairwoman handled all of the work, and her vice chair was strictly an honorary position."

"How odd. Usually it's the other way around."

I stared at her for a second. "Does everyone in the world know that but me?"

Grace said, "If you didn't go to bed by eight every night and took the time to join a committee now and then, you'd know it, too. I wonder why Peg didn't give up any of the responsibilities? It must have been a ton of work."

"That's the same thing Gabby and Janice Deal were wondering." I saw a patrol car approaching, and for once, it stopped in front of Gabby's shop instead of mine. As the chief got out and started to walk inside, he glanced over at us, and was clearly surprised to see Grace and me both on the couch watching him.

Without any formal plan, we both waved to him, nearly in unison.

He shook his head without responding, then walked into ReNEWed.

"Now what?" Grace asked.

"I don't know about you, but I'm not going anywhere until he comes out again."

"Sounds good. I just wish we had some popcorn while we're waiting," Grace said.

"This isn't a movie. It's real life."

"What, you can't have popcorn in real life?" she asked.

We didn't have long to wait. Less than ten minutes after he'd entered, we saw Chief Martin leave. This time, he didn't even glance in our direction as he got back into his patrol car alone.

"I wonder what that's all about?" I asked.

At that moment, Gabby walked outside, waved to the chief, and then ducked into the cruiser with him.

Grace came back to the door and saw them leave together. "What did I miss?"

"Gabby took off with him in the patrol car."

"He arrested her?" Grace asked, her voice growing suddenly louder.

I shook my head. "It didn't look like that to me. She appeared to go with him of her own free will."

As I reached for my telephone, Grace asked, "Who are you going to call?"

"I'm giving George a call to see if he can find out what's going on."

"He's talking to Burt, remember?" she reminded me as we got into her car.

I nodded as I slid my telephone back into my purse. "Actually, I forgot all about that. What are we going to do now?"

"We need to visit Patty Cakes," she said.

"Pull over and let me out then. You don't even have to come to a full stop. Just slow down enough so I can jump out."

Grace looked at me a second and said, "Don't be such a baby."

"This is going to be a nightmare. Janice Deal hates me," I said. "She's not going to tell me anything."

"Just charm her like you always do, Suzanne."

"I won't do it," I said.

She put the car into PARK, and said, "It's too late. We're already here."

I looked up and realized we were in front of Janice's cake shop. I wasn't sure the woman would throw a bucket of water on me if I was on fire, but I didn't have much choice. I had to find out what she knew about Peg Masterson's odd behavior just before she died, even if it meant I had to eat a healthy dose of crow to get any information out of her.

At least I didn't have to eat any of her cake.

"What are you doing here?" Janice asked as Grace and I walked into the cake shop.

"I felt bad about the way we left things," I lied. "It's no excuse, but I'm under a great deal of stress right now, and I took it out on you. I'm sorry."

She stared hard at me for a full ten seconds, then asked, "Does that mean you were lying about my cakes being bad?"

Oh, no. She wasn't going to make me eat one, was she? I wanted to find Peg Masterson's killer, but did I want to find out that badly? I hoped it didn't come to that.

"They're delightful," I said, barely able to choke out the words. If I were Pinocchio, my nose would have grown all the way out the door by now.

"I forgive you, then," Janice said. "After all, it takes a bigger person to forgive someone than it does to ask for forgiveness. I don't mind being the bigger person."

I couldn't take any more of that, no matter how

important it was that I get on good terms with Janice Deal again.

I started to say something when Grace stepped in. "We're both just so concerned about poor Peg. It's tragic, isn't it?"

"It's certainly unfortunate," Janice said, being careful not to commit one way or the other.

Grace went on, "We just spoke with Gabby Williams, and she told us about the dilemma you had trying to help her run the kitchen tour."

"I'm the vice chairperson," Janice said indignantly. "I should have had something to do besides signing checks."

"You'll have to do everything now, won't you?" I asked.

"Someone has to," she said. "We can't afford to cancel the next three weekends or we'll have to refund everyone's ticket, and there's not enough money in our account to pay people back."

"How do you know that?" I asked.

"These things always have expenses, the way Peg explained it to me. There are ads that have to be placed, flyers need to be made up, lots of things like that. You wouldn't think so, but it can really add up."

I had to bite my lip to keep my smart comments to myself, and when I thought I could do that, I asked, "Did you write many checks for the event?"

"Several," she admitted. "Some of them were for cash, too. Peg explained that a lot of the folks she dealt with preferred it that way."

"Could we possibly see the checkbook for the committee?" Grace asked.

"I'm not sure I should," Janice said. "It's really none of your business."

"You're right," I said. "We just thought we might be able to help you stay out of jail, but it's probably better to let the chief of police look at it first. Let's go, Grace, she doesn't need our help after all."

Janice moved in front of the door, blocking our escape. "What are you two talking about?"

I said, "We really won't know for sure until we see the books, but did Peg bring you receipts for the money she spent?"

"She told me it wasn't necessary," Janice said a little uneasily.

"Then you don't have any proof where the money's actually gone, do you?"

"A bit of it," Janice said as her frown became full blown. "Peg told me it was the way things were run, and I didn't have any reason not to believe her."

I said, "Do you happen to know who Peg used as a vice chairman before you took over the job?"

"Marge Rankin used to do it, until they had a falling out about something," Janice said. "Hang on a second. I'll go get the committee checkbook."

She ducked into the back room, and I asked Grace, "What do you make of this? It sounds fishy to me."

"Who takes cash for advertisements and flyers?" she asked. "I want to see the legitimate checks she wrote. That way we can see what's missing."

I walked to the window and pulled a flyer off the glass. "This isn't exactly state of the art, is it? It's not even in color, so it probably cost her a few pennies a copy."

"Then let's see how much she spent."

"Here you go," Janice said as she handed me the checkbook. I turned to the recording section and started scanning the withdrawals, keeping a running tab of checks made out to cash, and ones to legitimate suppliers.

Something odd struck me right off the bat. "There aren't that many checks made out to cash here, Janice."

"Peg said that it might look odd to the committee if we did too many of those, so she had me make most of them out to Party Enterprises Galore. That's a company of hers, and she said she could get us things at cost if we used her side business."

I looked at Grace and smiled. "I'm willing to bet all the checks read 'P.E.G.' I bet she thought she was hilarious."

As Grace took the checkbook from me, Janice asked, "Do you two honestly think I did something wrong?"

I wanted to tell her that she'd helped Peg swindle a charity by funneling money into a private account, but she looked so distraught I didn't have the heart to. "Someone else will have to sort it all out."

"You should call the chief right now and tell him everything you just told us," Grace said.

"Do I really have to? That man doesn't like me."

I said, "Grace is right. He needs to know. It could have been the reason Peg was killed."

"I didn't do it," Janice said fiercely.

"That's why you need to bring this to the police. They'll have an easier time believing you if you're the one who points this out to them."

"You two wouldn't hang around and stay with me, would you?" There was a look of abject terror in her eyes, and I wanted to agree, despite how I felt about the woman.

Grace surprised me, though. "We can't. It will look like we knew about it too, and the chief is already suspicious of Suzanne. She can't afford any more scrutiny, and if I stayed with you, they'd link it to her as well. I'm sorry, but you're going to have to do this on your own."

Grace handed the checkbook back to Janice, then said, "Let's go," to me.

Once we were outside, I said, "It's kind of harsh, leaving her to face Martin all by herself."

"I don't have any sympathy for her," Grace said as she got into her car. "She was stupid and foolish writing those checks, and she's going to have to answer for her behavior."

I nodded. "You're right, but I still can't help feeling a little bad for her."

"Suzanne, that's your problem sometimes. Your heart is bigger than your brain. Can you imagine it? Peg had the audacity to steal from the fundraiser, and Janice just went along with it."

"Why would she steal from charity, when she had so much money of her own?" I asked. "It just doesn't make sense."

"Maybe she had some sort of compulsion," Grace said.

I considered that possibility for a moment, then said, "I wonder if that's why Peg and Marge had a fight. She could have figured out what Peg was up to, but that begs one question, doesn't it?"

"Why didn't she turn her in," Grace said. "Unless."

I stopped and looked at Grace. "Unless what?"

"Is there a chance Marge wanted in on the scam herself?"

"It's possible," I answered.

"I thought she was rich in her own right," Grace said.

"Take one look at her kitchen remodel, and you'll get your answer. It must have cost her a fortune. And I'm beginning to wonder if she told me the truth about the house staging, or if it was just a way to cover for all of the expensive furnishings she's been buying lately."

Grace nodded. "But the question is, whose money paid for everything? Where does this leave us?"

I chewed my lower lip, then said, "It appears that Peg was skimming from the contributions, unless this P.E.G. was legitimate, which we both doubt. Over the years, she's headed every fundraiser in three counties. That's a golden opportunity to skim, especially if she was able to find naïve treasurers every time."

"You can bet she insisted on it," Grace said.

"But I still don't get why she'd risk everything for what must have been petty cash for her."

"I think we need to dig deeper into Peg and Marge's finances," Grace said.

"That's an excellent idea. I'm just not sure how we can manage to do that."

"Give me a little time to think about it," she said.

We pulled up in front of the donut shop, and Grace shut off the engine. "Maybe when the chief sees that checkbook ledger, he'll at least leave you alone."

"I highly doubt it," I said. "I'm just hoping it's enough for Jake to take me off his list suspects."

"Where is he, anyway?"

I got out of the car and looked in through the open door. "He had a family emergency, so he's back in Raleigh."

"I hope everything's okay."

I started to close the door, then said, "Me, too. Thanks for coming with me this afternoon."

Grace smiled at me as she started her car up again. "Are you kidding? I wouldn't have missed it. Now don't go snooping any more without me, okay? I don't want to be left out of this."

"Trust me, if I need a sidekick, you're the first name on my list."

"I'd better be the only name," she said as she drove off.

I thought about calling George to tell him what Grace and I had uncovered, but it was getting close to five, and I was hungry, and more than a little sleepy. With my hours, I didn't have the luxury of time in the evening that everyone else had. I had to start winding down early, or I'd suffer for it the next day.

I got into my Jeep and drove the three blocks toward home, a part of me wishing I could walk through the park instead of travel down the street, no matter how tired I was. That walk always used to invigorate me. At one time, I'd loved to stroll through the trees along the pathways, taking in my beautiful surroundings, but the park of my youth had been tainted somewhat by some things that had happened there recently, and I wasn't sure I'd ever be able to look at it with the wide-eyed innocence I'd once felt for the place.

As I parked the Jeep in our driveway and walked up to the porch, I saw Momma sitting out on the swing. She smiled and said, "It's a beautiful evening, isn't it?"

"Scoot over and I'll join you," I said.

As she moved over, I took my place beside her. After a few moments of swinging in the breeze, she said, "We don't do this nearly enough. Shall we have dinner out here tonight? We can set the card table up and dine al fresco."

"Why not?" I asked. "What are we having?"

"A little of this, a little of that," she said, and I knew it was leftover night. One night a week, we took everything we'd saved and had a buffet. It might include a bit of lasagna, some meatloaf, part of a chicken pot pie, and whatever else we had on tap. There was no hardship, though. Everything was always delicious.

As I set the table and chairs up on the porch, Momma added a tablecloth and some of our best china.

"Not paper plates?" I asked.

"We never use paper plates, and you know it," Momma said.

I picked up one of the fine china plates. "We don't exactly trot these out every day, either. What's the occasion?"

"We're alive, autumn is approaching, we have a

roof over our heads and a bountiful supply of food. Is there anything else we need to celebrate?"

"No, ma'am, that all sounds good to me."

As we ate, I was careful to keep our conversation away from Peg Masterson's murder, and what I'd been doing with my friends to solve it. Jake's name didn't come up, either, nor anything that might vex either one of us. It was as if we'd made a tacit agreement that, if not for more than a moment or two, we were going to forget the world's problems and focus on enjoying the time we had together. My mother could be the biggest thorn in my side, but evenings like this reminded me that she could be quite charming as well. We were just finishing our meal when I heard my cell phone laughing its summons inside the house.

"Just leave it," Momma said as she lightly touched my arm.

"I'm sorry, but it could be important," I said.

"More important than this? I know how much your friends mean to you, but just this once, don't answer it."

When I thought about it, there really wasn't anybody I had to talk to, at least not that instant. I did as she asked and ignored the laughter beckoning me from the other room.

After we finished eating, we cleared the table, and I returned the card table and chairs to the front closet.

That's when I remembered my cell phone, and the missed call.

I checked it, and heard Jake's voice. "Suzanne,

call me as soon as you get this. I need to talk to you."

Whatever it was, it didn't sound good. I excused myself, went up to my room, and called Jake back.

CHAPTER 10

"We've got a lot to talk about," Jake said.

"First things first," I said as I looked out the window at the park below. "How's your niece?"

"The fever broke. She had some kind of infection, but they think she's going to be all right."

"That's great news," I said.

"I'm sorry I took off like that, Suzanne."

"You were worried. I understand completely. When are you coming back?"

"I'm hoping to make it sometime tomorrow," he said.

I looked out my window and saw someone watching the house from the shadows of a large tree. There was still some light out, but I never would have seen them if I hadn't been looking out my window at that exact moment.

"Jake, I've got to call you back."

"What's going on?" he asked. "I can hear something's wrong in your voice."

"I'll call you later," I said, and then I hung up.

I quickly dialed George's cell phone number. "Somebody's watching my house. Do you still have your gun?" He'd told me once he'd kept his service revolver after he'd retired, too attached to it to give it up, so he'd paid to keep it instead.

"Sure. Don't go outside. I'll be right there."

"Should I call Chief Martin?" I asked.

"I can handle this myself," he said.

As soon as we hung up, I began to regret calling him. I should have dialed 911, and left George out of it.

When I tried to call him back, there was no answer.

A little belatedly, I dialed the police number and got Officer Grant, the cop who frequented my donut shop the most.

"I need a favor," I started off.

"Let's see. The going rate is a dozen donuts an hour. If you're ready to pay the price, I'm your man."

"This is serious. There's a prowler outside my house."

His jovial mood disappeared instantly. "Then it's not a favor, it's a police matter. I'll be right there."

"Hang on. There's something you should know. I called George Morris first, and he's on his way over here, too. He's armed."

"Suzanne, remind me to tell you how insane that was after this is over."

He hung up before I could defend my actions, not that there was a defense.

I kept my vigil for the prowler, but I had a sudden thought. Momma was still downstairs, and she had no idea someone was watching our house. I grabbed my softball bat and raced down the steps, just as my mother had one hand on the front doorknob.

"Stop," I shouted.

"Suzanne, what's wrong with you? I'm going back out to the glider."

"Not at the moment you're not," I said as I pushed myself between her and the door. "There's someone outside watching our house."

She peered around me and looked out the window. "I don't see anyone."

"I already called George, and the police are coming, too."

My mother shook her head. "That's an awful lot of firepower for just a prowler," she said. "Why did you call both?"

"I called George first, then I realized it was a mistake. If something happens to him because of me, I'll never be able to forgive myself."

"Don't worry, child, it will be all right."

"I wish I could be as sure as you sound," I said.

I looked out the window through the curtains, trying to see who would show up first. I couldn't see anyone from that vantage point, but then again, I hadn't figured I'd be able to.

In the distance, I saw George carefully approaching, and just behind him was Officer Grant. The police officer must have gotten George's attention, because I saw my friend stop, turn, and wave Officer Grant away.

When he wouldn't, the two had a brief discussion, and then I saw them approach together.

They peered into the undergrowth of several trees, and as I saw them stop at the massive tree where the prowler had been, I felt the muscles in my stomach tighten.

A minute later, they came out from under the

tree's canopy and walked out in the open toward the house.

I met them on the front porch. "He was right there. I swear it."

George said, "Well, he's gone now."

"Are you sure it wasn't just somebody out jogging?" Officer Grant asked.

"I can tell when someone's out for a run or standing there watching me," I said.

"Playing some softball later tonight?" he asked.

It was only then that I realized I was still holding onto the aluminum bat. "It's a girl's best friend," I said. "I'm not all that comfortable around guns, but I figure this will protect me well enough."

"I've seen you play softball," George said. "I'm pretty sure you're right."

Officer Grant nodded, then said, "I've got to get back to the station and fill out a report."

"Can't we just keep this between us?" I asked.

"No chance. I had to log it to get permission to leave the station. I've got desk duty tonight, and the chief watches us pretty close so we don't slip out."

"Thanks anyway," I said.

He tipped his patrolman's hat to me. "Part of the service, Suzanne. Good night, George." He started to walk away, then added, "The next time you try something like this, I'm going to do my best to get your gun permit pulled. You're not a cop anymore, remember?"

"You do what you have to do," George said, "and so will I. If one of my friends needs me, I'll take care of them first, and worry about getting permission later."

"Suit yourself," he said, and then headed back into the woods.

George and I watched him go, and then I said, "I'm sorry. I shouldn't have called you in the first place."

"I didn't need backup, Suzanne," he said. "I could have handled this prowler all by myself."

I patted his shoulder. "I know, but what can I say? I worry about you."

"There's no need to. I'm retired; I'm not dead."

"I get it," I said. "Since you're already here, why don't you come in for a cup of coffee?"

"Thanks, but I've got to be getting back home." He looked around the park filled with trees, then said, "If he shows up again, call me."

I didn't answer; I just smiled at him. I wouldn't make that mistake again, but I didn't have to rub his nose in it, either. "Good night."

"Night," he said as he left.

I walked back inside, and found Momma standing by the door. "They didn't find him, did they?"

"No. I've got a suspicion Officer Grant thinks it was in my imagination, but someone was out there, and they were watching us."

Momma shivered slightly, then dead-bolted the front door. "I think, for tonight, we'll sleep with our windows closed and our front door locked."

"I know you like the nighttime breezes, but I think that's a good idea," I said.

"What did Jake have to say when you two talked?" Momma asked as I started back up the stairs.

"His niece is going to be all right," I said.

"That's good news indeed." She hesitated, then asked, "But how about the two of you?"

"We're still working it out," I said.

"Give him time, Suzanne. Most good men are worth the effort."

"Was Dad a lot of work?" I asked.

"You're kidding, right? I had him nearly fully trained when he passed away, but it was a daily struggle." Her soft smile denied the severity of the words. It was clear to everyone who knew her that my dad had been the love of my mother's life, and it was easy to see that she missed him every day.

"Ninety percent is the best you can ever hope for, right?"

She nodded. "We have to leave them a little spirit, don't we?"

"I couldn't even get Max into double digits, so I'm not the one to comment."

I called Jake back once I got upstairs, debating whether or not to tell him about the prowler, but it was a moot point.

His phone went directly to voice mail. I left a message that said, "Sorry about that. We had a little excitement here, but everything's fine now. Call me tomorrow. I'm going to shut off my telephone and go to bed."

After the call, I did as I'd promised and I shut off my phone, turned out the lights, and tried to get to sleep, knowing that there might be someone out there watching me.

Surprisingly, I managed to nod right off, and by the time I got up, I was beginning to think that I might have misread the situation myself.

* * *

At 5:30 that morning, we were ready to open, but I was having trouble with the floor mixer again, so I asked Emma, "Would you mind getting the door?"

"Happy to do it," she said.

My assistant poked her head through the door, and then came straight back into the kitchen.

"Maybe you'd better do it," she said.

"Why? Is Jake out there?" Was that the kind of grand gesture I'd been hoping for?

"No, it's George."

"You're right. I'd better take care of him," I said as I brushed past her.

As I unlocked the door, I let George inside. "You're early. I didn't think we were meeting until noon."

As he took his seat at the bar, George asked softly, "Can we talk here without her hearing us? I don't want to drag Emma into this."

I said, "Don't worry about her. She's got her iPod on while she's working on the dishes. It's the only time I'll let her listen to it, and if I want to get her attention, I have to stand right in front of her and wave my hands in her face. Why, what's so urgent?"

George said, "This couldn't wait. First things first. Did the prowler come back last night?"

I shook my head. "No, we didn't see anything, and I'm beginning to wonder if it wasn't just some innocent jogger that I accused of watching my house. My nerves are more than a little on edge right now."

George said, "It's understandable if they are."

As I got him coffee, I said, "We've got some nice orange slice donuts today, if you are feeling like trying something different. It's a new recipe."

George said, "Why not? I'll try one."

I fetched him a donut from my latest recipe. I'd been working on incorporating different things into my donuts, and my latest attempt was mixing fruit or candy in with my batter. I thought this latest attempt was a winner that might go into my rotation, but I wanted to field-test it first.

I watched him taste his sample, and I got a grimace from George instead of the smile I'd been hoping for.

"What's wrong?" I asked him.

"Nothing," he said as he took a healthy swallow of coffee.

"George, I can't fix it if I don't know what's wrong with it."

He hesitated, then said, "It's a little sweet for my taste."

"They need a little more work then, don't they?"

"Hey, don't pull them on my account," George said. "I'm no donut judge."

"That's not true. I respect your opinion."

As I got him his usual fare, I said, "Is that why you came by, just to check up on me?"

"No, I've got some news to share," George said.

"I hope it's good. I could surely use some," I said as I took his sample donut and threw it away. I knew if I left it on the counter, he'd peck at it out of politeness, and donuts should be eaten for pleasure, not out of a sense of obligation.

"I've learned something interesting about Peg's late husband. It's true he worked for a large corporation, but he wasn't its CEO."

"What did he do?" I asked.

"He was a maintenance man," George replied. "His base salary was never much, and from what I understand, Peg was nearly broke when he died."

"But that was before the divorce settlement from her second husband," I said.

George shook his head. "That man never had five grand at one time in his entire life, let alone the fifty Peg supposedly got."

"What are you talking about, George?"

"That book you found should have been shelved with the rest of the fiction. From what I've been able to find out, Peg would have been lucky to raise a thousand dollars if she had to."

This was getting even more confusing. "She had nice things. Grace and I saw them in her house."

"I'm not doubting you. All I'm saying is that she was as close to broke as you could be. I don't know where she got her furnishings, but I'm willing to bet they're all copies instead of real antiques."

"Why would she do that?" I asked.

"People do the strangest things," George said. "I once arrested a man who claimed to be the real King of England. Talk to him about anything else, and he was perfectly rational, but when it came to his succession to the throne, he was so convincing I almost bought it. For whatever reason, Peg's ledger is full of what might have been, not what was."

"Then how has she supported herself? Peg's never had a job as long as I've known her."

"That is the question, isn't it? She lives in a modest house, and it's not even hers, most of it belongs to the bank. Still, with taxes, utilities, and pesky things like food and clothing, I have no idea how she managed to support herself."

"I think I do," I admitted.

George said, "Don't keep me waiting in suspense. How did she do it?"

Just then the front door chimed, and I looked up quickly, hoping again it was Jake. I was going to have to stop that, or it was going to drive me crazy.

It was Bob the pie man, ready to pick up his four fried apple pies. "I've had warmer greetings at the doctor's office," Bob said as he saw my face.

"I'm sorry. I was thinking of something else."

"Or was it someone?" Bob asked.

"Why do you say that?"

"I've seen that look of disappointment on a woman's face before when she realized it was me," Bob said, adding a smile to diffuse the bite of his own insult.

George swiveled on his stool and smiled at Bob. "I've been there a time or two myself."

Bob slid the money across the counter toward me and looked expectantly at the pies.

I handed him the box. "Enjoy them."

"You know I will," he said as he took his change. As he held the money aloft in one hand and the box of pies in the other, he said, "You're the best, Suzanne."

"That's nice to hear," I said, smiling.

"Even if it's just from me?"

I laughed. "Good-bye, Bob."

"Bye, Suzanne, and thanks."

After he was gone, I said, "Now, where were we?"

George said, "You were about to tell us how Peg managed to support herself after her husband died and she was out of money."

"I think she was stealing," I said.

"Honestly?" George asked. "From whom?"

"From the charities she chaired. I've found out some pretty interesting details about how she organized the committees she ran." I brought him up to speed on all of the checks written to P.E.G., and explained my theory of assigning only pliable treasurers and vice chairs.

George mulled it over, and then said, "I kind of find that hard to believe. Are you sure?"

"No, but I can't account for the way those checks had been written any other way. I convinced Janice to tell the chief about it, so we'll see what happens."

"Isn't he going to suspect you?" George asked.

"I'm hoping he doesn't connect me with it," I said, "but if he does, there's not much I can do about it, is there? So, what did you find out about Burt?"

George said, "It's not as good as what you uncovered. I had a few drinks with him, and I finally got him to talk."

"What did he say?"

"Burt's always been full of brash boasting when it comes to his conquests, and his stories about Peg were no different. He kept bragging about how he dumped her, which is what he told you, Suzanne, so I steered the conversation to Marge. That's when he shut up, and when I pressed him on it, the man walked out of the bar in a huff, even though I was still buying drinks."

I said, "That sounds reasonable enough. He was

finished with Peg, so why shouldn't he discuss her? Marge is a different story, though. From the look of things, they're right in the middle of their relationship."

George frowned. "That's the thing. Burt normally brags the most about the girlfriend he's got at the moment. I'm telling you, it's out of character for him. Something's going on there."

I said, "It's been my experience in the past that whenever someone changes their behavior pattern, there's a reason for it. We just need to find out what Burt's reason is."

George pushed a half-eaten glazed donut around his plate, then said, "Like I said, it's not much, but I'm not through digging yet." He looked at it, then added, "I can't believe Peg isn't loaded."

"She sure managed to look like she had more money than she did. Her wardrobe wasn't as expensive as it looked, though. Grace said she found Gabby's mark on nearly everything in her closet."

I knew from my own purchases that Gabby placed one single black line of stitching inside the clothes she resold. It was her way of tracking inventory as it came in and out of the store, and if you didn't know what you were looking for, it was easy enough to miss. "Now we know that she had every reason in the world to act frugal," I said.

Grace came into the shop, waving something in her hands. It looked like a 3X5 index card.

"You're not going to believe what I just found."

"I'm having a hard time believing you're even up yet," I said as I looked at the clock. It was barely seven, and for Grace, that was more like three A.M.

"I couldn't sleep, so I decided to go by Peg's to see if I could talk Heather into having breakfast with me so I could ask her for another chance to help her with her aunt's house."

"Why didn't you tell me?" I asked.

"I wasn't sure what you'd think," Grace admitted.

George asked, "What did you find?"

Grace held the card out to me, and I took it from her and read,

I'll be back at nine tomorrow morning. Heather Masterson.

I fanned the card in the air. "What's the significance of this? She's allowed to sleep in, isn't she?"

Grace shook her head. "That's not what's significant about it."

George had been looking at the note over her shoulder. "That's the same handwriting as the note you two found in Peg's coat."

Grace smiled. "I can see why you were a police detective. I have to admit, it took me longer than that to spot the similarities, and I was looking for it."

I looked at the card again and studied it. "I don't know. I'm not sure it's the same writing at all."

"That's because she jotted this one down in a hurry," George said. "Do you still have the other note?"

I reached into my pocket. "It's right here."

As I laid them side by side on the countertop, George said, "Look, there are some things that are unmistakable. Look at the way she makes her g's." He pointed to the *g* in *morning* and then the one in *change.* "That's not all. See the way she links the double ll's in 'I'll' and 'allow'? The same person wrote both notes, there's no doubt about it."

I was beginning to see his point. "Okay, let's say that Heather did write both notes. What did she mean in the first one? What was Peg trying to change her mind about? And what consequences could she have meant?"

I reread the first note. It said,

Peg,
    There's no use trying to change my mind.
    I won't allow it, and you should be prepared for the consequences.

Grace paused a moment, then said, "Could Heather have discovered her aunt's fraud, and was she preparing to turn her in to the police?"

"It's possible," I said. "In fact, it seems pretty likely."

George said, "Let's not rule out other possibilities so quickly."

Grace asked, "Like what?"

"It could be just about anything. Do we even know what kind of relationship the two women had? Could there have been something more sinister hidden in this note than we're seeing?"

I frowned. "I don't see how. The two of them were extremely close."

George tapped the two notes in unison, and I wasn't even sure if he meant to.

He said, "Think about it a second. Who do we

have to verify that at all?" He frowned, then added, "I keep wondering what terms they were on."

"She's been a part of Peg's life forever," I said.

"That still doesn't mean she didn't have something to do with what happened to her aunt," George said.

"Maybe we should all keep digging," Grace said.

"It might not be a bad idea if we all did," I added.

George finished his coffee. "I'm heading out. I've got to work a case this morning at the courthouse, but after that, I'll start back in on this."

"And I've got to go to Asheville," Grace said. "I'll walk you out, George."

After they were gone, business started picking up, and I was so busy filling orders that I didn't have time to digest all I'd learned that morning. We were getting a better handle on Peg and her life, but I wasn't so sure we were getting any closer to finding the murderer.

I hoped Chief Martin was having more luck, but from the sparse reports coming from the police station through George, I had a feeling he was hitting as many dead ends as we were.

By nine, it was starting to rain again, and I wondered what it was going to do to my business. Donuts weren't exactly a necessity in most people's lives, and sometimes all it took was a little bad weather to keep them away.

Three men braved the downpour, though, tumbling in through the front door as a particular bad patch of rain hit.

They were each dressed in hiking boots, canvas pants, jackets of various hues, and all of them wore baseball hats. Each man had a pair of high powered binoculars around his neck. For the life of me, it looked like the same man in three stages of his life; frozen in his thirties, his fifties, and his seventies.

The oldest took off his hat and hit it against his thigh, knocking some water off it as he settled in. "That's some bad weather you've got going on out there." He held out a hand and said, "Good morning. I'm Frank Stewart."

It was odd for a new customer to introduce himself like that, but I could tell from the twinkle in his eye that here was a man who truly liked women.

"Hi, Frank. I'm Suzanne. It's a bit wet for birding, isn't it?"

He chuckled and turned to the men he'd come in with. "I told you this was a great spot." Frank looked back at me and said, "Suzanne, I'd like to introduce my son Martin, and his son William. We were out spotting, and the downpour hit. Now most days I'm as willing to trudge through the underbrush as the next man, but I swear I could smell your coffee from the woods."

"Then you should have some," I said as I poured him a cup.

Frank took a sip, then said, "You are an angel of mercy." He looked back at his family and said, "Gentlemen, I'm not sure what you're waiting for, but I'm going to buy a donut and take a seat at the window."

Frank's son Martin said, "Dad, this isn't exactly what we had planned for today."

He put an arm around his son. "Thomas, sometimes the world laughs at our plans. Suit yourself, but I'm going to enjoy this rain from that couch over there."

William said, "You don't have to twist my arm, Grandpa. I'd kill for a cup of coffee myself."

Frank patted him on the back. "There's proof he's my kin. Suzanne, William is a doctor. He's single, too."

"Granddad, enough. Stop trying to fix me up with every woman we meet."

He looked at William, then said, "Maybe we should check to see if you really are my grandson. Suzanne, if I were forty years younger, you'd have an ardent suitor on your hands."

"Frank, if I were forty years older, you'd never make it out the door without the promise of a date," I said with a smile.

He laughed again, this one spreading through the room like a welcoming hug. "Forget the introductions to my offspring. You're too valuable a jewel to waste on such as these."

"Dad," Martin said with open disapproval.

Frank winked at me. "He doesn't approve of the genuine affection I have for women."

"Mostly just pretty women," Martin grumbled.

Frank smiled. "So, at least you noticed that she's pretty. I suppose that's a good beginning for you."

Martin looked at his dad, then at me. "I apologize, ma'am. My father's a bit of a rogue."

I said, "There's no apology necessary. Just coming in here, he made my day."

Frank nodded, then said, "And you made mine as well."

As I slid a yeast donut across to him, he added, "I hadn't ordered yet."

"This one's on the house," I said. "I needed a smile, and you brought one in with you." Then I turned to his son and grandson and added, "You two get to pay, though."

The senior member of the family laughed again, then clapped them both on the back and said, "I like it here, men."

Frank moved to the best couch by the window that overlooked the train tracks, taking his coffee and donut with him.

Martin said, "He's been this way his whole life."

"Is that an explanation, or an apology?"

"A little of both, I guess," he said.

"That's all right. I don't need either. What can I get you?"

After the two men ordered and took seats with Frank, I waited on new customers, but every now and then I saw the three of them pull out their binoculars and peer into the gloom. I wasn't sure how successful they were at birdwatching, but by the time they left, it was clear that all three of them had a wonderful time.

Frank actually tipped his hat toward me as he left, and I was shocked to hear myself giggling in response.

I was still smiling about it when Heather Masterson came in, and from the scowl on her face, it was pretty clear that I wasn't going to be very happy for long.

DEEP-FRIED CAKE SQUARES RECIPE

You can use large cubes of pound cake for this, but my family likes to use Twinkies™ like they make at the county fair! Some folks like to fry theirs on Popsicle sticks, but cutting the Twinkies™ into thirds and frying them that way works best for us. But go ahead and experiment, that's what it's all about!

INGREDIENTS

- 1 cup milk
- 1½ tablespoons plain vinegar
- 1½ tablespoons canola oil
- 1 cup all-purpose flour
- 1¼ teaspoons baking powder
- ¼ teaspoon salt
- Flour to dust Twinkies™ before battering them
- 4 Twinkies™

DIRECTIONS

Freeze your Twinkies™ for a few hours for best re-sults. When they're chilled, mix the milk, vinegar, and canola oil together in one bowl. Using another bowl, sift the flour, baking powder, and salt together. Add the dry ingredients slowly into the wet, mixing it in well as you work. Refrigerate this batter as your oil is heating. When the oil's ready (about 360–370 degrees F), dip each piece of cake into the batter, then quickly add it to the oil. Be very careful not to splash. The oil's extremely hot. Don't overcrowd the pot, and when the squares are brown on one side, flip them over so the other side can cook. Take them out when they're done, and let them rest for a few minutes before eating. You can dust the top with powdered sugar or eat them as they are. The filling becomes a marvelous white fluff that will leave you wanting more.

Yield: Makes 12 Twinkie™ Squares

CHAPTER 11

"Good morning, Heather. Can I get you something?"

"I've got problems," she said.

"What's wrong?"

She looked as though she was about to cry.

"It seems that my dear old aunt wasn't as wealthy as she claimed to be. I've got a stack of bills to pay, and there's not going to be enough money left after I'm through for me to buy a donut."

"I'm so sorry," I said.

"It's not that I wanted her money, but it would have been nice to be able to pay off my college loans, you know? That book you found got my hopes up, until her attorney started digging into it. I won't even be able to afford to pay him," she said.

I got her a cup of coffee and a bear claw.

She looked ruefully at them. "I'm not sure I can afford these."

"My treat," I said. "Think of them as a rainy day kit to cheer you up."

"Unless these things are laced with Prozac, I don't think they're going to help, but thanks for the thought."

While I had her here, it was a golden chance to ask her about her relationship with her aunt, and if the opportunity came up, about the note Grace had found in Peg's jacket. "Do you have a second?"

"I guess," she said.

"Come with me," I said.

Heather wasn't any mood to cooperate, though. "Where are we going?"

"We're just ducking back into the kitchen. I want to talk to you, but I don't feel like doing it out here. You can bring your breakfast with you."

She grabbed the bear claw and the coffee and followed me, though it was clear she was pretty confused about what was going on. As we walked into the kitchen, Emma looked up from her station at the sink, where her arms were buried up to her elbows in soapy water.

"I need you to cover the front for a few minutes," I said.

She nodded. "I'll take care of it as soon as I hear the door chime."

"Some of the tables need to be cleaned in the meantime," I said, signaling her that I wanted some privacy.

Reluctantly, she picked up a dishtowel, and as she dried her hands, she said, "Okay, Boss, I'll get right on it."

After she was gone, I said, "Heather, I'm sorry. I know it's a difficult time for you, but I need to ask you about something."

"You've got me curious," Heather said.

I desperately wanted to confront her about the note Grace and I had found, but if I came out and asked her about it, she'd know we'd been snooping when we'd offered to help her. Maybe there was another way to ask her about it without letting her know that we'd been rummaging through her aunt's things in search of clues.

"If you don't mind me saying so, you seem to be in an awfully big hurry to get things wrapped up here," I said. "Goodness knows she had a prickly side sometimes, so I can understand wanting to put all of this behind you."

She took a sip of coffee, then said, "Suzanne, I know most folks around here weren't all that fond of my aunt, but I loved her. When things got tight at college, she slipped me a few dollars to tide me over, and while it might not seem like much to anyone else, it was a lifesaver for me. She had her good points. Look at her charity work."

It wasn't the time or place to get into any theories that Peg had used them as her own personal bank accounts. "I'm not saying you don't have a right to mourn her. You do."

It looked like she was going to cry again as she said, "Do you know how hard this is for me? She's the last bit of family I have left. Had. I still can't get used to saying that. I just want to put this all behind me and get on with my life."

"Were you two having troubles in the end?" I asked softly.

"Why? What have you heard?" That certainly caught her attention.

"It's a small town," I said. "People talk."

"Okay, I admit it. We had some hard things to say to each other the last time we spoke."

"What were you two fighting about?" I asked.

"I tried to tell her she was wrong, but she wouldn't listen to me."

"Wrong about what?" I was getting close, and I knew it.

"We're all liable for the actions we take, the decisions we make," she said. "I'm not about to go into it with you, Suzanne, but my aunt did something wrong, something she showed no remorse for. I tried to talk her into making a clean breast of it all, but she refused. The last time we spoke, I said some truly awful things to her, and now I can never take them back." Heather dabbed an errant tear tracking down her cheek, then added, "I want to do what needs to be done here, clean out the house, and leave town. No offense, but after I'm finished, I never want to see April Springs again."

"I can understand that," I said. "I'm so sorry."

"About what?"

"Everything you're going through," I said. I believed her. The hurt in her eyes when she spoke about her aunt was too real to feign.

After Heather left, I kept wondering about where my clues were leading me. It seemed every time I turned one corner, another roadblock appeared.

Emma poked her head in through the door. "Is everything all right back here?"

"I'm fine," I said. "Why do you ask?"

"You've got customers waiting out front, and I have a sink full of dishes. Do you want to trade back, or should I get started again?"

"You go ahead," I said. "I'll handle the customers."

That was how we each preferred things. Folks

liked to see the owner greet them, since my shop was such a small one, and Emma was happiest buried up to her elbows in soapsuds.

Grace showed up at the donut shop ten minutes before noon.

"That was fast, even for you," I said.

"My boss is in New York at a conference, so I'm like a kid out of school for summer vacation. I just had to do a quick drop-in with a couple of customers, and then I was finished for the day."

"Won't your customers miss you?"

She grinned. "You'd think so, wouldn't you? Suzanne, I could always go somewhere else."

"Don't be a nit. I just don't want you to get fired."

She laughed. "That's not likely to happen. I know where all of the bodies are buried in my division." Grace thought about that a second, then said, "That's in pretty bad taste, given what's been happening around here lately, isn't it?"

"Don't worry, I won't hold it against you."

"Good." She looked around the deserted shop, and at the three dozen donuts still in the display case behind me. "Is business that bad?"

"You don't know the half of it. I've got four more dozen in back," I said. "It's more than I'd like to have on hand, but then again, it's not as bad as I've been afraid it would be. Things have slowed down some, but it rained today, and that might account for most of it."

"Are you telling me that a little rain is enough to kill your business?"

"Absolutely. When it snows, I'm tempted not to

even bother opening. You know how things are around here. We get a few flurries and folks stay home. An inch or two and the entire town goes into lockdown."

"And yet you don't miss a day at the shop," she said as she sat at a stool at the counter.

"Are you kidding? I get to walk across the park in the moonlight with snow falling all around me, or creep through town in my Jeep in a winter wonderland. It's like being in some kind of massive snow globe. What's the worst that could happen? If we get a ton of snow and I can't drive back to Momma's, I'm never more than a brisk walk away from home. Besides, if my dear, sweet mother and I are cooped up together for too long, we tend to get on each other's nerves."

Grace nodded as she rocked gently back and forth on the stool. "So, what are we going to investigate after you finish up here? Are there any new suspects we can confront?"

"To be honest with you, I'm not sure what we should do next."

Emma came out of the kitchen. "Suzanne, I was wondering . . . oh, hi, Grace. I didn't hear you come in."

"Is your iPod cranked up again?" I asked.

"You had the front covered," she said a little too defensively. "All of the dishes are done, except for the last few trays. Can I take off early?"

"What's going on? Do you have a big date?" Grace asked her before I could warn her off the subject.

"I'm not sure," Emma said.

"New developments?" I asked.

She shrugged. "Paul called. He wants to talk."

"Go," I said. "And good luck."

"Thanks," she said as she raced out the door.

"What was that all about?" Grace asked after we were alone.

"Emma's having trouble with her new boyfriend."

Grace laughed. "There must be a lot of that going around."

I looked at her. "Why do you say that?"

I had my back to her, collecting the last of the donuts from the display trays.

"Maybe you should turn around," Grace said.

"What are you talking about?"

"Unless I'm mistaken, someone's walking up the sidewalk with some flowers for you."

It was Jake.

So he'd decided to make a grand gesture after all.

Grace slipped off the stool. "I'll catch up with you later. Call me when you're through here."

"You don't have to leave," I said as Jake neared the door.

"I won't go far. Come by the Boxcar after he leaves and we'll have lunch. That way we can eat as we plan what we're going to do next."

"Sounds good. See you soon."

As Jake opened the door, Grace slipped out. She said a quick hello, then left us. "She didn't have to leave," Jake said. "I can only stay a minute."

"She didn't go far. How's your niece?"

"She's much better. It's almost like she was never sick, you know? I get the sniffles and I'm down for a week. I just don't get it."

I said, "She's young, and we're not." He wasn't going to say anything, so I looked at the roses in his hands. "Are those for me, or are you just taking them out for a walk?"

He started to redden. "Sorry. I've warned you enough times that I'm not very good at this. Of course they're for you."

I gladly took them. They were lovely, crimson buds that held the promise of bloom tightly within their clinched petals. "They're exquisite." I leaned forward and kissed him on the cheek. "Thank you."

"You're welcome."

I was smiling at him, but it quickly vanished when I looked out the window.

Jake picked up on it in an instant. "Was it something I said?"

"No, I thought I just saw a ghost." It was true, too. Max had been walking toward the donut shop, but when he'd spotted me with Jake—and the roses in my hands—he'd turned white and rushed away. By the time Jake turned around to look, Max was gone.

But my ex-husband managed to kill my good mood.

"Can we talk again tonight?" Jake asked.

"Over dinner?"

"I'd honestly love to, but I can't," he said. "I've already missed too much work. I need to catch up on what's been going on."

"You know, if you really want to get back in my good graces, there is one thing you could do."

"Forget it," Jake said, laughing. "I'm not sharing police business with you."

I smiled at him. "Hey, it was worth a shot."

He leaned forward and kissed my cheek. "Thanks. I've really missed you lately."

"Me, too," I said.

After he was gone, I took out a large vase from the back and filled it full of water. The roses looked lovely on the counter, but before I went home, I'd collect them and take them with me.

If for nothing else, it would be fun seeing the look on my mother's face.

I found Grace sitting at a booth in the Boxcar.

She waved me over to her and said, "Hurry up. I look like a pig hogging this booth all to myself."

"I came as fast as I could," I said. I pretended to study the menu as I said, "Let's see. What looks good today? I feel like something different."

Grace knocked the menu out of my hands. "I don't think so. What just happened? I want details."

"You mean with Jake?"

She said, "You're not funny, you know that, don't you?"

I laughed, something I hadn't done much of lately. "We're both going to try harder," I admitted.

"At least he's making some effort."

"That's true." My stomach grumbled. "I'm starving, but don't let me forget, I've got four dozen donuts back at the shop I need to get rid of."

"What are you going to do with them?" she asked.

"I'm sure we'll think of something."

Trish came over and smiled. "Good afternoon. Are you two ladies ready to order?"

After we told her what we wanted, Trish said, "By the way, those roses were beautiful, or so I heard."

"How on earth did you hear that? Grace, have you been spreading rumors and lies about me again?"

She nodded. "Of course I have, but I didn't say anything to her about the roses. I swear."

Trish laughed. "Sarah from the flower shop came in for a quick bite, and she told me how long it took your policeman to pick out the right bouquet for you."

Grace said, "It's tough to go wrong with roses."

Trish shrugged as she said, "I don't know, I like daisies myself. They're so happy."

I said, "He really spent some time thinking about it?"

Trish nodded. "Sarah said it took him half an hour."

After she was gone to place our orders, I looked at Grace and saw her grinning at me. "What's that about?"

"You're happy about this, aren't you?"

I laughed. "Getting flowers is better than being called names," I said. "Who wouldn't be happy getting them?"

"I can't remember the last time a man brought me flowers," she said wistfully.

"You can have half of mine," I said, joking.

Evidently she took me seriously. She thought about it a few moments, then said, "Thanks, but it just wouldn't be the same, would it?"

"No, I don't think so. I could send you flowers myself, if you'd just like to get some."

"Again, thanks, but no." She played with her fork,

spinning it lazily on the table, as she asked, "So, what's next on our agenda?"

I said, "Let's enjoy our meal, and then we'll talk about the case."

"Good enough," she said. "Here it comes right now."

We ate, chatting about nothing in particular, and after we finished, I felt like I was ready to take on the world again.

And that included finding Peg Masterson's murderer.

As I got out the money to pay for our meal, I said, "If you're up for it, I've got an idea of what we can do next."

"I'm ready," she said.

"Don't you even want to know what I have in mind?"

Grace shook her head. "If you like the plan, that's good enough for me."

"Okay, here's what I had in mind. I want to take another run at Marge, and I need your help," I said. "I think between the two of us, we can break her down and find out the truth about what happened between her and Peg."

Grace looked up from her plate and asked, "Suzanne, do you honestly believe that Marge could have had anything to do with killing her? We've both known her forever; she's not a murderer."

"I realize it's hard to think of her that way, but honestly, how do we know that for sure?" I asked. "What's a murderer look like? Maybe Marge thought she had a good reason to want Peg dead."

Grace took another sip of her iced tea. "I just can't believe it."

"Do you like Burt better as a suspect? We've known him our whole lives, too. How about Peg's niece, Heather? Do you think she looks like a killer? Honestly, I can't see anybody killing Peg, but the woman didn't poison herself, did she? I know this is a hard concept to believe, but a killer's out there somewhere in April Springs, and I need to find whoever did it. There are too many folks who are going to believe that donut left my shop already poisoned, and I can't have that."

"I get it, believe me, I do," she said. "You're right. I guess I feel a little squeamish digging around in other people's lives like this."

"We've done it before," I said.

"I know, but it didn't seem as real to me, for some reason."

I shrugged. "That's because this is the first time we've done it where we know the suspects so well. If you want to back out, I understand completely."

Grace frowned as she pushed her fork around on her empty plate. "No, I said I'd help you, and I meant it. Let's go tackle Marge and see if we can break her."

"Hang on a second," I said as I put my hand on hers. "I'm not trying to ruin anybody's life. I'm just looking for the truth."

"And you honestly don't believe we're going to do some harm when we're looking for it?"

I stood. "I guess there's bound to be collateral damage, isn't there?"

"Funny, the way you put it sounds a lot nicer than ruining innocent lives."

We headed to Marge's in silence, each left to our own thoughts. As Grace drove, I looked out the window, studying our small town, wondering how a community that looked so peaceful and idyllic could harbor so many secrets. As a child, I'd felt safe growing up in April Springs, leading a gentle existence filled with fireflies and long, summer days, but as I'd grown older, I'd come to realize that there were secrets everywhere, jealousies, anger, and pain lying just below the surface. And sometimes they managed to work their way to the surface, contaminating whatever they touched. I still loved my town, and its collection of odd birds, but that didn't mean I was blind to its flaws.

"What do you two want?" Marge was obviously pretty unhappy to see me, and I wasn't sure I could blame her. We hadn't exactly left things on good terms the last time we'd spoken.

She wouldn't even open the door when she saw it was me, staying behind the latched screen door that separated us instead. It wasn't a solid barrier by any stretch of the imagination, but the symbolism of the closed door wasn't lost on me.

"We just want to chat," I said.

"Like last time? I think not."

"I'm sorry if I was rude before," I said. "I'll be on my best behavior this time. I promise."

Grace added, "If she gets out of line, I'll rein her back in." She had her charm turned up to its highest level, but it was clear Marge wasn't buying it.

I repeated my request, "May we come in?"

"I'd rather you didn't."

"Are you here alone?" I asked.

"Burt is at the hardware store, if that's what you're asking," she said. "He told me not to speak with you again without him present."

"I said I was sorry."

"I'm not talking about it," she said adamantly.

"Then at least you can listen. We know what Peg was up to with the finances for her charities, and we found out that was the real reason you two fought. It had nothing to do with your fathers."

Marge's eyes narrowed. "Who have you been talking to?"

"I keep my sources confidential," I said. "That way, you can be sure that whatever you tell me won't get spread around town either."

Marge didn't look pleased with us at all. "There's no need to tell me; it had to be Janice Deal. Whatever she told you, she's lying."

· I was stumped as to how to handle that when Grace said, "Don't worry, I'm sure the audits from the past ten years will clear everything up."

"What audits?" Marge asked, the same question echoing in my own mind.

"Those fundraisers were set up to generate money for good causes. The police have been informed of Janice's suspicions, so full audits are naturally the first thing they're going to do. Any treasurers of committees Peg chaired in the past will be held accountable for their actions."

That hit the mark dead on as it got Marge flustered. Her hands were shaking as she said, "I wrote the checks she told me to. That was my job."

"Let me guess," I said. "A lot of them were made out to P.E.G., weren't they?"

"She told me it was a business she'd created to get our supplies and materials at cost," Marge explained.

"And you weren't suspicious?" I asked, "not even when you found out the company moniker matched Peg's first name? Come on, Marge, you're smarter than that. Did she give you a cut of what she was skimming? What happened? Did you want a bigger share? Is that what you two were really fighting about?"

"Suzanne Hart, you shut your mouth!" she yelled at me.

"Is that what happened, Marge? Tell me now, or tell the police later. I noticed that as soon as you got your inheritance, you dropped Peg like a hot cookie sheet. What's the matter, didn't you need the money anymore?"

"I didn't take a dime from her, and I didn't do anything wrong," she insisted, her voice starting to break with the intensity of her emotions.

"Then why did you quit being Peg's vice chairman?"

"Because I knew she was doing something she shouldn't have been doing," Marge said, her words tumbling out in a rush.

Grace asked, "If that's true, why didn't you tell anybody?"

"Who was I going to tell? Peg ran everything in April Springs, and if I made waves for her, she'd kill my reputation around town. I confronted her with my suspicions, and she said if I told anyone what I'd uncovered, she'd place the blame squarely on me. After all, it was my signature on all of those checks. She never signed one, just stamped it FOR DEPOSIT ONLY, then put it into another account. Peg claimed she had two sets of records, one that told the story she wanted the world to see, and another one laying all the blame on me."

It appeared that Peg lied about her finances in more places than the fake ledger she'd been filling out since her divorce. Knowing what she'd written in the log I'd found, it didn't surprise me that there were at least two sets of books for every charity she ran.

"If that's true," I asked, "then why on earth did you agree to have your kitchen featured on the tour?"

"I didn't want to! She blackmailed me into doing it," Marge said, the tears starting to track down her cheeks. "I had no choice."

I was about to press her further when Burt pulled up in his truck. As he rushed toward us, he asked, "What's going on here?"

"We're just talking," I said.

One look at Marge was all he needed. "You'd both better leave."

Grace and I stood our ground.

I gestured to Marge and said, "Not unless she tells us to go."

Marge looked from us to Burt, and then back again. "You'd better leave," she said softly.

Burt looked at us triumphantly.

I wasn't about to let him have his moment of victory. "That's fine, we were finished here anyway. We got all we needed. Let's go, Grace."

We were nearly back at her car when Burt approached us. There was a look of anger on his face that I'd never seen before. "I need to talk to you."

"Make up your mind," I said as I opened Grace's car door. "First you want us to leave, and now you're ordering us to stay."

"What did she tell you?" he asked, his voice barely more than a low growl.

"Ask her yourself," I said as Grace started the car.

"You're not going anywhere," Burt said.

"How are you going to stop us? Are you going to throw yourself in front of the car? Don't tempt us, Burt."

He shook his head. "Suzanne, what's gotten into you? This doesn't concern you, and yet you keep butting in where you don't belong."

I put a hand on Grace's arm. "Hang on a second." Then I turned to Burt and said, "It concerned me the second someone poisoned one of my donuts. That makes it my business. And, you know what? There's probably no one in town with more access to rat poison than a man who runs a hardware store." As I stared at him, I said without thinking, "I just realized that your hair color is close to matching the person I saw at the crime scene right before Peg was murdered." It was true; it could have easily been Burt I'd seen hiding near the courtyard of Marge's home.

His eyes flared as I said it. "You're out of line. Leave us alone."

"You should worry about me coming after you next, not Marge."

"Is that a threat, Suzanne?"

"No, sir. It's more like a promise."

I turned to Grace and said, "We're finished here. Let's go."

CHAPTER 12

As Grace drove off, I looked back to see what Burt was doing. He'd made no move to rejoin Marge on the front porch. Instead, he stood there in the driveway, watching us until we disappeared from sight.

Grace said, "If I were you, I'd find another place to shop for my hardware from now on."

I shrugged. "I'd already planned on doing that." I let out a lungful of air, then added, "That was certainly interesting, wasn't it?"

"I wonder if Marge realizes yet that she just gave us a great motive for her committing the murder."

"If she doesn't know by now, Burt will understand the ramifications as soon as she relays our conversation with her, you can believe that. You want to know something that's funny?"

Grace said, "Sure, I could always use a good laugh."

"Not funny that way, funny odd," I said. "Neither one of them ever mentioned calling the police, no matter how belligerent we got with them."

"*You* were belligerent. I was sweet," Grace said.

"Whatever. Don't you find that strange?"

"No, Marge admitted she had something to hide when she said Peg had threatened her."

"That's the thing with secrets. They always have a way of coming up to the surface if you give them enough time."

Grace asked, "So, who should we talk to now? I wonder if Father Pete's around. We can take a swing at him, while we're going after people in April Springs."

"Believe me, if I thought he had something to do with Peg Masterson's death, I wouldn't hesitate."

My cell phone laughed at me, and I saw my mother was calling. Before I answered it, Grace said, "I thought you were going to change that ringtone to something normal."

"I was, but I've kind of gotten used it." I opened the phone and said, "Hi, Momma, what's up?"

She nearly screamed at me, "Suzanne Hart, have you completely lost your mind?"

"Probably. Why do you ask?"

She said, "I just got off the phone with Marge Rankin, and the poor woman was in tears. What did you do to her?"

"I just asked her a few innocent questions," I said.

I saw Grace's eyebrows go up at that, and I frowned at her.

A bit mollified, Momma said, "That's not the way I heard it."

"Who are you going to believe, Marge or your own daughter?"

She paused way too long for my taste.

I said, "I'm waiting."

"I'm thinking," my mother said.

"When you figure it out, give me a call back," I said as I hung up on her.

Grace said, "Oh, you're in trouble now."

"I'm a little too old to be grounded," I said. "She's just going to have to deal with it."

"I admire you. Your mother scares the pants off me. She always has."

"That's because you let her," I said.

"So, all of the drama aside, what do we do next?"

"I'm not exactly sure," I said. "Let me get back to you on that. In the meantime, why don't we just drive around until something comes to us?"

Grace kept looking at her watch, and I finally asked, "Is there somewhere you need to be?"

"I've kind of got a dinner date, but I can cancel it if you need me."

I said, "Pull over."

We were a block from the donut shop, and she did as I asked.

I got out of the car and said, "Have you lost your mind? If you've found someone crazy enough to ask you out, you should go."

"That's kind of what I was thinking," she said with a smile.

"Who is it? Anybody I know?"

"No, he lives in Union Square. I'm meeting him at Napoli's for dinner."

She knew that was where Jake and I had gone when we'd eaten out on those rare times he was in town. No wonder she hadn't wanted to say anything to me about her plans.

"Go on, then, get out of here," I said. "Don't be late on my account. Have fun, okay?"

"I'll try. Call me if anything comes up, I mean it."

"I will," I promised as I watched her drive away.

At least one of us had a social life. I wondered what Jake was doing for dinner. No doubt he was having takeout at police headquarters as he caught up on any progress Chief Martin had made in his absence. I couldn't imagine the file being very thick, but then again, I didn't have a great deal of faith in our fair chief.

As I walked past Two Cows and a Moose, I decided to pop inside. The three stuffed animals the newsstand had been named for were on their shelf of honor above the register, and I saw that they were each decked out in Halloween costumes. Cow had a vampire cape on, Spots was wearing a cowboy outfit, and Moose had on a superhero ensemble. Emily Hargraves had taught me early on that the way to tell the difference between the two cows was the green ribbon tied to Spots's tail.

Emily, the pretty young brunette who owned the place, saw me admiring her stuffed friends. "They look positively resplendent, don't they?"

I nodded. "Where did you find costumes that fit them?"

She smiled. "I have a sewing machine and an imagination. What more do I need?"

"I'd need someone to use them both," I said. "Do you have the latest issues of *Ellery Queen* and *Alfred Hitchcock* mystery magazines?"

Emily went to a rack and grabbed one of each. "Sure thing. Can I get you anything else?"

I shook my head as I paid for the magazines. As Emily handed me my change, she said, "I'm so sorry about what happened. Why on earth someone would take something as full of joy as a donut and turn it into a bad thing is beyond me. It's just not fair."

I nodded. "You're preaching to the choir."

As I was leaving, I saluted the stuffed animals and said, "Happy Halloween."

I half-expected them to respond, but they kept their vigilant watch over the place, never shirking their duties.

I got into the Jeep, and as I drove home, I realized that my mother hadn't called me back after I'd hung up on her. That meant she was still angry that I'd cut her off so abruptly, and I debated about whether to go back home at all.

But I'd have to face her sooner or later, so I realized that I might as well get it over with.

At least there'd be food there, and I was starving.

"Dinner's almost ready," my mother told me as I walked in the door. I looked at her, searching for some clue about her mood, but from the way she was acting, it was clear she'd decided to ignore our previous exchange.

That was fine with me. I'd had enough drama today to last me a while.

"It smells great," I said. "Lemon chicken?"

She nodded. "With mashed potatoes, green beans, homemade cranberry sauce, and cherry pie for dessert."

"Wow, I feel like a queen. When did you have time to make pie, too?"

"I've been home cooking all day," she admitted.

"Just for the two of us?" It wasn't odd for my

mother to cook elaborate meals for both of us, but this was a little over the top.

"I thought Jake might join us," she said. "Is there any chance you could call him and issue an invitation?"

"Sorry, Momma, he's busy," I said. "Do I still get to eat?"

"Of course you do. Set the table, and we'll go ahead."

I washed my hands first, then set the table for two. So that was why my mother had gone into "extreme cooking" mode.

As we sat down to eat, I realized just how hungry I was.

As I piled my plate up with food, Momma said, "Maybe it's just as well Jake couldn't make it. You eat like a lumberjack sometimes, Suzanne."

"I've got the appetite of one," I said. "Besides, Jake's already seen me eat. He likes the fact that I don't pick at my food."

She could tell that I was in no mood for her verbal jabs, and after our truncated telephone conversation, I realized she was a little touchy, too. We dropped the sparring, and I was surprised to find myself enjoying her company as much as the meal. My mother could be charming when she set her mind to it. Of course, I'd heard her say the same thing about me. Maybe it was true about the apple not falling far from the tree.

I was ready for bed, and reached for my telephone to turn it off when it laughed in my hands. It was Jake.

"I didn't wake you, did I?" he asked.

"It's not even eight o'clock," I said. "I'm still awake."

"For how much longer, though? You're ready for bed, aren't you?"

I looked out the window. "Why? Are you outside watching me?"

"No, but that's why I called. Why didn't you tell me there was a prowler outside your house last night?"

He was upset; I could hear it in his voice.

"There was nothing you could do about it, Jake. You were in Raleigh. I handled it," I said.

"I heard you called George, and then the police," he said. "You weren't crazy enough to go outside yourself, were you? I don't care if you do have a baseball bat, it's no protection against someone out to get you."

"I'm happy with it," I said. "I don't like guns, and it seems a little odd if I carry a sword around with me."

I put the phone down for a second and stared outside. Had I heard a twig snapping, or had it been my imagination? I was the first to admit that my senses were on overdrive, looking for possible danger where it might not exist. But I also knew that the woods made their own noises at night, and a lot of it, particularly in the silence of the evening, when the rest of the world was settling down.

Try as I might to see into the shadows though, I couldn't spot anything untoward.

I heard Jake talking loudly as I put the telephone back to my ear. ". . . coming over right now!"

"What? Why would you do that?"

He said, "Suzanne, what's going on? Are you all right?"

"I'm fine. I heard a squirrel out in the park, and I immediately envisioned a prowler lurking in the shadows."

"Is that what happened last night?" he asked.

"No, that was probably just a jogger bending over to tie his shoe. My imagination's getting the better of me lately; I'm the first to admit it."

"I'm coming over, anyway," he said.

"Jake, it's nothing, trust me. Besides, I need to get some sleep if I'm going to be up in five hours."

"You don't have to invite me in and entertain me, Suzanne. I'll come over, look around, and make sure everything's okay. You won't even know I'm there."

"You don't have to do this," I repeated.

"I know I don't have to. But I want to."

He hung up, and I walked downstairs to tell Momma not to worry if she saw a flashlight in the park.

She was watching a television program, something that she rarely did.

As she looked up at me, Momma almost appeared to look guilty. "I just turned it on," she said.

After a second, she asked, "What are you doing up, anyway? Isn't it past your bedtime?"

I nodded as I double-checked the locks on the front door and the windows, to be sure they were all secured.

"Jake's coming over," I said.

"So you're making sure he can't get in? Suzanne, I've heard of playing hard to get, but you're taking it to entirely new levels."

"He's not coming for a visit. I made the mistake

of telling him I heard a squirrel in the park, and now he's going to rush over to check."

"So, we should get something ready for him. How about some of that cherry pie? I think there's some vanilla ice cream in the freezer, and I can make some coffee, too."

She started to get up when I said, "Momma, sit down. Jake's not coming in, so there's no need to make him a snack. He's going to look around outside, and then he's going home. Period, that's it, no visiting, no conversation."

"That sounds harsh," she said.

"I can't let him in even if I didn't need to get some sleep. I forgot his flowers at the donut shop."

That certainly got her attention. "He sent you flowers? What kind?"

"Roses, a dozen of them," I admitted.

"And you just left them at Donut Hearts?"

I nodded. "They really brighten the place up, but I don't know how to tell that to Jake. I bet he was expecting me to bring them home."

"As well he should," my mother said. "Now, shouldn't you be getting off to bed?"

Why was she rushing me all of a sudden? Then I knew. "I'm not asking him in, and don't you invite him, either."

"Suzanne Louise Hart, this is still my home. I can invite whomever I'd like into it, and there's not a thing you can do about it."

I shook my head. "Okay, let's back up a second. You're right, you can have him in if you'd like. I'm just asking you not to. It's late, and fast getting to be past my bedtime. I need my sleep, so it's a lot easier all the way around if we don't invite him in for dessert."

I started for the stairs, and she said, "Of course I wouldn't have anyone in you didn't approve of."

"Momma, I don't approve or disapprove at this very moment. I just want to go to bed."

"Understood," she said.

I walked upstairs, then listened carefully, and heard the sound of the TV show coming back on. I stayed outside my door for a few seconds, trying to figure out what on earth she was watching, but to no avail.

I went back into my bedroom and turned off the lights. I meant to get to sleep, but I found I couldn't do it, not with Jake out there trying to protect me. After a few minutes of searching out my window, I saw his flashlight bobbing up and down in the darkness. He checked every tree and bush within two hundred yards of my house, then approached the front porch. As he neared the front steps, his flashlight caught me fully in the face up in my window.

"What are you still doing up?" he asked.

"I was watching to be sure you were safe."

"I looked all over, but I didn't see anybody."

"See," I told him. "It was all in my head. It was probably just been a squirrel after all."

"That's not entirely true, either. Come downstairs and let me in. We need to talk."

I grabbed a robe and hurried down the stairs. He hadn't been joking; that much was clear. So what had Jake found?

When she saw me, Momma said, "For goodness'

sake, Suzanne, make up your mind," as she shut off the television. She had been watching something again, and from a single glance, I could see that it had been repeats of a British comedy—*As Time Goes By*—we'd both watched a few times. Jean and Lionel were her favorite couple on television, and I had to admit, the times I'd watched, I'd enjoyed their adventures as well.

I opened the door, and Jake stepped inside.

My mother looked thrilled. "Jake, how lovely to see you. We were just talking about you. Would you like some pie?"

"No thanks," he said.

Jake turned to me and said, "I called Chief Martin. He'll be right here."

"What's this all about?" I asked as Momma said, "I'll make coffee."

Jake said, "Somebody's been watching your place after all. It wasn't your imagination."

"Did you see someone, too?"

"No, but I saw where he was standing."

"Take me out there," I said.

"We'd better wait for the chief."

"Feel free to," I said as I got my dad's old flashlight out of the hall closet, a huge black steel monster that would club a grizzly. "I'm going out to see for myself."

He followed me outside, and as I started for the trees, Jake said, "I'm not telling you what I found, or where it was."

"That's fine," I said. "I watched your flashlight bobbing in the dark. I've got a pretty good idea where you were."

As I approached a dense blue spruce, he said, "Stop right there."

"Getting warmer, am I?"

"You're about to contaminate a crime scene," he said.

I stopped dead. "There's not a body under there, is there?"

"No, but there might be a clue about who is watching you, and that might mean a murderer's been in there."

I was about to try to get a look anyway when Chief Martin drove up to the house, and after a moment, he joined us by the tree.

He looked at me and said, "What are you doing out here?"

"Is there any chance you'd believe me if I said that I was just out taking my nightly stroll?"

"Dressed like that? I doubt it."

"You caught me," I said, grinning as I held my wrists out to him. "I was peeping on my own house."

Martin shook his head and turned to Jake. "What's this about?"

"Over here." He pulled a couple of branches of the tree up, and used his flashlight to illuminate the ground.

He led us around the tree, where I saw a freshly cut branch. "Whoever was in there cut this branch to get a better view of the house."

"Have you checked it out?" the chief asked.

"No, sir. I was waiting for you."

Martin nodded, then studied the needles shed underneath the tree. "We won't get any footprints there." Taking out an evidence bag, he disappeared into the heart of the tree, and after a few moments, came back out.

"You should take a look," he said.

I started to duck under the branches when I felt a hand on my shoulder. "Not you. I was talking to Jake."

Jake ducked in before I could protest, and after a minute, he reappeared. "Chief, she should see this, too."

"Why?" he asked gruffly.

"Because she has a right to know."

"What is it?" I asked. "You two are scaring me."

Jake looked at the chief, who nodded after a moment's thought. "Go ahead."

I ducked under the branches before he could change his mind, and found that someone had built a little nest in there. It was tight, and whoever had done it hadn't been claustrophobic, but I couldn't see much more than that.

"What am I supposed to be looking at?" I asked.

"Sit down on the ground, and then look toward your house."

I did as Jake instructed, and was surprised to find that the missing branch had afforded the perfect view of my house. Worse yet, my window was perfectly framed in the brushy opening.

Someone wasn't just watching my house.

They were watching me.

I crawled back out from under the tree, then said, "Okay, now I'm scared."

"I told you it was a bad idea to tell her," the chief told Jake.

"No, I'd rather know what I'm dealing with," I said. "It's the unknown that's the scariest of all."

Momma came out and joined us.

"Phillip," she said as she saw the chief. "What are all doing standing out here? I've got fresh coffee, and there's enough pie for everyone."

"Thanks, but we've got more to do here," the chief said. "Someone's been watching your place, Dorothy."

My mother bit her lower lip, then said, "And I'm sure you two will find him. In the meantime, I'll bring you your coffee out here. Come along, Suzanne, you can give me a hand."

"Thanks, but I'm staying right here," I said.

"Nonsense. You aren't going to miss anything. Will she, Phillip?"

"No, ma'am. We'll take a few photographs, but there's really not much else we can do. I'll have two of my men canvass the park again, but I doubt we'll be able to come up with anything. Whoever did this wasn't a professional."

"How do you know that?" my mother asked.

The chief and Jake both shrugged in perfect unison.

Chief Martin said, "We'll find out who's behind this, don't worry."

"I don't see how," I said, without realizing that I'd spoken the words out loud.

"We're not entirely incompetent," the chief said, "no matter what you might think. We actually manage to solve a crime or two around here without your help, Suzanne, believe it or not."

I caught Jake fighting to hide his grin. He was enjoying this way too much for my taste. I turned with as much dignity as I could muster and started back toward the house. "Coming, Momma?"

She nodded, and we went back inside. Why was someone watching me? Was it related to Peg Masterson's murder, or did it have an even more ominous meaning for me?

The next morning, I was just getting ready to snip the long-john dough blanks into pinecones when there was a banging on the front door. It was four A.M., a good hour and a half before we were due to open.

Emma looked up at me and said, "I vote we ignore it."

"Somebody might be in trouble," I said as I wiped my hands on a towel.

"If you let them in, it could be trouble for us. Call the police and let them deal with it."

I approached the door between the kitchen and the dining area. "I'm going to at least look to see who it is."

I peeked out through the barely opened door and saw Jake standing there.

"I'm letting him in. It's Jake," I said.

I opened the door, careful to look behind him, just in case someone was lurking in the shadows.

"What are you doing here?" I asked as I dead-bolted the door behind him.

"I've got to go back to Raleigh. My niece's fever is back, and now it's worse than ever. I just wanted to come by and tell you in person before I took off."

"Thanks, but go. I know you need to be with your family."

"I'll call you as soon as there's anything to report," he said. Jake hesitated a second, then he kissed me with a quick but affectionate buzz, hitting my lips this time instead of my cheek. At least his aim was improving.

"Bye," he said as I opened the door again for him.

After he was gone, I turned around and found Emma watching. She was grinning broadly.

"What's that look for?"

"Me? A look? I don't know what you're talking about."

I shook my head, and with a slight smile, I said, "Let's get back to work."

"Yes, ma'am. You're the boss."

I swatted her with a towel that had been sitting on the counter, and after we got back to work making pinecones, I couldn't help but be pleased by Jake's response to an emergency this time. I dearly hoped that his niece would be all right, but I was glad he'd come by the shop to tell me what was going on in his life before he took off again.

"Suzanne, I know you've been investigating Peg Masterson's murder. I'm just wondering why you haven't asked me to help," Emma said as she glazed the yeast donuts I'd just pulled out of the fryer.

I'd been waiting for her to make the request, and I had an answer ready for her. "You've been tied up with your own life this past week," I said. "I didn't think you'd have time to help me."

"Don't worry, that's over," she said.

"You two didn't break up already, did you?" I asked as I flipped the current batch of yeast donuts in the fryer with my long, wooden skewers.

"We never got serious enough about each other to call it a breakup."

"What do you think went wrong?" I asked as I

pulled the donuts out of the hot oil. We often held postmortems on Emma's relationships as we worked. She claimed it helped her gain perspective on what had happened, and if she'd made any mistakes, she'd work to correct them the next time around. I had to give her credit for her optimism. Emma constantly lived her life based on the premise that new opportunities were everywhere. Her job was to be ready for them when they appeared.

"I know what happened," she said, focusing more attention on pouring loaf pans full of glaze than was strictly necessary.

As I delicately dropped another round of donuts into the fryer, I said, "So, tell me what it was this time."

"He was a jerk," she said.

"Come on, I met him. What made him such a jerk?"

"If you must know, Paul wanted me to quit my job," Emma finally admitted.

I was shocked by the news. "Why? Doesn't he like donuts?"

"It's the hours I keep that he hated. He kept saying how ridiculous it was for me to have a nine P.M. curfew."

I nodded. "I know, it must sound crazy to the rest of the world. Emma, if you want to quit so you can have a more normal life, I won't stand in your way."

She looked surprised by my statement. "You mean you don't want me working for you anymore?"

"No, that's the farthest thing from the truth," I said. "Honestly, I don't know how I'd run the place without you."

She appeared to be at least a little mollified. "That's more like it."

"I meant what I said, though. I'd hate for you to . . ." I stopped before I finished that particular thought, but she knew what was on my mind.

"What were you going to say, end up like you?"

I admitted it. "Life's hard enough without making things more difficult with an insane work schedule like we've got."

"You know what? I have faith that I'm going to find someone who wants me, despite my crazy hours. And until I do, I'm going to focus on making donuts with you, and I'm going to keep taking classes in the evenings whenever I can. I don't have time for men in my life right now, anyway."

"Still, they can be a lovely distraction, can't they?"

"Absolutely," she agreed. "Now, why don't we try a new design with this dough? I'm getting tired of making pinecones."

"What did you have in mind? You know me; I'm always up for an experiment when it comes to donuts."

"I was thinking that if we cut them on the diagonal, we can do a fancy braid instead of spiking the dough up. I don't mean like a cinnamon twist. I was thinking more along the lines of something like this."

She took one of the rectangular long-john shaped pieces of dough and attacked it with our stainless steel scissors. After mangling the dough, Emma wadded it back up and put it with the rest of the scraps. "Okay, that's not quite what I was going for."

"Sketch it out on paper this afternoon, and we'll see what we can do to make one tomorrow."

"You're awfully forgiving of my mistakes," she said as she started making pinecones again with me.

"It's only dough, and it's not like we have to throw our misfires away," I said. "We'll recycle them into fried pies. If nothing else, Bob will be a happy man."

"He does love your pies, doesn't he?"

"Bob's a man with simple tastes," I said. "We could both do worse finding men like him."

"But not him, right?" Emma asked as she smiled at me.

"No, I'm afraid Bob's on his own there."

By the time we opened for business, I was in a decent mood again. I knew that Jake wasn't anywhere near Raleigh yet, but I couldn't help worrying about what he might find when he got there. He loved his niece like she was his own daughter, and the drive must be agony for him.

Unfortunately I couldn't do anything to help him, I had problems of my own, though they weren't on the scale of his.

I had barely unlocked the doors when I was surprised to see Janice Deal approaching the donut shop at a quick pace. From the expression on her face, I kept looking behind her to see if someone was following her, but if they were, they were adept enough to escape my detection.

"You've got to help me," Janice said as she burst in. "Now someone's trying to kill me, too."

FRIED BANANAS

This one's not for the faint of heart! It's an acquired taste, and it took me quite a few tries to find a blend my entire family likes. It's not a standard offering, but it might be something fun for you try on a rainy day when you have too many ripe bananas on your hands!

INGREDIENTS

- 1–2 ripe bananas
- ¼ cup flour
- ½ teaspoon baking powder
- ¼ cup granulated sugar
- ¼ teaspoon cinnamon
- ¼ teaspoon nutmeg

DIRECTIONS

Smash the bananas with a fork, something the kids love to do to help. In a bowl, sift the flour and baking powder together. Spoon the banana puree into the flour and mix it all together well. Then add the sugar, cinnamon, and nutmeg, and mix it all together again. Drop this batter into a pot of canola oil (360 degrees F) and turn once when it browns.

Yield: One; or several smaller pieces

CHAPTER 13

I looked behind her as I reached for the telephone to dial 911.

"I don't see anyone chasing you," I said. "Are you sure?"

"Who are you calling?" she asked.

"The police," I said.

"Hang up the telephone, Suzanne. I didn't mean that they were after me this very second."

I hung up, then drew her a cup of coffee. "Take a sip, draw a deep breath, and then tell me what's going on."

She nodded as she did as I asked. After a few seconds, Janice said, "It's not my imagination. Someone really is trying to kill me."

"What happened?"

Emma came out of the kitchen, where she'd just started on the dishes. "Is something going on?"

"No, everything's fine out here," I said.

It was pretty clear Emma didn't believe me, but she went back into the kitchen anyway. I was afraid that Janice wouldn't talk as freely to me if Emma was there as well. And right now, I really needed her to focus.

"You were saying?"

In a voice that was anything but steady, Janice said, "I was unlocking my front door a few minutes ago when I got the weirdest feeling that someone was watching me. When I turned around, I saw someone ducking back into the shadows, and when I started toward them, I heard a shot."

"What? Somebody took a shot at you?"

"Yes, and I've got proof."

As I started to reach for the telephone again, I asked, "Did you see where the bullet hit?"

She frowned. "No, but there was a witness. Someone was driving by in a beat-up old car. He had to have heard the shot, too. It's not my imagination."

I put the phone back down. "Was the car blue, by any chance?"

"Yes, how'd you know?" she asked.

"That was Happy Cane. He delivers the morning papers around town, and his car backfires every twenty feet. You're not used to coming in this early, are you?"

"No," she admitted. "It sounded like a shot to me."

"Don't feel bad," I said. "The first time I heard it, I dove to the pavement and ripped a hole in a brand-new pair of jeans." I hesitated, then said, "I'm curious about something. What made you come here?"

"I knew you were open, and I didn't want to be alone," she admitted.

"You could have called the police on your cell phone," I said.

"I don't have one. I don't believe in them."

I dug mine out of my purse. "They're real enough."

"I don't mean I don't believe they exist, Suzanne.

I mean I don't feel obligated to be available whenever anyone wants to call me. Those things are dreadful."

"Most of the time, I agree with you," I said as I put mine back into my purse. "But they can be handy in cases of emergency."

Janice frowned. "Point taken. Maybe I'll get one of the horrid things after all."

"Here's an idea. Don't give anyone the number, and just use it if you need to."

She nodded. "I could do that, couldn't I?"

"I don't see why not," I said. "Should we call the police anyway? If someone's stalking you, Chief Martin should know about it."

Janice took another gulp of coffee, then said, "The more I think about it, I'm not entirely sure I saw someone. It was dark, and there were shadows everywhere. I don't know how you do it, coming into work in the dark every day."

"You get used to it after a while," I said.

"Well, I'm not going to. I've decided to abandon the idea of offering donuts to my customers."

I was glad not to have any more competition no matter how bad hers would probably be, but I was curious about how she'd come to the decision.

"Is it out of loyalty to me?"

She barely chuckled. "No, the profit margin isn't enough to justify all the effort you have to expend. I don't know how you manage."

"Some months it's a struggle," I admitted. "How did the police take your news about Peg?"

"With Chief Martin, who knows? I'm not sure, but I suspect he thinks I'm guilty and I'm just trying to lay the blame on someone who can't defend her-self."

"Yeah, I get that from him all of the time."

She finished her coffee, and I offered her more.

"No, thanks. I've got a big order to fill. I'd better be going. Thanks for the coffee," she said as she reached for her wallet.

"Don't worry about it. It's on the house."

Janice just shook her head and laid a one-dollar bill on the counter. "With your profit margin, I couldn't accept it in good conscience."

I laughed after she was gone, and the second Emma heard the door, she came out of the kitchen. "What was that all about?"

"Janice thought someone was trying to kill her," I said.

"Who would want her dead?"

I frowned. "That's the same question I keep asking myself about Peg."

Ten minutes after we opened, the front door chimed, and I walked up front to help our customer.

I was surprised to see Burt come in, with Marge practically in tow.

"Good morning," I said. "What brings you two out here this early? Come by for some fresh pastry treats?"

"We want you to leave us both alone," Burt said. "Enough is enough."

"I don't know what you're talking about," I said.

Burt reached into his pockets, but evidently couldn't find what he was looking for. He turned to Marge and asked, "I can't find it. Do you have it?"

"It's right here, "she said as she dug into her purse. Marge pulled out a note and handed it to him.

"What's that supposed to be?"

"Don't act dumb," Burt said.

"It's not an act," I said with complete candor. "I honestly don't know what you're talking about."

He shoved the note under my nose. It said MUR-DERER in big, black letters.

I waved it away. "I didn't do this. Where'd you find it?"

Burt frowned. "It was in her mailbox last night. Are you trying to tell us that you didn't write it?"

"That's exactly what I'm saying," I said. "Since you're here anyway, is there anything I can get you?"

"No, thanks. I don't like what you use for toppings," Burt snapped. "Come on, Margie, let's get out of here."

Marge at least had the decency to say, "I'm sorry about this."

"I understand." I paused a moment, then asked, "Is that new?" as I pointed to her ring finger. She was sporting a brand-new golden wedding band, and a quick look at Burt's hand showed the matching ring.

"We got married at midnight," she said. "Isn't that romantic?"

"Marge, we don't need to tell everyone we see, do we?"

"You picked an odd place to spend your honeymoon," I said. "Aren't you going anywhere besides my donut shop?"

"I'm not sure going away is the best idea right now," Burt said. "There's too much to do around here."

"I still think we should go to Hawaii, Burt," Marge said. "It's not every day you get married."

He looked at me, and I could almost see the wheels spinning in his head. A slow grin started to creep across his face as he said, "You know what, Marge? You're absolutely right. Neither one of us is getting any younger. We've got some money to burn, and I can turn the store over to Pete Evans until we get back. Let's go pack. We can be out of town by noon."

Marge looked absolutely delighted. "Do you mean it? We're actually going to Hawaii?"

"Maybe we'll do just that. Wherever we go, we won't be back here anytime soon."

"Congratulations," I said to them both, not meaning a word of it.

As Burt dragged his new bride out of my shop, I began to wonder why they'd had such a hasty wedding. Was it out of love, or could it have been motivated by a wife not being able to be forced to testify against her husband? Or for that matter, was it so the husband couldn't testify against his wife?

Had all of April Springs suddenly gone insane?

On another front, why would someone leave that terse note in Marge's mailbox? And more importantly, why would Burt automatically assume it was from me?

I was still mulling it all over ten minutes later when Heather came in.

She said, "Good morning. Suzanne, I don't know how you do this every morning. I got up at five today, and it's killing me."

"I've been up since one," I said. "Would you like some coffee?"

"I'll take a gallon if you've got it. And how about some donuts, too? Mix them up. I need them to go. I have a big morning ahead of me."

"What happens this afternoon?" I asked as I prepared her order.

"I'm leaving, whether I'm finished or not, and the house is going on the market, as is. This is the last morning I'm ever going to spend in April Springs. No offense, but there are just too many memories here."

"I understand," I said as I handed her a coffee and the box of donuts. Heather paid for her order and left.

After she was gone, I collected a few plates and mugs from the empty tables and put them into the sink, and as I walked back to the front, my foot hit a caramel candy wrapper on the floor by the register. I reached down to pick it up, and then—before I touched it—I realized it was the same brand that was discovered near Peg's body. Since I'd done a good job sweeping the floor the afternoon before, I realized that one of my visitors this morning had most likely been the same person who'd been near Peg when she'd been murdered. My list of suspects was now firm, and it was down to Janice, Heather, Burt, and Marge. Unfortunately, I couldn't eliminate any of them yet. But I knew in my heart that Peg's killer had been in my donut shop that morning.

Now I just had to narrow the list down to one.

I wished Jake was still in town so we could discuss this latest development, not that I was a hundred percent sure he'd talk to me about the case even if he was here. Still, it would have been good having him around. I knew Emma would love to talk about it, but so far, I'd done my best to keep her out of my investigations, and if I could help it, I'd keep shielding her from the ugly side of life in our little North Carolina town.

By eight, George still hadn't shown up, and that was beginning to worry me a little. I knew that George had a life of his own, but I still liked to see him spend part of his day with me at Donut Hearts.

I wondered where Grace was today, or where she was scheduled to be, at any rate. On a whim, I finally broke down and called her to see what she was doing.

Her phone went straight to voice mail, something odd for a woman who worked in sales and had to be accessible to her customers all the time.

It appeared that I was all alone in my sleuthing, at least for the moment.

Since business was slow half an hour before we were due to close, I grabbed a pad of paper and a pencil and started a list of my suspects, and why any one of them in particular would kill Peg. I had Janice and Heather down for money as a motive, Burt was listed for love, and Marge qualified for both motives. There weren't many reasons anyone could justify killing someone else, in my opinion, but love and money were certainly at the top of the list.

I was doodling my thoughts on the page when the front door chimed and I looked up to see Chief Martin approaching. Before he could get to the counter, I flipped the pad over and hoped he hadn't spotted my musings.

"Good morning, Chief. Did you come by for a donut?"

"No, but it's not a bad idea. What's good today?"

I couldn't help myself as I said, "The lemon-filled ones are particularly nice."

He frowned as he shook his head. "No, I don't think so. How about a cinnamon cake donut and a small coffee instead?"

I nodded. "To go?"

"No, I'll sit right here while I eat it," he said.

In all the time I'd run Donut Hearts, the chief had never eaten a donut there on the premises. Something was going on.

As I delivered his coffee and donut, I asked casually, "How's the investigation coming?"

He nearly choked on his donut, but somehow managed to swallow. "Do you really think I'm going to answer that?"

"Not really," I admitted.

"Why ask, then?"

"It's odd to have you eat here, not that all customers aren't welcome at Donut Hearts."

He shrugged. "Sometimes I like to shake things up." After taking a bite of his donut and washing it down with coffee, he added, "Since I'm here though, you might be interested to know that we just cleared Janice Deal of the murder."

"Why?" I asked.

"Why did we clear her, or why am I telling you?"

"Take your pick. I'd love to know the answer to both questions."

The chief finished his donut, then stood up. "We

cleared her because she had a tight alibi. I'm telling you this as a favor to your friend."

Neither one of us had to say Jake's name to realize that was who he meant.

"What was her alibi?" I asked.

"Don't push your luck, Suzanne," he said. "I'll see you around."

"I'll be here," I said to him as he left.

I would have loved to know what Jake had said to him, but I doubted he would tell me. And what was Janice's alibi that so convinced them she was innocent? Since I didn't know, I couldn't very well verify it myself. For now, I was going to trust Jake and the chief, though the former more than the latter, and mark her off my own list.

That left Burt, Marge, and Heather as my main suspects.

I wondered if the chief knew Burt and Marge had just gotten married.

He was still out in his cruiser, talking to someone on the radio, so I was going to return the information favor.

I called out to Emma, "Back in a few minutes," then darted out the door.

I tapped on his window, and I didn't realize that he hadn't seen me until I noticed his startled look.

As he rolled his window down, he said, "You almost gave me a heart attack. What do you want?"

"Did you know that Burt Gentry and Marge Rankin got married at midnight last night?"

He nodded. "I heard about it over at the courthouse. Judge Hurley said he thought it was kind of rushed, but they wanted to get hitched, and evidently Burt had arranged for the license last week. Marge was surprised, but she was happy enough to do it."

"Do you think they're really in love?"

He shrugged. "It doesn't matter what I think. What business is it of yours? Do you have something against marriage all of a sudden?"

"No, and you know that's not it. I'm just surprised you're letting two of your suspects leave your jurisdiction without even a fight."

He said, "Don't be so sure. Burt told me they were staying in town for their honeymoon, so I'll be able to keep a close eye on them both. I'm aware of their motives in wanting Peg dead." I must have looked startled by the confession, because he laughed, and then added, "You'd be amazed what all I know."

"Did you know they were on their way to Hawaii?" I asked. "I talked to them thirty minutes ago. When did you see him last?"

"It's been about two hours," the chief said. "Suzanne, are you sure about that?"

"They made the plans right in the donut shop," I said.

"I'd better go see what's going on," he said.

As he pulled away, I wondered if maybe the chief wasn't as dull as I'd thought. From the sound of it, most of his list matched mine.

But that still left Heather.

If I was going to talk to her, now was the time. Soon enough, she'd be gone for good, and if she'd killed her aunt, most likely she was going to get away with it.

Back inside, I said, "Emma, it's nearly noon, so I'm taking off. Just lock up and I'll clean everything up when I get back."

"Can't we just close now?" There was a plaintive note to her voice, and I could tell she was disappointed.

"What's going on? Don't tell me you're going to try to get Paul back."

She rolled her eyes. "Come on, Suzanne. I think I always knew in my heart that was doomed from the start."

Still, there was something about the way she looked. "There's somebody you're not telling me about, though, isn't there?"

"While you were on your break, the nicest guy came in. His name is Patrick, and he wants to be a doctor. He's so sweet, Suzanne, you just wouldn't believe it. He's meeting me after work so we can get to know each other better."

I thought about warning her about moving too fast, of falling in love before she knew what she was getting herself into, but I was her boss and her friend, not her mother. "Go on, take off. I can hang around till noon myself."

"Are you sure?"

"You'd better go before I change my mind."

She was out the door before I even finished talking.

I might as well have shut down when I'd sent Emma on her way. No other customers came in, and the phone didn't ring.

I boxed up the remainder of the donuts, rinsed off a few things, then collected the carafe of coffee and carried everything toward my Jeep.

David Shelby approached me as I neared my vehicle.

"Can I give you hand with those boxes?" he asked.

"No, but you can get the passenger-side door for me."

As he opened the door, he said, "I can't believe you don't keep this thing locked."

I put the boxes in the seat and said, "Yeah, I know, because vinyl windows are such a good security system on their own."

"You've got a point," he said.

I closed the door, then asked, "Was there something you needed?"

He frowned, then said, "No, it's not important. I don't want to keep you."

"I just closed up the shop. I have time for you right now." I'd been wondering about the man since he'd first walked into my shop, so I wasn't about to pass up on the opportunity to talk to him when he was in the mood. Heather was just going to have to wait.

I leaned against the grill and said, "So talk."

He ran a hand through his hair, then said, "I just wanted you to know I'm not always this way around people."

I pretended to study him. "I don't know what you're talking about, unless you mean you're aloof, cryptic, and just a little acerbic at times."

That made him smile. "Okay, you got me. Honestly though, deep down, I'm a pretty good guy."

"Why is it so important to you that I believe that?"

He looked down at his hands, then into my eyes. "I'm not sure. I've got this feeling that we've met before, but I don't believe in déjà vu, do you?"

I said, "You know, I've had the same feeling about you since the first time you walked into my shop."

"Maybe there's something to it after all," he said.

"I don't know about that. Did you ever go to school around here when you were a kid? Did you visit April Springs growing up?"

He shook his head. "No, the closest I ever came was Camp Camelot up in West Virginia. It was a summer camp for kids—"

"—of Union Carbide employees," I finished for him. "I was at the girls' camp, Carlyle. I can't believe you spent your summers on Blue Creek, too."

"Four in a row, until we moved away. How about you?"

I grinned. "My grandfather worked for Carbide, so I got to go, too." I studied him another moment, then said, "I think I danced with you one summer."

"You know what? I think you're right. That explains a lot."

"I feel better about it, too."

David smiled at me, then said, "Since you're off work, do you want to go grab something to eat? We can hash over old times around the campfire."

"I'm sorry, but I can't," I said.

"I understand," he said. "There's somebody else, isn't there? Of course there is. Why wouldn't there be?"

"There's just somewhere else I need to be."

"So then you're saying that there's not somebody?"

"No, you were right. There's somebody in my life right now. I'm sorry."

"Don't be sorry. That's a good thing. See you later, Suzanne."

"Good-bye, David."

I hoped I still had time to catch Heather before she left. I doubted I could get her to confess if she did it, but maybe I could make her sweat a little before she took off.

"Hi, Suzanne. What a surprise," Heather said as I walked into Peg's house. "I was just getting ready to leave."

I looked around the living room and saw a lot of things boxed up and ready to go. There was a lot left, though. "What happens to all of this?"

"The Girl Scouts are taking care of it for me. I'm giving them a pretty nice donation, and they're having a yard sale with everything that's left. I've taken a few things with me, mostly sentimental stuff."

I nodded. "Peg would have approved." I unscrewed the top of the coffee carafe and asked, "Would you like some for the road?"

"Sure, that would be great. Just let me grab my travel mug. It's in the other room."

She went into the back bedroom, and I decided a little coffee would be nice as well. As I moved to a box near the kitchen in search of a mug, I inadvertently hit Heather's purse, spilling its contents to the floor.

"What happened?" Heather asked pointedly as she came back into the room.

"I'm so clumsy," I said. "I didn't mean to knock over your purse. Sorry, it was an accident."

I started to gather her things together when Heather

pushed me aside. "That's all right. I'll take care of it myself." She must have seen the expression on my face, because she suddenly asked me, "Suzanne, what's wrong?"

"What? Oh, nothing. I just feel a little faint. I think I stood up too fast."

"Let me get you some water," she said as she moved into the kitchen.

There was a clear path out, and I started for the door. "That's all right. I just need a little fresh air."

"I don't think so," Heather said behind me. Her voice was calm and clear, but I could tell that something was wrong.

When I turned back to look at her, she was holding a knife on me.

CHAPTER 14

Heather was moving closer toward me as she asked, "You saw something in my purse, didn't you?"

"I don't know what you're talking about," I said, doing my best to sound believable.

Heather laughed. "Suzanne, you're not that good an actress. You might as well tell me what you saw. Lying isn't going to do you any good at this point."

I couldn't believe I'd allowed myself to be caught just as I'd figured it all out.

"It was the candy," I admitted.

"You're kidding me, right? I don't know many women who don't have some kind of candy in their purse."

"Not that particular brand of caramel," I said. "I checked, and they don't sell it in April Springs. I'm willing to bet you got it while you were away at college."

"So what?" she said. "It's not illegal to eat candy."

"No, but it is incriminating. I found a wrapper near Peg's body, and everybody knew her weakness was my donuts. This morning I found one at the donut shop, but I never linked them to you until I saw them in your purse."

She shook her head. "So, you figured it out because I'm addicted to caramel. I don't believe it."

"There was a lot more to it than that," I said. "You dyed your hair at Peg's after you realized I'd spotted you at Marge's when you were waiting for your aunt to come outside. I'm willing to bet that a lab will confirm that your hair was dyed red before the recent change. When you weren't arrested right after the murder, you must have realized that I hadn't seen your face, but that I could have easily seen your hair. That was pretty clever of you to dye it before you came to see me at the donut shop. Grace even found the box you used in Peg's trash can, but we both just assumed it had belonged to Peg and not you. I didn't think a thing about it when I saw that your hair tint matched hers perfectly. I just assumed it was genetic, and not out of the same bottle of dye."

"Nobody else will get it."

I said, "Don't kid yourself. If I put it all together, the police are sure to be able to as well."

"I doubt it," she said. "By the time they make the connection—if they ever do—I'll be gone. There's not nearly as much here as I'd hoped, but I did manage to find Peg's hiding place, so I'm not leaving empty-handed." She took a banded stack of money from a hidden section in her purse and fanned the money with her free hand. "I thought for sure you saw this, and it would be a little hard to explain, given how broke Peg and I apparently were."

"You're not going to kill me, are you?"

"Don't be ridiculous," she said. "If I were going to do that, you'd already be dead."

There was something in her eyes that made me

realize she was lying to me. I was going to have to fight for my life, or I'd never make it until sunset.

"Why me? I didn't do anything to cause you to come after me, yet you've been hounding my steps for days."

She laughed. "If you can believe it, I thought you were on to me. That's why I started watching your house, but you never put it together, did you?"

"You were on my list," I said, defending myself.

"With Peg gone, now you're at the top of mine."

"Did you bring the poison with you from school? It must not have been that hard to steal one of my donuts the morning I wasn't at the shop, but the poison has me puzzled." I had to stall her. Maybe someone would come back before Heather stabbed me. If anyone did, I had to be ready to act. I'd only get one chance, and I had to make it good. As I talked to Heather, a plan started to formulate in my mind. It was a long shot, but it was the only chance I had of getting out of this alive.

Heather said, "It was in her shed out back. You know how she felt about your lemon-filled donuts. It was the one thing I knew she couldn't turn down, so I took one from her stash."

"I still can't believe you killed your own aunt. She was family."

"Some family. I don't have to tell you that my aunt was no angel. When I needed help with tuition, she turned me down, even though I knew she had money. Look at the way she dressed. And she didn't have to work. She had time to run all of those charities. It wasn't fair. I figured I'd just speed up my inheritance a little when it could still do me some good. When I slept over here a few months ago, I found her ledger in her office after she was asleep. I still can't believe she tricked me like that!"

"I think she was lying to herself more than anyone else. She bought most of her clothing used," I said, "and she was skimming off charity proceeds to finance her standard of living."

Heather bit her lip, then said, "You don't think I found that out as soon as I started really looking at her bank accounts and her credit card statements? I realized I'd made a mistake pretty quickly after I killed her, but by then, it was too late. I had to salvage what I could, so I took the jewelry and some of her nicer things, but I knew she had money squirreled away somewhere around here, and I was right."

"Why did you agree to have Grace and me help you, if you were looking for Peg's hidden money?"

"I wanted you to be the one to find the ledger, and it took you long enough," Heather said. "I nearly had to help you myself."

"But why did you need me?"

"I figured it would look better for me if someone else found it. Fat lot of good it did me."

"But you're not coming away empty, are you? Where'd you find that cash, in the cookie jar?"

She frowned at me. "My aunt was a lot craftier than that. It took me forever to find it, but I finally did. One baseboard came off at my touch, and I realized she'd used magnets to secure the trim in place instead of nails. That's where I found the money."

"Are you sure you found it all?" I asked.

"What are you talking about?"

I was stalling—that was pretty clear—but I hoped

her greed would supersede her caution. "I just discovered this morning that your aunt skimmed over three hundred thousand dollars in the past two years. The chief of police came by my shop an hour ago and told me the audit was complete. Did you find that much?"

It was all a lie, but I knew Heather couldn't exactly call Chief Martin and ask him. "No," she said a little warily. "Nowhere near that, but after all, she had expenses."

"That much? Peg didn't live in luxury, that's pretty obvious. My first thought is, what did she do with the rest of it?"

Heather scowled. "After I've taken care of you, I'll keep looking."

So much for that tactic. For all I knew, there might still be money hidden in the house, but it appeared that I wasn't going to live long enough to see it.

If I was going to make it out of there alive, I needed to do something, and do it fast. I looked for anything nearby that I could use as a weapon, but the only thing within reach was a stack of old books. Not much of an arsenal, but it was all I had.

Before Heather could stop me, I lunged for the book on top, an old mystery.

At least it was a hardcover.

My movement was all the incentive Heather needed to strike. She made a hard backhanded swing in the air at me with the blade, nicking my hand as the knife flew past. I felt a brief sting, but I couldn't let that stop me. I swung the book at her head, trying my best to break her nose with it.

She was too quick for me, though.

With a sudden jerk, Heather ducked enough for

the book to glance off the top of her head instead of making a solid impact with her face.

Even worse, the book slipped out of my hands and fell when it failed to find its target.

Heather looked at me with a new level of rage.

I could rush her and take my chances, but that meant facing the blade in her hand with no weapon of my own, and the way she was looking at me, she was ready to kill me.

I really had only one option.

I had to run.

I started for the other room, and as I did, I heard her just behind me.

Heather lunged again, and if she hadn't stepped on the book that I'd just dropped, I knew I would have been dead. Fortunately for me, she pulled up at the last second as she lost her balance, but her stabbing attempt was still close enough to tug at the back of my shirt. My adrenaline was pumping so hard at that moment that I had no idea whether I'd been cut again or not.

I looked wildly around for something else to defend myself with, and I saw that I was close enough to my coffee to grab it, but how could I possibly use it to go against a crazed woman with a knife?

Out of the corner of my eye, I saw movement on the front porch. It was George!

I had to stop him from coming inside. I wasn't about to let her kill my friend.

As the front door started to open, I shouted out a warning to him.

Heather pulled the knife off me and started swinging it toward George.

I knew I had to act fast.

I reached over and grabbed my hot coffee and threw it on her hand. She jerked it back, and the knife clattered to the floor. The coffee hadn't been scalding, but it was hot enough to catch her by surprise.

We both fell to the floor as we scrambled for the blade. Heather and I were still fighting for it when George said, "Drop the knife or I'll shoot you. I swear I will."

Heather immediately loosened her grip on the knife, and I picked it up and pointed it at her.

George said, "Sorry I was a step behind you."

"Better late to the party than never," I said. "How did you know to come here?"

"It finally made sense, once I realized what was going on."

"Did the wrappers clue you in, too?"

"No," he said, looking more than a little confused. "I suddenly realized that Heather hadn't known that ledger was a fake. She might not kill her aunt for the little bit she got out of her inheritance, but what if she thought it was worth a million dollars to see the woman dead?"

"I'm glad you made it," I said.

George looked down at Heather and said, "Would you mind calling the police for me? I don't want to take my eyes off her."

"I'm happy to. What should I tell them?"

"Let the chief know that we found Peg Masterson's killer," he said.

After Heather was in custody, I was still at the house, waiting to talk to Chief Martin once he'd dispatched his prisoner to another patrol car. It was his request, not mine. All I wanted to do was go home, take a long, hot bath, and go to bed for a week. I still couldn't believe how close I'd come to getting stabbed worse than I had been, and my nerves were more than a little shaky.

Finally, the chief had time for me.

The first thing he did was gesture toward my hand, which was now wrapped in gauze. "You okay?"

"I got lucky. She barely scratched me." The blade had barely nicked me on the first pass, and it had missed my back completely, thanks to Heather slipping on the book I'd tried to clobber her with.

I'd have to replace my top, though. It had been that close.

The chief nodded. After a moment, he scowled at me, then ordered, "Okay, from the beginning, tell me what happened."

"I don't know when the beginning was," I admitted.

"When did you know Heather killed her aunt? Suzanne, I swear to you, if you knew when you sent me off on a wild goose chase looking for Marge and Burt this morning, I'll lock you up out of pure spite."

I confessed, "I didn't know it until I saw her purse fall open. She had a handful of the caramels and freshly dyed hair, so I knew she had to be somehow involved."

"Why kill her aunt, though? Was it really for the money? Peg didn't have all that much."

I nodded. "We all know that now, but she talked a good game, didn't she, and that ledger she kept made her look like a success in her niece's eyes. I can't imagine that she'd realize it would be the motive for her eventual murder."

"People do the most awful things for money," the chief said.

"That and love," I replied.

At that moment, my telephone started its laughing summons. I glanced at it and saw that it was Jake, so I asked the chief, "Are we done here?"

"For now, but don't wander too far off," he said.

"I'm just going out onto the porch. There's better reception out there."

"Sure there is," he said.

I didn't mention more privacy as well, but it was pretty clear he already knew that.

Once I was outside, I said, "Hey, Jake. How's your niece?"

"This bug's a little nastier, but they think they have it whipped, too. She must have picked it up while she was in the hospital. What's going on with you?"

"Nothing much," I said. "Oh, there's one thing. I solved Peg's murder while you were gone."

"Yeah? Are you going to work on world peace next?"

"I'm not joking," I said. "I figured out who did it and caught her." It might have been stretching things a little bit, but it was still within shouting distance of the truth.

There was a moment or two of hesitation, then Jake said, "Suzanne, you're not joking, are you?"

"No, and you can talk to the chief when we're through if you don't believe me. Care to guess who did it?"

He said, "I don't have to guess. I finally figured it out myself. It was either Burt or Heather."

It was my turn to be surprised. "How on earth did you know that?"

"Heather and Burt both thought Peg was rich, and they needed money. Heather is in debt up to her eyeballs with loans, and Burt's hardware store is losing money at an alarming rate. I would have proved one of them did it, but I needed more time."

"Well, I just saved you the trouble," I said.

He said, "I'm proud of you, even if you shouldn't have been meddling in police business. What gave it away? Did you find the poison she used? Did you track a clue down that I missed? What was it? Don't be shy, I'd really like to know."

"I saw some candy in her purse, and as soon as I realized that her hair was freshly dyed in the exact same shade of her aunt's, everything fell into place."

"Good work, Suzanne," Jake said softly.

I asked, "How long will you be staying in Raleigh?"

"Amy's not out of the woods yet. The thing is, you wrapped up the case, so there's no real reason for me to come back."

"I can think of one or two," I said.

"Really? What did you have in mind?"

"You're the detective, you figure it out."

He laughed, then said, "I'll see what I can do. In the meantime, try to stay out of trouble, okay?"

It was my turn to laugh. "Now what fun would that be?"

After we hung up, I looked in through the porch window at Peg's possessions boxed up and ready to go, and I wondered if she had any idea what kind of legacy her life of lies would leave behind. She'd stolen more than money from some worthy charities that needed it. And she'd lied her way into her own murder.

This time, karma's bite was strong, swift, and deadly.

I just wished Heather hadn't used one of my donuts as a murder weapon.

A thought occurred to me, something that made me smile.

I hadn't realized Chief Martin was standing outside with me until he asked, "What is it? If you can think of something funny, I'd love to hear it."

"I just decided I'm going to send Heather a care package as soon as she's tucked safely away in jail."

The chief frowned. "She tried to kill you, and now you're going to give her a treat?"

"Who said anything about her enjoying it?" I asked.

"What exactly did you have in mind?"

"If I brought a dozen lemon-filled donuts dusted with powdered sugar over to the jail, would you be sure she gets them?"

He nodded seriously, but I could see a slight smile on his face. "Suzanne, you can count on it."

I normally hated making more than one batch of donuts in a day, but at the moment, I was willing to make an exception.

Heather was going to get her donuts as soon as I could make them, and they'd be ready for her before she spent her first night in jail.

With every bite she took, I hoped she thought

about her aunt, and about where her own greed had led her.

It was a taste of justice by lemon-filled donut, the best kind, in my opinion.

Here's a look ahead at

SINISTER SPRINKLES

the next Donut Shop mystery, coming soon from

Jessica Beck and St. Martin's / Minotaur Paperbacks!

I heard the first scream just as I gave a warm apple-spice donut and change to Phyllis Higgins from the booth outside my shop, Donut Hearts, during the nineteenth annual April Springs Winter Carnival. There had been whoops of great merriment long before then coming from the crowd of folks out enjoying the displays and vendors' offerings, but there was a quality to this particular shriek that chilled me to my toes, despite wearing two layers of thick woolen socks and my most sensible shoes. I wondered for a second if it had been some kind of aberration, but then there was another scream, and yet another.

When I heard someone in front of the courthouse shout, "Muriel Stevens has been murdered," I knew the Winter Carnival—and Muriel—had come to a sudden and abrupt end.

Christmas is my favorite time of year. I love the way my neighbors decorate their homes with icicles of light and erect trees overloaded with ornaments and tinsel inside. It's no accident that my attitude is reflected in the selection of donuts at my shop, offering treats adorned with red and green icing and glistening sprinkles that overload the display cases in honor of the holidays.

Our Winter Carnival—balanced precariously around Thanksgiving, Hanukkah, and Christmas—offers the residents of my small town in the North Carolina foothills of the Blue Ridge Mountains the opportunity, even the excuse, to go outside and enjoy the brisk weather. During most years of the festival, we haven't experienced our first snow of the season yet, but at the moment, the streets of our quaint little town were covered in a glistening layer of white. It was like everything was topped with icy frosting, a place nearly everybody in the world would visit if they could.

But now all that was ruined.

Phyllis dropped her donut in the snow when she heard Muriel's name.

"Suzanne, is it true?" she asked me.

"I was standing right here beside you when we heard the first scream," I said. "Let me get you another donut, and then we'll go see what's going on."

"Don't bother," she said. "I couldn't bear to eat it now. Poor Muriel." I knew Phyllis was shaken. She'd never passed up the chance at a donut in her life.

As she waddled away toward the courthouse, I turned around and rushed into Donut Hearts. It was handy having my booth right in front of my business, and I'd asked my friend and the carnival coordinator, Trish Granger—owner of the Boxcar Grill just across the street from my donut shop—for the favor, which she'd gladly granted me. There had been some grumbling from a few of the other vendors when they learned of my coup, so to be fair, Trish decided to scrap the previous year's plan and start completely over. Business owners in April Springs got their first choice of spots, and vendors from out of town had to make do with what was left. It made sense, especially for me. If I was going to supply my customers with fresh, hot donuts, I needed to be as close to the source as I could manage. I had my assistant, Emma Blake, inside, ready to add hot glaze to some of the extra donuts we'd made that morning as we needed fresh supplies. I would have loved to make the donuts themselves as they were needed, but the process didn't lend itself to sudden orders, and the warm glaze still managed to give the donuts an air of instant creation.

"What's going on?" Emma asked as she peered outside at the people hurrying by the shop window. Barely out of her teens, Emma had a petite figure I envied, though I didn't covet her flaming red hair. If it meant hanging onto my twenty extra pounds to keep my chestnut-colored hair, I was willing to make that trade.

At least we could watch what was going on outside from where we stood. My donut shop was housed in an old railroad depot, and it afforded plenty of views of the abandoned tracks beside us, as well as Springs Drive through the front windows, the main road in our little town.

"I need you to watch the booth," I said. "Somebody just screamed that Muriel Stevens is dead, and I need to check it out."

Emma reached for the telephone. "Should I call 911?"

"No, from the sound of it, it came from in front of city hall. I'm sure Chief Martin is already there."

Emma frowned at me as she asked, "Suzanne, you're not investigating another murder, are you?"

I shook my head. "No way. I've had my fill of that. I just want to go check on poor Muriel."

"Fine, but come back as soon as you hear anything. Promise?"

"I'll get back as fast as I can," I said as I left the shop again.

The snow was falling again, picking up in intensity, and I wondered if that would affect the crime scene. I'd been thrown into an investigation or two in the past, and I'd been forced to learn a little about police techniques, if for no other reason than to keep myself out of jail as I dug around the edges of cases that impacted my life.

Muriel's murder wasn't going to be one of them, though. She was a regular customer of mine, but nearly every other business owner in April Springs could make that claim as well. Muriel Stevens was the grandmother-figure everyone loved, and I couldn't imagine what would drive anyone to kill her.

As I started toward the courthouse, I felt a hand grab my shoulder from behind, and I wondered for a split-second if I was next on the killer's list.

Then I heard Gabby Williams speak, and almost found myself wishing it was the murderer instead. At least then I could be openly hostile, something that I could never afford to do with Gabby. She was the town wag, spreading stories and rumors at a speed that put satellite relays to shame, and worse yet, her used clothing shop was right next to mine.

Getting on her bad side was a form of character suicide, and I always tried to tread on her good side, though at times it was a tough line to toe.

"Suzanne, where are you going in such a hurry?"

I tried to brush her hand loose, but she had the grip of a longshoreman, despite her prim and petite appearance. It would be easy to underestimate the woman, but I'd made that mistake before, and wasn't about to make it again.

"It's Muriel Stevens," I said.

Gabby's face went ashen. "What about her?"

"I heard someone say she was dead. Murdered," I added softly.

Gabby frowned. "Why are we standing here, then? Let's go."

Her grip barely eased as we hurried up the sidewalk toward the courthouse. There was a crowd gathered around the town clock mounted on an ancient cast-iron pole, but it was clear no one was all that interested in the time. As Gabby and I fought our way through the mass of people to get a better look, her grip on my shoulder finally eased, and I broke away from her before she could reattach it.

I saw George Morris, a loyal customer and retired cop who helped me with inquiries from time to time, so I pushed through the crowd toward him.

"What's going on?" I asked as I finally reached him.

"Hey, Suzanne," George said. "At this point it's still too hard to tell, but someone shouted that Muriel Stevens had been murdered, so of course everybody in town rushed right over here. I tried to help with crowd control, but the chief sent me over here."

He looked miffed by the thought of his dismissal, and I didn't blame him. "I thought I might be of some use is all."

"It's tough being a retired cop, isn't it?" I said as I patted his shoulder.

"I admit it, 'Serve and Protect' kind of gets in your blood." As George spoke, his gaze stayed firmly on the body in the snow. When folks nearby shifted from foot to foot, I caught a glimpse or two of Muriel's coat, and I knew that there'd been no mistaking her, even from that distance. The jacket was a patchwork whirlwind of reds, yellows, oranges, and blues, something as distinctive as the woman herself had been.

Then I saw a touch of gray in the murder victim's hair—which made me look closer—and said softly, "That's not Muriel."

"What are you talking about, Suzanne?" George asked. "No one else in the world has a coat like that."

"I'm telling you, it's not her," I repeated, staring again at what had to be a wig. The black and gray hair had skewed a little—maybe in the attack—and I could see blonde hair beneath it, pinned down. If there was thing Muriel was prouder of than her coat, it had to be her lustrous black hair. Whenever a gray hair dared to appear, it was quickly either plucked or dyed out of existence.

Before he could ask me more, we were interrupted by a voice behind me.

"There you are," Gabby said as she joined us. I moved instinctively away from her, but if she noticed, she kept it to herself.

After a moment, Gabby said flatly, "That's not Muriel," leaving no room for debate.

For once, and maybe the first time in my life, I was startled to realize that I agreed with her. "That's what I've been trying to tell George. It's the hair, isn't it?"

Gabby didn't even look back at the body as she spoke. "No, that's not it. She brought a bag of clothes into the shop yesterday, and three hours later she was pounding on my door, a good thirty minutes after I was closed for the day. It seemed that she was under the impression that she had put her favorite coat," she paused and glanced briefly at the body, "that coat, in the bag by mistake. She wanted it back, and I mean instantly. The problem was, though, when we went through the bag, the coat wasn't there. She claimed someone stole it from my backroom, but I've never had anyone ever take any of my merchandise."

"At least not that you're aware of," George said.

She put her ferret-eyed gaze on him. "Sir, I know my business, and I know my inventory. If I say something about my shop, you can believe it."

George was suppressing a smile, though I could see it, but he somehow managed to keep her from noticing. "My apologies, ma'am." I swear, if he'd had a hat, he would have tipped it to her.

"Can you even be sure the coat was there in the first place? Did you go through the bag the second it arrived?" I asked.

"Suzanne, I don't have time to evaluate the things I'm offered immediately," Gabby said. "I categorize and price the items at my leisure, not my clients'."

"So you can't be sure the coat ever made it to Re-Newed," I said.

Gabby frowned. "I just told you, it was never there." She paused, then added, "Though Muriel was absolutely certain of it. She accused me of keeping it for myself, as if I'd ever wear something as garish as that, much less display it in my store." Gabby Williams made a nice living reselling some of the nicer clothing items in our part of North Carolina. I'd bought a dress there once myself, and with our shops next door to each other, I saw her inventory more often than I liked. She was right, too. I couldn't imagine Gabby ever selling something as, well, for lack of a better word, colorful as Muriel's coat in her shop.

Chief Martin was shouting for everyone's attention, and we quieted down to listen to what he had to say.

"Folks, it's pretty obvious this year's Carnival is over. We'd appreciate it if you'd give your names and addresses to one of the deputies standing by as you leave. Have a driver's license ready to show them, or some kind of photo identification so they can confirm your information."

"Who killed Muriel?" a voice from the back shouted.

"We're not ready to disclose what happened here yet," he said. "And I'm not going to answer any questions until I've got a better handle on what's going on."

I couldn't help myself. "How about a statement, then? It's pretty obvious that's not Muriel Stevens. Why don't you tell us who it really is under that wig?"

Chief Martin met my gaze, then said icily, "Suzanne Hart, get up here. Right now. Everybody else, do as I said. Now." The last word was delivered with an explosive forcefulness that got the crowd moving, albeit reluctantly. Deputies were posted on both sides of Springs Drive with clipboards, and I noticed folks digging for their IDs as I walked up to the police chief.

That's when I realized that George was right behind me.

I stopped in my tracks and said, "I appreciate the show of support, but I don't want to make him any madder than I already have."

"Don't sweat it," George said. "I'm not going to let him bully you."

I shook my head, but I didn't say anything else as I walked toward the chief. If he wanted to get rid of George, let him try. Honestly, I was kind of glad he was there beside me, despite my effort to convince him otherwise.

"Just Suzanne," the chief said when he saw him.

"Sorry, that's not happening," George said.

He and the chief locked glares, then Martin waved a hand in the air. "Don't push me, George."

"I won't any more than I have to," my friend said, and I had to wonder how much of his bridge to the April Springs Police Department he was burning on my account. As a retired cop, George enjoyed nearly free access to his old workplace, but we all knew that it was at the whim and will of the chief.

Chief Martin seemed to forget all about him as he focused back on me. "Suzanne, how did you know it wasn't Muriel, especially from that far away?"

"Gabby Williams told me Muriel lost her coat yesterday, so I figured it couldn't be her. Plus, I saw that black-haired wig with touches of gray on that poor woman's head, and I knew it without a doubt. You know how proud Muriel was of her black hair. She never wore a wig in her life, especially not one with gray hair in it. Whoever was killed was a blonde, you can see that, if you look closely enough. So, who was it?"

"You seem to know a lot about this," the chief of police said, still refusing to answer my question.

"She's observant," George said.

"Who was it, Chief?" I asked again, hoping he'd tell me, though I knew he had every reason in the world not to.

"We're not releasing that information at the moment," he said as he turned his back on me and dismissed me.

I tried to get another look at the body, but there was still a cluster of folks blocking my way, so that was pointless. I turned to George and said, "Let's go."

As we walked toward one of the deputies, I told George, "I didn't mean for you to get into trouble because of me."

He shrugged. "If it wasn't you, it would be something else. I seem to have a knack for it lately." As our gazes met, George added, "You need to stay out of this investigation."

"I'm not disagreeing with you," I said. "I just wanted to know what happened, so I asked."

George didn't respond to that, and after we gave our names to one of the deputies and showed our IDs, we went our separate ways.

I walked back to my booth, thinking about what I had to do to shut it down for another season. The

Carnival still had a few hours until its official closing time, but I had to agree with Chief Martin. It
was no longer a time for fun and frivolity.

When I got back to Donut Hearts, I found Emma
peering out the front window toward me.

She said, "What's going on? Is it true? Is Muriel
dead?"

"No, it was someone else," I said as I took off my
jacket and hung it on the coat rack. I looked around,
happy to be back in my shop where I felt safe and
happy. The front dining area was filled with couches
and comfortable chairs, while the walls and harsh
concrete floors were painted with a pretty plum faux
finish. All in all, it was a lovely place to spend my life.

Emma asked, "Who was it, then?"

"The police aren't saying," I said.

"And you're going to let it go at that?" she asked.
"That's not like you, Suzanne. What's happened to
you?"

"I've decided to keep my nose out of it, for once,"
I said. "Do you want to help break down the booth,
or would you like to stay inside where it's warm?"

"Thanks, but the snow's still coming down pretty
hard. I think I'll cover the front," she said.

Emma wasn't a big fan of the cold, and one of her
constant threats was to move as far south as she could
until she could see the outline of Cuba in the distance.
I'd been to Key West once—had even rubbed the colorful marker at the southernmost point of the US for
good luck—and I didn't have the heart to tell her that
Cuba was invisible from there, still nearly ninety miles
away. Emma added college brochures of schools in

warmer climates whenever the temperature dropped below forty degrees. I knew my assistant would go off to study somewhere soon enough—and I dreaded that day like a root canal—but I couldn't expect her to be my helper for the rest of her life.

"I'll take care of the booth, then," I said as I grabbed my jacket and headed back outside. The sooner I got everything dismantled, the faster I could forget seeing that body lying on the cold, snow-covered ground. I for one loved the snow, relished the way it decorated the world with a fresh, new coat of promise. Even the ugliest things took on a new perspective with the brush of winter.

I was just beginning to take the vinyl banner down from the top of the booth when I heard a familiar voice beside me.

"Need a hand with that?"

It was my ex-husband Max, more handsome than he had any right to be, with wavy brown hair and deep brown eyes. He also had a voice that could melt my toes when he put his mind to it.

"No, thank you. I've got it," I said as I reached up for the banner and managed to grab one corner of it.

"Here, let me get that," he said as he brushed past me and took the edge from me. From his proximity, I could smell Max's subtle cologne, and despite my feelings about the man, I was ashamed to realize that I had to fight the urge to lean toward him and savor his presence.

He easily plucked the banner off its hooks, then folded it before handing it back to me. "Here you go. You must have sold out fast."

I shook my head. "No, there are dozens of donuts inside that I don't have a clue what to do with."

"Then why are we taking the banner down?" he asked.

"I don't need it now that the Carnival's over."

Max looked around, and seemed to realize that most of Springs Drive was deserted. He looked at his watch as he shook his head. "What happened? It's supposed to run another two hours."

"Did you just get here?"

Max shrugged. "You know I like to sleep in whenever the opportunity affords itself," he said. "I haven't been up all that long. So, what happened?"

"Somebody was murdered under the town clock," I said.

It was pretty clear that Max was hearing this for the first time. "What happened? Who was it? Come on, Suze, give me some details."

I hated when he called me Suze, but he was too upset for me to correct him. Max, though his exterior was always cool and urbane, was a soft cookie on the inside, one of the things that had first drawn me to him.

"A woman wearing Muriel Stevens' jacket was killed. I'm not sure how; nobody really said."

He frowned. "How do you know it wasn't Muriel? And why was someone else wearing her coat?"

"The murder victim had a gray-haired wig on, and Muriel never wore one in her life. Besides, Muriel told Gabby Williams she lost her jacket yesterday, so it couldn't have been her."

"If it wasn't Muriel, then who was it?"

"I don't know," I said as I handed him a set of

empty trays. "Make yourself useful since you're here, and take these in to Emma."

"Yes, ma'am," he said, adding a grin. "I'm your man."

"You used to be, but you quit on me, remember?"

Max groaned. "Don't bring Darlene up again, would you?"

"I won't if you don't," I said. "I have no desire to ever talk about that woman again." I'd caught my ex-husband in bed with Darlene Higgins, thus the end of our marriage and the beginning of life for me as a single woman again. I'd reacted quickly to finding them together, divorcing my husband, moving in with my mother, taking back my maiden name of Hart, and buying a rundown shop and converting it into Donut Hearts.

Max took the trays inside, then returned to help me break down the actual booth itself. It was made of plywood, two-by-fours, and enough bolts to keep it up, but still easy enough to erect and disassemble when needed. I worked a few fairs a year selling my donuts, and it was handy having a nice place to work from when I was away from my shop.

Max and I had just carried the last piece into the shop and put it all into my storage room when the front door chimed.

"Do you need to get that?" he asked, once again standing more than a little too close to me than I liked.

"No, Emma's covering the front," I said.

"Then there's no reason to rush back up there."

He was definitely pushing his luck now, and he knew it.

I said, "Tell you what. I'll buy you a donut and a fresh cup of coffee for helping me break down."

"How about two donuts, and a hot chocolate?" he countered.

I couldn't help smiling. "You never know when to quit, do you?"

"I like to think it's part of my charm."

I patted his cheek. "You would, wouldn't you?"

He followed me back to the front, and I was surprised to find Chief Martin talking to Emma there.

"I said I was sorry," I said the second I saw him. "I didn't mean to give anything away. It was just a gut reaction."

"I'm not here to see you," the chief said.

"What did I do?" Emma asked.

"You, either."

Max took a step forward. "Then you must want to see me, though I can't imagine what it could be about."

"Let's go somewhere we can talk," the chief said as he glanced over at me.

"If you have anything to say to me, you can say it in front of these ladies," Max said. "I've got nothing to hide."

"I'm not so sure about that," the chief said.

"What's this about?" Max asked, the usual playfulness in his voice now gone.

The chief glanced over at me, then said, "There's no use keeping it a secret anymore. Your ex-wife was right. It wasn't Muriel Stevens."

It was all I could do not to say, "I told you so," but I managed to contain myself. "Then who was it?" I asked.

Chief Martin ignored me. He asked Max, "Do you mind telling me where you were for the last hour?"

Max frowned. "I was sleeping—alone, unfortunately—and then I grabbed a quick shower, got dressed, and came out to see the festivities. Why do you ask? Are you just naturally curious, or do I need an alibi?"

"Why do you ask that?" the chief said.

"Because I've got the feeling you think I had something to do with whoever got killed. I can assure you, I didn't do it."

The chief frowned. "Save your assurances for someone else. Did you see anybody along the way from your place to the donut shop who can vouch for you?"

"No, I was surprised how deserted the streets were. Everyone was at the carnival, no doubt."

The chief frowned, then said, "Everyone but you."

I was amazed at Max's patience, but I knew it couldn't last much longer. I blurted out, "Get to the point, Chief."

"Stop telling me what to do, Suzanne," he snapped at me.

I took a step back from the force of his protest.

Max noticed it too. "She's right. Why are you grilling me?"

"You have an intimate relationship with the victim," the chief said. "That automatically makes you someone I need to speak with."

"The only person I care about in all of April Springs is standing right over there," he said as he pointed to me.

"She's not the only person you've been with in your life, though, is she?"

I knew what he was going to say next before the words left his lips, but his voice still fell like muted thunder as he added, "The murder victim was an old girlfriend of yours. Somebody murdered Darlene Higgins."